# I Am
# Sheffrou

## An Alien Love Story

## Cami Michaels

*I Am Sheffrou*

Paperback ISBN: 979-8-9850772-2-3
Second Edition

Cover design by Miblart.com

# The Sheffrou Trilogy

*I Am Sheffrou*

*Sheffrou Betrayed*

*The Sheffrou's Gambit*

# Contents

# Author's Note

Welcome to the sci-fi fantasy world of *I Am Sheffrou*. To enjoy this novel to the fullest, please refer to the glossary in the back.

Thank you,

*Cami Michaels*

# Chapter 1

I had another argument with my husband this morning. Sometimes I wish I could change my life. Be somebody else. Be somewhere else.

I stomped out on the back porch, fuming. I climbed down the steps leading to the yard careful not to dirty my new sneakers, stopped on the landing, and pondered the future of our relationship. Under the warm April sun, I surveyed the lowcountry marsh in the horizon my jaw locked tight with frustration. The Nate I knew had changed into someone I didn't recognize anymore.

A pelican took flight with long slow sweeps. The fog had lifted, and the sun shone over the tranquil water of the creek chasing away the shade from under the trees.

Today was Saturday and I would be alone most of the day. Again. My son David had left early to study with friends and my daughter Allison was upstairs organizing a shopping trip. Jonathan, the youngest at sixteen, was still dreaming in bed.

My husband Nate had disappeared in the den, like he did every weekend, to catch up on work. We rarely spent time together anymore, and boredom had replaced passion and adventure in our life as a couple.

"Don't you get enough excitement at work? I'm sure the Emergency Room offers plenty of action," he said when I commented on his total lack of enthusiasm.

Yes. At the hospital we dealt on occasion with complex cases like gunshot wounds, or vehicle accidents with multiple trauma, but mostly we treated patients with the flu or other respiratory ailments, minor lacerations, broken bones, etc. Being an Emergency Room physician was stimulating but not nearly as exciting as he thought.

I strolled in my backyard along the path leading to the live oak and admired the various shades of green of the budding boxwood and the vibrant pink of the azaleas. Spring was later than usual this year and I was happy to get a chance to enjoy the sunshine before the suffocating heat of the summer settled in.

Perhaps this year would be different: the whole family could travel down to the Keys and my husband and two sons could go fishing with my brother. I knew he would be thrilled with the idea of spending quality time with his nephews. For my part, I would explore the shops in downtown Key West with my daughter and Trish, my sister-in-law. There were so many things to see and we could sample the fresh local seafood with a cold glass of iced tea in one of those outdoor cafes.

I surveyed the grounds and, way in the back, an odd-looking piece of trash caught my eye. It shone between the shrubs at the base of the big live oak, less than ten feet away from the neighbor's hedge.

Plastic bags and other trash were often blown in our yard by the wind, so I automatically went towards it to pick it up. As I got closer, a sudden wave of nausea stopped me in my tracks, and I coughed several times. I held my stomach and waited for the feeling to dissipate even though I couldn't smell anything offensive.

This wasn't a plastic bag. The bushes grew around an area devoid of grass that glittered in the sunlight. Intrigued, I stepped closer. The ground swayed violently under my feet. I extended my arms to keep my balance and the hard rocking stopped. Right in front of me, a circle about two feet in diameter glistened and rippled as if it was alive. I looked up at the sky to confirm it glowed from within. I bent over to examine it and I fell downward in a long bright tunnel. The world around me disappeared and was replaced with bright flashes and long streams of light.

I screamed but couldn't hear my voice. My heart drummed in my chest, my breathing became more and more labored. The sensation of falling endlessly was terrifying. The pressure circling my head and chest increased and I thought every breath would be my last. I lost consciousness.

The loud ringing in my ears drowned out all sound. I was lying flat on my stomach with my face pressed to the ground. I fought the intense pressure on my head and shoulders, pushed hard, and stood. I took a few steps forward and then stumbled in circles unable to comprehend what I saw. Every familiar landmark had vanished; my house, the trees and grass in the backyard, our street lined with live oaks, even the neighborhood had been replaced by wide open space. Only dirt and rocks remained.

What could have caused this? A bomb? An explosion? A tornado? I didn't see any debris, torn metal, or charred wood. I ignored my spinning head and called out. "Nate? Allison?

Jonathan? Where are you? Is anybody there?" Only the wind howled in the distance.

Bewildered, I pushed my sore frame ahead, each step more difficult than the last under the sun's oppressive heat, and searched for my children, my neighbors, anyone. I couldn't hear any familiar sounds, no bird calls, singing cicadas, or buzzing bees. All around, the horizon remained the same: a deserted landscape without vegetation, houses or roads.

I refused to believe everyone and everything I once knew was gone. I walked and searched in a daze, blinking tears. I dragged myself forward for hours, ignoring the fatigue, willing my feet to continue. Stopping was admitting defeat, acknowledging the impossible. There had to be someone somewhere. After a long while, I dropped to the ground, and retreated in the shade of a boulder the size of a small car, one of many scattered across the area like pebbles on a beach.

What was I doing before this? Where was I?

I recounted the minutes leading up to that awful event. I had gone in my yard to investigate something shiny. Everything after that was a blur. A visceral fear, unlike anything I had felt before, rattled my very core. Throughout the day's search, I had pushed it away but now, with the sun finishing its long course across the sky, it seeped through my pores and invaded my mind. Prostrated in the shade, my head throbbing with a bone-crushing headache, I watched the miniature vortexes in the sand that swirled in the hot air and dissolved into nothingness. I picked up a handful of the fine soil and let it trickle between my fingers and disperse in the breeze.

Something terrible had happened, a devastation so massive the world I knew was gone.

Why was I still here? What happened to the others?

Tightness grew in my chest and tremor shook my hands and legs. I closed my eyes and blocked everything out. My mind drifted to the soothing splashes of pink and fuchsia in my yard and the vivid green of the spring grass. Dreamless sleep carried me away.

>———< < ● > >>———<

Awakened by a blast of orange glow, my body stiff and sore, I struggled to make sense of what I saw. In the light of the new day, a massive orange sun shot fierce rust and crimson rays in the navy-blue sky. I rubbed my legs and got up, put one foot ahead then another and called again and again. No one answered. Only my voice echoed in the distance.

After a few hours, my scalp throbbed as if pricked by thousands of pins and needles. My tongue felt dry and worn like and old leather boot. I collapsed with my back against a rock and wiped my brow. Fine dust covered my face and hands, stuck to my eyebrows and eyelashes, and made my eyes water. My white polo shirt had turned into a dirty rag and reeked of sweat.

I rested until the sun's intense rays decreased and the breeze cooled then I rose and searched for water. My throat was parched. Fluids would help me find a solution, survive. Denial wouldn't change what happened.

I needed a new perspective.

Spotting hills in the distance, I chose one at least eighty feet high, strode towards it, and climbed. It was rough going, each step had to be carefully planned lest I lose my footing and fall.

On one side, the slope wasn't too steep but, amid the crisp dry soil and smooth rocks, the climb close to six stories high was a challenge for a city girl like me. I had to crawl and use my hands to keep from tumbling down. Ignoring my fear of heights, I kept my gaze upward on my way to the top. Twice I stopped. Bright twinkles of light twirled around my head. Loud ringing filled my ears. I gritted my teeth, held on tight to the rocky surface, and waited for the symptoms to subside, ignoring the anguish and the fear.

The effort of climbing sucked my last bit of energy. Beads of sweat dripped from my forehead. Every exposed inch of skin burned, and my neck throbbed. Fearful of falling, I kneeled when I got to the highest point and steadied myself with my hands. Hot and panting, I shielded my eyes from the sun and evaluated the horizon. There used to be small lakes not far from our house. I looked for a stream, a pond, anything suggesting water. The land appeared desolate. Monoliths of all sizes were scattered about, nothing else. My hopes of finding water close by were crushed. Perhaps there was water somewhere, but too far for me to see or reach. Struggling to keep my footing, I climbed down.

How long could I last without water?

A week? A day? A few hours?

I felt panic, the kind that rises hot and salty in the back of your throat and I knew I had to fight it. Being out here alone in a destroyed version of my world was scary enough. I had to stay in control of my mind.

I staggered to a shady spot and plopped down in the dust. I spotted a flat rock, the size of a large kitchen knife, with a sharp edge. With the improvised tool, I dug a hole behind the boulder. Sometimes water would spring to the surface after a few hours. I had seen a documentary on survival in the desert about using a piece of clothing to draw water from the soil, so I removed my shirt and put it in the hole. Even a little might keep me alive.

Night fell and a purple curtain stretched across the sky. The hot breath of the second day vanished, replaced by a cold unforgiving breeze. I shivered and huddled against another monolith which had absorbed the sun's heat. I thought of my family, my children. What happened to them? Where were they? Were they alive? Tears filled my eyes. I wiped them off one by one. I had to stay focused, keep my wits about me, fight to survive.

Alone and miserable, too worried to relax, I kept listening but there was no other sound than the whistling of a cold breeze. I watched for small insects but there were none, not even cockroaches or Palmetto bugs. It was as if my world had vaporized, and had been replaced by a silence so deep, so complete it felt ghostly.

Overwhelmed with dread, my thoughts drifted to Nate and the difficulties we faced in our relationship. How I wished I was back with him, in the safety and comfort of his arms, nestled against his body, inhaling his masculine scent. But Nate along with my children were gone and I couldn't see anything that reminded me of them.

Normally, I was a calm and focused person: trained to identify problems, assess situations, ready for the unexpected, and always working with a team to find possible solutions. My life as an Emergency Room physician had a routine and a familiarity to it. Now my world had disappeared. Terror accelerated my breathing and I gasped for air. I slumped on the ground, put my head in between my knees, and gripped my legs. I forced myself to focus on my shoes coated with reddish dust. I visualized my parents' beach house. How tranquil it used to be in the evening and how beautiful the sunset was. After a long while, I regained control. Fatigue dulled my senses and overcame my will to stay alert. I slept. During the long night I woke up numerous times

and stared wide-eyed in the darkness only to find I was still
stranded in the unknown.

The next morning, I woke up early. I opened my eyes to a
world of contrasting shades of ochre, purple, and rust. Over the
horizon, a crescent moon hung like a jewel amid the fading stars,
and a second, fat gibbous moon, sat suspended in mid-air over
rocky formations the size of mansions.

Two moons.

I stared at the rising orange sun flanked by those two moons
and held my breath as terror invaded my thoughts. This wasn't
Earth. It was another world. How was this possible?

I blinked and held my legs to stop their shaking. Fear
gripped me and reached a new height. Nauseated, I threw up. I
scrambled to stand but couldn't move. I screamed but my throat
made only a chocked croaking sound.

The heat quickly became intolerable. Sunburned from the
previous day's trek, I had to find another shelter since the large
rock behind which I had spent the night didn't offer enough
protection against this harsh sun.

Thirsty and dizzy, I broke down and sobbed. Maybe this
was a huge desert that stretched on for miles and miles and I
would never find water. I wiped my face with the back of my
hand. How did I get here? I had heard stories about space travel,
but this was surreal, ridiculous, illogical.

I lacked the energy to move and hid in the last bit of shade,
and then I saw a puddle under my shirt. I touched it with my
fingers and tasted it. I licked all the water, savoring the cool
wetness. Even though it was a small amount, it brought some

relief. The air hung thick and dried out all moisture from my lungs. I forced myself to take a deep breath every few minutes to make sure I got enough oxygen because there was no way to know if the atmosphere here contained the right elements to survive.

I massaged my stiff limbs and wobbled over to a boulder three times my height and settled behind it. I wiped my watch. It had stopped at 10:35am, the tenth of April, two days ago. Tears stung my eyes and dripped on my cheeks. I thought of Nate and my children. Our life as a couple was locked in an unyielding position, each one stubbornly refusing to make concessions. My children struggled to live amidst the tension between us. Now, transported in this strange world, all communication was impossible.

Doubt crept in my mind. If I walked all day and found water, what next? This might only prolong my agony. How long would I survive without food? I touched my cracked lips with my tongue and tried swallowing what little saliva I had. My brain struggled to explain my arrival in this wretched place.

The shiny circle.

Yes.

The peculiar shiny circle in my backyard. Glossy like a clear sheet of plastic and glowing from within, it had caught my eye. I should have suspected something. How careless I had been to bend over it. But how could I have known the circle was dangerous? Perhaps it was a portal of some kind, an open door to another world, created by intelligent aliens hoping to lure unsuspecting visitors. A trap?

I remembered the eerie sensation of standing in it and over it. Then my body lifted off the ground, floated in mid-air, and dropped down a deep hole.

I recalled the insane endless falling sensation, without ever reaching solid ground. I had screamed loud and hard but couldn't hear my voice. The pleasant sounds of my backyard, the bird songs and the rustle of the breeze in the trees vanished. The yard twisted, turned, and disappeared. My body plunged faster and faster, spinning until my stomach rose in my throat. Unable to move or breathe, I had drifted into unconsciousness.

My thoughts wandered to my children. Each one of them had to be sick with worry. I knew David, the eldest at twenty-two, would search for me endlessly, but would remain strong and support his father. My sweet and gentle Allison would cry and cry and summon her friends to share her grief. Jonathan would hide his fear and retreat in his room and in his music.

I shook myself. I concentrated on a round pebble about a foot away from where I was. Its roundness suggested there had been water in the past. I owed it to my family to hold on and continue looking for a way home for as long as I could if only for their sake. I had to keep fighting to stay alive. The thought of dying alone, in the middle of nowhere, was appalling. Revolted, outraged by the cruelty and senselessness of it all, I cried out at the top of my lungs. I scrambled to my feet and screamed and pounded the rock behind me with my fists. I bruised my knuckles and growled in disgust. I wailed and my voice echoed far and wide onto the empty land. Exhausted, I dropped on my knees. My legs hurt too much to continue. Severe stomach cramps made me roll up in a ball. I waited.

I watched the sun drag its huge mass across the sky leaving the parched land begging for a reprieve from the heat. Sometime later, out in the distance, partially hidden by the long shadows of the boulders, I saw tall figures. With big broad shoulders, they walked on two legs with an easy stride.

They were not human.

Instinct pushed me to retreat against the boulder, making myself as small as I could. My mind was swimming in fear. My teeth clattered out of control. What should I do? They might be my only chance of survival. Fascinated and terrified, I couldn't keep my eyes away from the creatures. My pounding migraine made their shapes dance and move like puppets suspended in an orange glow.

They were closer now. I could see four, walking side by side in a synchronous steady gate.

A new level of terror seized me. My heart pounded so hard in my chest that I thought my ribs would crack. I watched them and my lungs inhaled and exhaled in short spurts as if they were oppressed by an immense weight.

I couldn't make out their faces but their skin, a warm tan brown, was visible through their transparent clothing. They didn't wear hats or head coverings. They weren't carrying weapons or bags, or any item resembling a tool. Perhaps they had a base close by or had traveled aboard a vehicle of some sort. Their feet stirred the dry soil and a small cloud of dust followed them. A moment later, they stopped and changed direction. I choked.

They were headed toward me. . .

One of them moved his arms up and down and emitted loud clicking noises. Petrified with fear, my hair stood on ends, my legs froze in place. I brought up my knees and braced for our first contact. When they were a few feet away, I stared into their oval eyes.

"Don't hurt me," I said, my voice hoarse, a mere whisper. "Please."

I hated the pleading tone in my voice. That wasn't me. I used to be the one who gave orders. I was the voice everyone listened to for direction. Now, my life was on the balance. I had no choice but to let them take me.

The closest one bent down and made a sound, something soft. He inserted his arms under me and lifted me up as if I was weightless. The creature's face became blurry, its eyes bigger and bigger. I blacked out.

# Chapter 2

A long time later, repeated clicks woke me up. I blinked and looked around to assess where I was. A bluish glow filled the surrounding darkness with hazy shadows.

Something stirred close by. An elongated hand with three slender fingers and a thumb reached in my direction. My blood froze. I shrieked, moved back as fast as I could, and hit my head on the wall behind me. I kept my eyes riveted on the strange hand. I had to muster all my willpower to avoid a full-blown panic attack. I pressed my mouth shut and put an arm against my chest to shield my body.

The alien uttered soft clicks then grew quiet. It pulled its arm away. A faint odor that reminded me of wet soil after a spring rain lingered. I lifted my head and stared at it. His large chocolate brown eyes set under a pronounced v-shaped brow looked down at me with an expression which I couldn't decipher at first, but after a moment, concluded it was more like concern than anything else.

It moved closer for a second time.

I broke out in a cold sweat and watched its every move.

The creature put a few small containers on the ground in front of my feet and waited. I stopped breathing and remained motionless. It mumbled something with 'sh' sounds as if it expected me to respond. Then it raised his large oval head, stood, turned, and went back to join a group of five others sitting twenty feet away on large ottomans.

Inhaling a long breath of relief, I sat still and made no sound. I examined my surroundings. I was resting on a thick spongy carpet the size of a yoga mat in one of many alcoves in a dark cave. The rocky walls were dark brown and bare. I didn't see any doors.

The aliens emitted loud clicks when the first one came back. Gathered in a circle, the group seemed to be engaged in an animated discussion with a lot of waving and slapping at each other with big muscular arms. On the ground in front of them, a cube the size of a basketball shed a dim blue light on each one. They wore light khaki clothing: a simple shirt with long sleeves and pants fastened around the ankles. Once the first one joined them, they ignored me.

I turned my attention to the jars which contained a pale orange gel. There was also a tall bottle of clear fluid with an oval opening and something that looked like a miniature scooper.

My stomach cramped and twisted at the sight of the jars. My instinct prompted me to refuse the alien's offering, but I couldn't resist the fluid. I discarded all caution and grabbed the bottle. I held it with shaky hands and brought it to my mouth. I sniffed the clear liquid and touched it with my lips. It was water. I took a sip and let the tepid fluid moisten my tongue and palate then drank more. I picked up the scooper and took a mouthful of gel from each container. It had a fresh fruity taste. I ate everything and lay back on the thick carpet. After a few minutes my eyelids closed, and I fell sound asleep.

I woke up with a sharp stabbing pain just below my ribs. I held my stomach with both hands and waited until it subsided. I was alone in the cave except for one bright blue cube on the rocky ground beside me. The ottomans and the other cubes were gone. My sneakers were missing. A horrible thought crossed my mind.

I was their prisoner.

I ate the food in new jars deposited by the aliens. I stood and walked around on my socks on the cold bare floor. A beam of light from small recessed areas on the walls shone on me when I approached that part of the room and turned off when I moved further away. The cave was elliptical with four paneled doors at the end. The high polished walls bore no visible writings or signs.

I stood in front of each of the oval doors. Only one opened as I stepped close. Its two overlapping panels slid apart, and I jumped back, startled. I peeked in the room lit by blue globes and noticed a round bowl made of a smooth material not unlike plastic, on the far wall, four feet off the floor. I approached it and saw my reflection on the glossy wall. My hair looked dirty and tangled and my face presented a worn and sad expression. I clenched my jaw, stretched my arm and touched the bowl. A stream of clear fluid came out from high above, trickled down the container, and disappeared. I let the liquid drip on my fingers. The water was cool, refreshing. I washed my hands, my face, and my neck multiple times to relieve the pain of my sunburned skin. I bent down and rinsed my hair over and over until it felt straight and smooth.

A thousand thoughts raced in my mind. The aliens had offered food and water. Why did they bring me here? What were their intentions? I swallowed with difficulty the lump in my throat. Was I alone in this forbidden place? Did any others travel here? Was this a trap of some kind? If so, I had to escape. If not, I had to find a way communicate with them.

I went back and sat in the small alcove. On Earth, Nate and the children had to be shocked by my unexplained disappearance. There would be a search party, investigators, police. Unless they searched the back yard, and assuming the shiny circle hadn't disappeared, it was unlikely they would ever find what happened to me. Tears rolled on my cheeks. I sat on the hard floor, pulled up my knees, and cried in silence.

After what seemed to be two days in the cave my situation hadn't changed. The creatures didn't harm, attack, or eat me. In fact, the aliens treated me as a guest. They brought food several times and provided a light blanket woven with long strands of fine hairs with a musky odor. Each day, I heard far away sounds, loud grinding and drilling noises. I concluded this was a mine, and they were workers.

Fear overwhelmed me every time one of them approached. At the hospital I was trained to deal with emergencies and unusual circumstances but here, no matter how much I wished to initiate contact, every time an alien came close, I panicked. I cowered and averted my eyes as if expecting them to harm me.

With my back pressed against the wall, I watched when they came in from their outings. They were an odd bunch. They strolled in the large cave at a leisurely pace, hugged and slapped each other while clicking non-stop, sat and slurped liquids from tall glasses but never seemed to eat anything. They wore the same lightweight beige clothing with a multicolor sash around the waist like a uniform.

I couldn't understand why they would bring me here, feed me, and then ignore me. What were they planning?

On the third day, a new alien came in; he was slender with golden tan skin, a much lighter color than the others. He wore a loose light blue shirt open in the front, revealing a hairless chest and faint markings. His sash was a warm butter yellow and his olive pants, tied at the ankles and made of a fine silky material, floated around his legs.

He moved with grace and swiftness like a feline. A less prominent brow and high cheekbones with smooth features gave him an air of nobility. He bent down and sat on the floor about fifteen feet away from me and tapped on a little gadget that reminded me of a miniature computer which traced strange diagrams, (holograms?) in mid-air. I noticed he gazed in my direction a few times and turned his head the other way when I retreated deeper in the alcove.

After about thirty minutes, he came closer and sat six or seven feet away from me, his long legs stretched out in front of him. Across the room, he looked striking but nonthreatening, so I felt safe. Up close, his alien figure filled the cave with a powerful presence.

I summoned all my courage and ignored the fear creeping in my bones. He appeared to be their leader. I had to communicate with him. My mouth went dry at the thought of saying something. I took a long breath and tucked my legs under me so he wouldn't notice how much they shook. My plan was to keep my words as clear and simple as possible. My life might depend on what I said.

As if he had anticipated my move, he turned and looked right at me with large oval eyes.

This was my chance. I lifted my right arm and lightly pressed on my chest with my hand. "Tamara," I said in a clear voice and then repeated, "Tamara."

His facial expression didn't change, but he responded without hesitation. He also lifted his arm and touched his chest. His voice had a strange musicality. He said, "Maashi."

This is what I had been hoping. I gathered my courage and repeated the same gesture, "Tamara." Then I pointed at him and said, "Maashi."

I held my breath and waited.

He repeated, "Maashi" and extended his arm towards me and uttered, "Tamara."

The tip of his fingers brushed mine in a light and reassuring gesture. His features changed. His brow faded, his pupils enlarged, his eyes paled and became two clear pools.

Overwhelmed and grateful, I nodded and blinked back the tears that welled in mine. My survival depended on our ability to communicate. Even though we had exchanged a single word, this was the first step in establishing a meaningful connection.

I couldn't believe how easy it had been. I wanted to laugh and cry out in happiness. Perhaps all my fears were unfounded. Would this alien be able and willing to send me home? I needed to make him understand I had to go back to my family as soon as possible. My mind was going at a thousand miles per hour, but even though I tried, I could not speak another word. It was as if they had all betrayed me and vanished from my brain.

The alien didn't make another sound either. He sat without changing his position or his expression and his eyes remained colorless. He returned to his hologram for a few minutes and then stood and left.

The next day, when the alien came, things progressed faster than I expected. He repeated his name, Maashi, his voice echoing in the cave. Then he pointed at my hand.

I said, "hand," and he repeated after me, "hand". He continued and pointed at my arm, my shoulder, my face, and each time, he repeated the word. Then, he stretched his arm and turned his palm upward, brought it close enough for me to touch.

I looked at him. He sat very still, waiting. I brought my hand forward and touched his fingers.

He slid his hand under mine. It felt warm and soft like kid leather. He emitted soft clicks.

I sensed a warm glow climb up my arm and tensed up but didn't pull away and break the contact between us.

"Friends," I said, "friends. Is this what you mean?" I whispered.

He bent his head a little to one side and his eyes changed to a honey color. "Friends," he said and held my hand in his. He blinked and the color of his oval face lightened.

I relaxed my shoulders and swallowed. As I grew more comfortable in his presence, I decided he wasn't so scary, and his smooth golden skin and small round ears gave him a certain masculine charm. When he left, I felt hopeful for the first time since my coming to this wretched world.

That night I stayed awake for hours while my mind churned on my misfortunate arrival in this place and how to approach the subject with him. I needed to make him understand my presence here was a big mistake. I couldn't stay here. My husband, and my children needed me. I had to go home, to my house, to my family. I needed to touch the trees and smell the flowers, to reconnect with the sand and the ocean of my world.

As the night progressed the temperature in the cave dropped until icicles hung from the ceiling and the bare walls glistened with frost in the pale light of the cube.

My breath formed white puffs inches from my face. I rubbed my arms and thighs, swaddled in the blanket they had provided but to no avail. I couldn't get warm. In the morning I felt chilled to the bone and feverish, and my teeth clattered non-stop.

I was convinced I had developed a kidney infection. The signs and symptoms were clear: my back just below my ribs hurt and throbbed every time I took a deep breath and, even with the water provided by the aliens, my urine was dark, opaque, and had a strong smell, a sign of dehydration.

When Maashi came, I lay exhausted and cold, on the verge of tears. I couldn't think of a way to make him understand I was sick. I had been so close to finding a solution to my quandary and now, I might lose everything and die in this awful cave far from my family and my loved ones. The thought was too much to bear. Tears trickled down my face and I couldn't stop them.

The alien looked at me and produced a long series of clicks. He drew me close and pressed his mouth on my cheeks and kissed the wetness on my face. He cradled me against his chest and whispered strange words, his head resting against mine.

His embrace, although gentle, was overwhelming. As much as I welcomed his soothing presence, I couldn't tolerate his body this close to mine. The surrounding air grew hot, and I suffocated. In a mere instant, the alien energy he generated tampered with my senses. Vivid hallucinations invaded my brain. I stood helpless, alone, on the edge of a tall cliff. I stared down a terrifying black pit and felt an irresistible urge to leap to my death. Desperate to escape the horrible vision I moaned and fought to free my mind. I pushed on his chest and cried out, "go away, don't touch me, leave me alone."

The alien clicked and massaged the nape of my neck. His words froze my blood.

"Do not be frightened, little one. Let me hold you."

The vision dissipated in seconds, my fear eased off, replaced by a sense of peace and calm.

He pressed his lips on my forehead and I reeled in shock and surprise when the odor of warm caramel, my favorite candy, filled my lungs. I couldn't help inhaling deeply and the tension inside me slowly melted away.

"I will not hurt you," he said, "Let me help you."

He traced the outline of my face with kisses. He kissed my temples, my cheeks, my nose, my chin. I couldn't move but instead of being alarmed I closed my eyes in utter contentment and the world disappeared in a sweet blue cloud.

I woke up later, warm, comfortable, and chuckled to myself. What an incredible dream. I reveled at the power of my own imagination. I recalled the alien's powerful embrace and shook my head in disbelief. Time to rise and check on Jonathan. School started at eight thirty. Eyes closed I patted the mattress beside me only to find Nate wasn't there. I opened my eyes and reality came rushing back. I was in the cave, wrapped in a much thicker fuzzy blanket, my back well supported by a large pillow. My fever was gone. I felt much better.

A cold sad chill ran up my spine.

Right then, I heard a musical voice which was becoming familiar. "Good morning, Tamara. I think this is the appropriate greeting."

I turned around and there he was, immobile, watching me like a cat. He sat on the floor a few feet away, his long limbs resting in front of him, his head bent sideways, his eyes two large amber crystals.

How could this be?

"Are you hungry?" Maashi said in a soothing voice. "I hear your belly making noises." His tone, as if we had been conversing like this every day, his behavior, proper and concerned, were astonishing.

Too shocked to answer, I pulled myself up and stared.

He held up something and then put it close to my hand. "For you," he said.

I stared at it, dumbfounded.

"Take it. You may eat it."

With my eyes riveted on him, I grabbed the fruit. Hunger had become my constant companion and I couldn't resist any offering of food. It was a beautiful tangerine color, firm and oval, like a blend of apple and pear. I took a bite. It tasted fresh. He then set in front of me a few of the jars I was familiar with.

He waited for me to begin.

"You speak English," I said, my mind blank with disbelief.

He put down a few more containers with a thick creamy mixture like pudding.

"I don't understand," I said, "How did you learn?"

"Yesterday," he said, "I licked your tears. This gave me access to your memory and your language."

My eyebrows raised in alarm. I stopped chewing. "You learned all this by licking my tears?"

Maashi put his hands together in front of him. "I focused on your language, not on your personal emotions and feelings. There is much to learn."

I paused and took a deep breath. He was some sort of telepath. "Can you read my thoughts now, without touching me?"

"I can reach them, but I need to be in close physical contact to understand anything meaningful. Your mind works in many different paths." He added, "You should eat."

This was extraordinary. The fact that we could discuss any subject opened incredible possibilities. My stomach grumbled. I scooped up a little more pudding. It tasted like coconut cream.

"Are you going to eat something?" I said between mouthfuls.

"No," he answered. "You need to learn more words in my language."

I remembered how sick I was the day before and put down my scooper. "Did you give me medication? My pain is gone. I'm not feverish anymore."

"Close contact with me reestablished your body's wellness."

I frowned. What did he mean by that? How could he heal my fever so fast? This was fascinating, and I intended to discuss this with him at the earliest. For now, my main concern was to find out why they brought me here. I wanted answers.

"Where am I?

"We call this planet Chitina. We are Chamranlinas."

"Listen to me. This is very important. My arrival here is a big mistake. I need to go home to my world. Why did you bring me here?"

Maashi stared at me for a few seconds and his brow seemed to darken. He said, "We did not bring you here. We are trying to find out how and why you came here."

"What?" I gasped. "What did you say?"

He lowered his voice, "We do not know where you are from."

I stared at him speechless. This couldn't be true.

"You need to learn a few more words. Let's start with important words, yes, no, and definitely not."

I couldn't believe it. If they didn't bring me here, then how would I go back home?

"Those words are a key to your safety. You may need them since you appear to be fragile and needy."

My mind exploded. He had to be lying. How dare he? Anger swelled in my chest and my neck felt fiery-hot. I said in a solid voice, "You're lying to me. Don't underestimate humans."

Maashi observed me for a moment. "You said humans, are you referring to your species?"

"Yes."

"Why do you say, "don't underestimate"?"

I spoke, emphasizing each word, "Humans appear weak and defenseless, but they are resourceful and possess a strong will to survive."

"I agree," he said. "You have already proven this. But you are also a weak species. You need air and warmth, must ingest large amounts of food every few hours, and require a long period of sleep every day." He tilted his head to the right and said, "It is important for me to learn what you require for survival."

Survival? Yes. I agreed with that.

What I should say? I explained the basic human needs as best as I could; oxygen, moderate temperatures, food and water and how important it was not to be underwater, even though I hadn't seen any large body of water so far.

He bent his head, first right then left, as if not understanding my answer. Then he replied, "Since breathing air is primordial, it is logical to conclude you cannot stay underwater at all. However, cleanliness is very important for us Chamranlinas. A place to soak and wash your body, adequate for your size, will be available every day from now on."

A bath sounded good. I smelled awful.

His earlier statement, "We do not know where you are from", echoed over and over in my head. I had to make sure he understood I wanted to go home. I stated in a firm and clear voice, "I'm from Earth, planet Earth. It's the third planet out of nine from our sun. From space it looks blue and white."

As an educated person with a scientific background, I understood the absurdity of the statement. How in heaven's name was I going to explain where Earth was? An astronomer would find this a daunting task and my description sounded so inadequate, my cheeks burned with shame.

Maashi stared at me for a few seconds. "Tamara," he said, "There are no planets in proximity to Chitina which correspond to your world and could sustain a species like yours. We cannot transport you anywhere until we find your own world."

"What???" My lower jaw dropped. I turned my head away to hide my tears. Where was this place? Where was Earth?

On a small console that appeared on the floor, Maashi pressed on a series of buttons. He soon produced a multicolored flexible bracelet and snapped it on my right wrist.

"What are you doing?" I asked. "What is this for?"

"This is to inform all the other Chamranlinas about your physical needs. The black color is to warn them you will cease to live if anyone holds you underwater. This area is devoid of underground water but there are significant reservoirs in the other sectors. You must keep these on you at all times." His eyes had transformed into black onyx. "Your life will be in danger if you remove them."

I looked down at the bracelet. He had just confirmed there were rivers and lakes on this planet, and all I could think of was I wasn't a good swimmer.

He added a royal-blue and gold bracelet.

"This one is a sign you belong to me. These are my colors. This bracelet will protect you."

"What do you mean?" I said in a loud voice, "I am not your property or anyone else's."

Maashi's brow widened.

"Forgive me," he said, "if my words sounded offensive. I only want to offer you my protection."

Were there other aliens who might hurt me?

He continued. "There is also a single command you must always obey. "Come", means you must come to me at once. Your life may someday depend on it. Do you understand?"

This conversation seemed pointless. Emptiness filled my heart, my head throbbed like when I sensed the onset of a migraine. My only wish was to return home.

"Do you understand?" he repeated.

"Yes, I understand," I said in a voice almost inaudible.

"Tell me what part of your body I can and cannot touch. We Chamranlinas communicate by touch and kisses. You do not seem to tolerate this well."

After yesterday's hug and my reaction, I agreed. I said, pointing to my shoulders and knees, "Anything between just below the shoulders down to right above the knees is a no-touch zone."

He was still sitting on the floor close by. I had just finished my last words when he extended his arm and opened his hand. "Friends," he said.

I hesitated, then put my hand in his.

"I am pleased," he said. He caressed my fingers and released my hand. "You are not an enemy. You are Ishkibu, a traveler." A hint of softness appeared in his eyes. "I will care for you."

He rose and strolled out of the room. The doors closed behind him with a dull swishing sound.

I watched him leave. His words echoed in my mind, "We do not know where you are from". Was this the truth?

As he stepped out, I ran toward him. "Wait. Wait. Don't go. You don't understand. I have to go home." I screamed, "Maashi. Maashi. Maashi come back. I can't stay here." I pounded on the door and kicked at it. I cried out and yelled and still the door wouldn't open.

I thought of my children, my world, now far out of my reach. Why? Why did this horrible thing happen to me? Would I ever go back home? I grabbed another fruit and bit a large chunk out of it then threw it so hard it splattered against the wall.

# Chapter 3

We traveled all night to reach the Central Compound.

The day before we left, Maashi came to sit with me and explained we would move to an area a long distance away from our current location. "We will march in the tunnels. I will carry you and provide a blanket to keep you warm."

"No," I said, "I don't want you to carry me. I can walk." The thought of being held in his arms, even for a short time, filled me with apprehension.

He insisted. "You are small. You will not be able to keep up."

"Why do we have to leave? I want to remain close to the place where I arrived. If we find that shiny circle, I'll go home."

"This place is not safe." Maashi's eyes darkened. "You and I cannot stay here."

The light of the cube cast a blue sheen on his skin. I fisted my hands in frustration.

"Why are we traveling at night?" I asked. "Why can't we use a vehicle instead of walking?"

"We are leaving during the night for our safety. We cannot use underground vehicles in this sector."

"Why aren't we going on the surface, then?"

"It is safer underground."

I stood and paced back and forth in the room, my hands resting on my waist. Although annoyed with the arrangement, I couldn't think of another alternative. I turned and faced him, "No kissing, and no touching."

Maashi's brow softened. He said, "You will be treated with respect and no one will touch you."

I agreed with reluctance. "Okay. I'll let you carry me."

"I will come and pick you up later." He stood and strolled out, leaving me alone and frustrated.

The hours dragged on. With nothing else to do, I walked the length of the cave to stretch my legs and calm my worries. I was afraid the shiny circle, if it was still there, would disappear in a short time, perhaps just in a few days. I had regained my strength and wanted to search for it but Maashi left me no choice. I had to leave.

The group marched on through the night. New aliens, bigger and taller than the miners, escorted a group composed of Maashi, I, and several others, in the tunnels. They wore black clothing; thick rubber-like fitted shirts and pants with short black sashes at the waist. Their faces were set in cold, impassive stares.

Maashi carried me in his arms wrapped in a thick blanket. Even though I was well covered, the stale odor of the tunnels filled my nostrils and the damp air gave me chills. The rhythmic pace of the trek made me drowsy, but sleep didn't come. The same emotions of anxiety and dread invaded my senses as they used to when I worked the graveyard shift in the Emergency Room, and we were expecting trauma patients.

The Black guards kept their distance as soon as they saw the blanket's deep blue color with specks of gold, the same combination as the second bracelet on my wrist. I concluded the colors held a special meaning for them. Once, I peeked from under the blanket and after several minutes my eyes adjusted to the dark. The Chamranlinas marched one behind the other in a winding rocky tunnel carved by some ancient fast-flowing river. There weren't torches or lights to show the way. Either the guards possessed exceptional night vision, or they were familiar with the path.

After a long while, we reached another section bathed in dim yellow light that created strange shadows which stretched along the walls and followed our steps as if hundreds of ghosts were marching with us in the tunnels.

Twice we halted. The two closest guards surrounded Maashi and I and locked their arms around us. After a moment we heard sharp clicks, and the march resumed.

"What's going on?" I asked keeping my voice low even though I didn't think the others understood my question.

"At each intersection," Maashi explained, "we must scan ahead for any threat before we can advance further."

Hours later, we arrived in a warm area where the tunnels shimmered in gold and turquoise. Small sconces flashed on and off every five or six yards, signaling the way. We walked through a series of oval doors that closed with two metallic panels like the ones I had seen in the cave. We entered a well-lit khaki room and I saw furniture for the first time: huge couches, twelve feet long and six feet wide covered by a thick quilted mattress reminding me of lounge chairs with adjustable backs. They were accompanied by crescent-shaped side tables made of gray stone.

The walls lacked any pictures or sculptures. Overall, the decor appeared to be spartan yet comfortable.

Maashi put me down and removed my blanket. He directed me to another smaller chamber and said, "You may refresh yourself in there, then come back to the receiving room."

I gave him a questioning look, "Where?"

"We call the first area where we arrived the receiving room. It is where we gather and spend time together."

When I came back, Maashi was sitting on a couch working on a screen that hung in mid-air a foot in front of him. He touched it now and then with the tip of his finger, and the colors and signals changed.

A Chamranlina, most likely a guard dressed in gray with a light fitted shirt with long sleeves and a brown and gray sash, stood at the door.

Maashi was busy with his virtual screen, so I went to another couch further away.

He waved his hand, and the image disappeared. "Come," he said. "Come, Tamara."

He was testing me. I came with reluctance and stood by his side. He opened his arms, signaling me to sit on his lap.

I was treated like his little pet, being trained to come when called. I stared at him, and said, "I will sit here beside you."

"You may do so if you wish," Maashi said and his head bobbed sideways a few times.

As soon as I settled on the couch and he put his left arm around my waist as if afraid I would dart off.

I was uncomfortable close to him. It wasn't fear anymore but an unsettling, disquieting feeling, which made my heart race and my face blush. A fragrant aura, faint but powerful, surrounded him like a veil and followed him everywhere he went.

I couldn't tell if he wore cologne or if that lingering sweet scent emanated from his own body. All I knew was that my knees shook, and my body tingled with anticipation like a teenager on a first date.

I remembered my husband's embrace and how in our years together I had become so accustomed to his body and his touch. Filled with sadness and longing, I wished I was back in my house surrounded by familiar sounds and smells, sharing a tender moment with Nate. Then I recalled his indifference and moodiness, and my lips tightened in annoyance.

A slight movement from Maashi brought me back to reality. I looked up at him and saw he was scrutinizing me. Was he reading my thoughts?

Maashi bent his head and gave me a light kiss on the forehead. This caught me by surprise, and I responded with a quick smile.

Damn. Why did I do that?

What was wrong with me?

I needed to be in control of my reactions. That alien knew more than I assumed, and his keen eyes noticed everything. I had to be careful.

Maashi's expression changed. "I will teach you more words today," he said, "and in the next few days."

Great. More schooling. He sure was persistent. Well, I consoled myself, this may be useful later. I tried to pry information from him.

"Maashi," I said, "why did you bring me to this place?" I hated the fact that this long trek might crush my hopes for a quick return to Earth.

"This area is safer."

"Why are there so many guards here?"

"The guards are here for our protection."

"Why do we need protection?"

Maashi's face paled, his eyes narrowed. "We require protection against our enemies."

Why was he answering this way, disclosing so little information? I sighed, exasperated. I didn't trust him.

I tried another line of questioning. "Did any other human come here?"

"We have never heard of or been in contact with your species before." He stood as if ready to leave.

"Don't go. Listen." I said. "Listen to me."

He tilted his head and looked at me.

"I have to go back home. I can't stay here." Could he see how distressed I was? Did he understand my anguish?

Maashi's face paled. His cheeks, his forehead and even his neck faded to a light ivory color, and a gray shadow covered his eyes like summer clouds heavy with rain.

"I wish to help you reach your home world, but I cannot do so without knowing how you came here and where you are from." With that, he sighed and left. The guard followed him.

His words hit me as if I had been slapped. I clenched my hands and locked my eyes on my feet to stop the spinning in my head. Perhaps he wasn't interested in helping me. It would be impossible to find the exact place where I arrived without his help. What if I never went back? I couldn't bear the thought of being unable to leave this planet and never seeing Earth again. I closed my eyes, wishing this world would just vanish and everything would change back to normal. Why did this terrible thing happen? Why did it happen to me?

I blinked my tears away. I had to stay vigilant and explore all avenues that could lead back home: pay attention to detail, watch for clues, and learn more about Chamranlinas and find out if they were responsible for my arrival here.

Over the next two days, out of boredom and to keep my sanity, I kept practicing their language by repeating their strange sounds. I pushed far away in my mind thoughts of my family and my home. I decided the best way to deal with my current situation was to gather as much information as possible and devise a plan of escape.

To Maashi's dismay, even after a lot of intense repetition, I wasn't learning his odd language as fast as he expected. "I have repeated and explained the same sound several times," he said, his brow darkening, "Why do you keep forgetting what you learned the day before?"

I agreed. "To make any progress, I need to record your words," I told him. "I need a pen and something to write on or I'll never be able to learn your language."

Pen and paper appeared just as alien to him as his virtual computer was to me. Maashi looked at me, his brow wider and more pronounced as if he was pondering this, and said, "I will see what I can find."

Minutes later, he came back with something like a writing pad and a stylus. Even though he had only four fingers in each hand, one thumb and three long fingers, he manipulated the pen with impressive skill and with either hand. With a lot of patience, he taught me how to use it. The little device had several functions. It let me write in English and translated in their language as a color code or a sound. Maashi showed me how to make it appear out of thin air or from the floor with a few rapid flicks of the wrist. The device was easy to work with and I played with it for hours until I dozed off on the couch.

The next day, he brought me to his quarters. His section was close to the first one. His receiving room, with polished granite walls the color of warm sunsets, was much larger and lead to a series of smaller adjoining chambers. A ten-foot high banner with a bold blue wave ran along the length of one of the walls. On the frames of the two main doors, gold and silver vines climbed and reached the ceiling. At the far end of his quarters rested an odd-looking egg-shaped structure.

"The encounter room," said Maashi matter-of-factly. "You can enter through this door." He demonstrated the mechanism by stepping closer to a large circular door that opened and closed with a suction noise.

There were several Chamranlinas in the receiving room sitting on rectangular couches overflowing with big teardrop-shaped cushions in shades of blue, green and gold.

They rose as Maashi walked in. Each one wore a loose shirt with brown or gray pants and sash with two or three lines of another color. The aliens emitted clicking noises, kissed his hands and his neck, and patted him on the back. Maashi's face lit up, and he settled on a large couch.

One of them stood out from the others. He was tall and wiry with a bony face, and hair cropped short, military style. He wore an olive-green sash with a thin gray line and a charcoal braided belt crisscrossed his chest.

The Chamranlinas stared at my hands then at my face and hair. A few tried to touch me but Maashi clicked and shielded my body with his arm, so they kept their distance. I sat still by his side. They continued their conversation and ignored my presence. Only the one with the bony face shot furtive glances in my direction with mocking brown eyes.

I studied the room, surprised by its elongated shape. The furniture was sparse, but I noticed they summoned more from the walls or the floor at will. Did the couches and tables exist and were just pulled out of wherever they were, or did they materialize on demand?

Time dragged on. On Earth, as a health care provider, I worked hard and was busy all the time. I saw multiple patients in the Emergency Room every day, performed minor procedures, and supervised subordinates and students. Forever rushing from one task to another, I never stayed in one place for prolonged periods. Here, bored and with nothing to keep me occupied, I squirmed and fidgeted, stretched, crossed and uncrossed my legs.

At some point, the aliens ceased clicking. I asked Maashi, keeping my voice low, "Everyone has a different color sash. Do the colors have any specific meaning?"

Maashi gave me his full attention. "I am pleased to see you noticed all Chamranlinas dress according to their color. We call the ones present with us today Multicolors."

Mildly interested, I lifted an eyebrow. "I see."

"The color of each one's sash," Maashi continued, "correlates with the individual's personality and skills. The individuals present in the receiving room are part of my personal guard. They dress in similar clothing but each one wears a different sash."

"What about the other bands on their sashes, what do they mean?"

"The other colors represent minor traits: orange for sociable and outgoing, green for strength and courage, pink for kindness and empathy."

"Why is it important for everyone to wear their colors this way?"

"Wearing one's own colors promotes unity and stability. In our society, we assign everyone a function compatible with one's abilities."

"You have a khaki sash. What does it represent?"

"Khaki is neutral. My real color is blue." Maashi paused. "I display it on special occasions only. It would not be appropriate to wear it every day."

"Why not?"

"Blue indicates I am Sheffrou," Maashi said in an unexpected grave tone. "It is not advisable to show my color. I must remain inconspicuous and avoid being detected."

"Because of the enemies?"

"Yes, because of the enemies."

He turned his head away and spoke in his language to one of the other aliens. I reclined on the couch. What was a Sheffrou? Why did he need to conceal his identity?

Maashi stood up and said, "Come, Tamara." He took my hand to make sure I followed him into the strange egg-shape structure. He bent down low to enter. The tube leading inside was five feet high, too low for me to stand upright. A singular black and white diamond-shaped pattern, each diamond delineated by a thin gold border covered the floor, the ceiling and the walls, and created a strange optical illusion. Bigger than my hand in the middle of the room, the diamonds became smaller and smaller closer to the extremities. It looked as though the oval room flowed endlessly. I had never seen anything like it. The room was just big enough for the alien to lie down, approximately ten feet long and six feet wide.

Maashi sat on the floor with the only source of light behind him and waited. He motioned for me to sit down.

The diamond pattern on the floor shimmered and rippled when I walked. I lowered myself on it with care. A few ripples ran to the base of the walls.

"Do you like this room?" he asked, his eyes fixated on me.

"Yes," I answered, "It's unique."

"We call it the encounter room or the timeless room because of the uninterrupted pattern which makes it appear to continue on forever. Neither space nor time matter in this chamber."

Maashi bent down and touched my forehead with his lips. In this narrow space he could reach me without moving from his spot. I tried to slip away but before I knew it, I was in his arms. He pressed me to his chest while his left hand rested in the middle of my back.

Irritated by his move, unwilling to experience the fear I felt the first he kissed me, I shook my head. "Don't do that. Let me go."

Maashi's amber eyes shone. "Do not be frightened, Tamara," he whispered, "I will not hurt you." He touched my hair, picked a strand, and let it slide between his long fingers. For an instant, he rested his hand on the nape of my neck. He touched my cheeks with his palm then he slid it under my chin and lifted my head. He gazed at me with eyes the color of honey and emitted soft clicking sounds.

His fragrant aroma and the delicate caress of his fingers made my knees feel weak and shake uncontrollably. In just a few days, my fear of him had morphed into an unexplainable attraction. The simple action of being held in his arms had an intoxicating effect and heat crept up along my chest and neck. I sensed my resistance melt away and turned my head but as much as I tried, I couldn't contain my agitation.

A powerful yearning I hadn't experienced in a long time with my husband Nate stirred inside me. Our relationship had suffered because of his aloofness and indifference. He had become more involved in his job, increased his workload, neglected his time with me, and we had grown apart. I didn't think he was seeing another woman, but his indifferent manner had left me wanting. Sex had become such a dull exchange between us that I didn't care for it anymore and we hadn't been intimate for months. Now, Maashi's gentle touch reawakened my body.

A troubling surge of emotions and wild thoughts raced through my mind. I wanted to hold him, caress him, kiss him. I was overwhelmed, powerless to curtail my desire.

Maashi kept his eyes locked in mine and tilted his head. His face came to rest inches away, his sweet breath against my ear. He said in a soothing voice, "Stay calm Tamara." Then, still holding me, he reclined on his back.

Laying on top of his sensuous body was intolerable. Dizzy with desire, the room spun around me, and my mouth filled with saliva. I lifted my head and shoulders, pushed on him as hard as I could, and cried out, "Maashi, let me go. Let me go now!" He loosened his hold, and I wiggled out of his arms. I sat a foot away, my back set against the wall, shaking, panting, fighting to recover from what felt like an assault.

Maashi sat back up, his expression unchanged, his eyes gentle. He showed no surprise or annoyance at my refusal to be held. He waited a minute, then asked, "You are female, are you not?"

"Yes." I said in a guarded tone.

Maashi bent his head sideways. "Our females are long and slender," he said, "You are short with round body parts."

I was five foot two but otherwise of average size and shape. Their women were most likely tall and thin like models. Piqued, I readjusted my posture and just stared at him.

"Your brown eyes are round," he declared in a mellow voice, "your breasts and your buttocks are round."

Annoyed by his comments although they weren't likely meant as insults, I said, "Women have curves."

"You are very different," Maashi rested his hand on his thigh, "but beautiful." His amber eyes shone, and his mouth stretched in an odd smile.

Was he trying to seduce me?

"I reached in your thoughts and found that on your planet you have lived with the same male for many years. Do you have offspring?"

He could reach in my thoughts much more than I expected.

"Yes," I answered in a dry tone, "I have three children, two boys and a girl."

Maashi nodded and his face glowed. "Three offspring. Congratulations. Did you mate each time with the same male?"

"What difference does it make?" I blurted out, my voice sharper than intended.

"Please answer my question," Maashi said in a tone so calm I shivered. "This is an important detail for Chamranlinas."

I hesitated. "I wasn't involved," I blinked, "with anyone before my husband, and I've been faithful ever since we wed." It was true. I married my high school sweetheart. My husband's arms were the only ones I had ever known. Some days I wondered if I had made the right choice, but that wasn't a subject I was willing to discuss with an alien.

Maashi commented. "Our females are paired with a different male every year. The Council of Elders decides who among the Pure Colors will be chosen for mating." He added in a decisive tone, "We need to meet tomorrow."

I held my breath. A meeting? What did he mean by that?

Maashi stood and stepped through the strange paneled door. He paused, making sure I followed him back to the receiving place, then turned toward me and said, "We will meet in the encounter room. It is the only area that is not monitored. It is an important meeting. Be prepared."

# Chapter 4

After long hours of sleep, I woke up in my new quarters. Lights along the base of the empty walls bathed my receiving room and my adjoining bedroom with a pleasant glow. Furnishings were comprised of only three pieces: a large bed, a lounge-chair with a multitude of pillows and cushions, mostly cream or sandy color and a small grey table made of stone and shaped like a "C". The chambers had two doors, one led to the hallway outside, and the other to a narrow corridor connected to a series of "water-rooms".

The open concept of the quarters provided maximum visibility with disregard for privacy, seemingly a low priority for the Chamranlinas. Was this design a means to facilitate detection of the enemies or were they a species which lived at ease with nudity and in close quarters?

My thoughts wandered back to what happened with Maashi in the encounter room. Maashi seemed to possess a distinctive body chemistry which stimulated my senses. I didn't expect such an intense physical attraction every time he touched me, especially considering he was an alien.

I was determined not to let his pheromones, or whatever it was, affect my judgment. I needed to keep a cool head and focus my energies on finding a way out of here. Today's "meeting" would be different.

Maashi came early. "Come, Tamara," he said, "it is time."

I followed him in the encounter room. Dressed in light khaki pants and ivory shirt, a stunning royal blue sash circling his waist displayed his color. A wide gold bracelet with an intricate design adorned his left wrist. He sat down and the patterns on the padded floor came alive and rippled around him.

"First, we both undress and then we can meet," he said with a solemn voice.

My heart jumped a beat. "What?" I must have misunderstood. What was he planning to do? I scanned the room, intending to bolt if needed.

Maashi's brow lightened. "Little one," he said, "a meeting does not mean mating. It is a way to learn more about your body and its normal physiology. It is a gentle and harmless process. I touch you all over and you touch me all over. Then we kiss each other and let our minds meet."

Although relieved to find out this wasn't sex, the touching-all-over part and the joining of the minds didn't reassure me. To make matters worse, my previous state of uneasiness in his presence came rushing back. I was amazed to see how sitting close to him made my head spin.

I debated my options. I didn't think he would coerce me to proceed with this meeting but then what would he do if I refused? His behavior had been unreproachable until now, but he was seven-foot tall and I was no match for him. What if I accepted and then couldn't tolerate his touching and panicked or worse, succumbed to an irresistible urge to jump in his arms? With the strange way I felt from the moment I stepped into this odd room, everything seemed possible. I didn't want to anger him, but my reactions scared me.

I took a deep breath in a futile attempt to clear my head.

Where was the self-assured woman I used to be?

In the Emergency Room, I took charge. I decided on the most appropriate course of action to produce the best results for the patient. My feelings didn't cloud my judgment. I refused to succumb to the influence of wild emotions and unbridled desires, so I gritted my teeth, straightened my shoulders, and forced myself to focus.

Maashi reached for my right hand, bent down, and kissed my palm. "Tamara," he said, "tell me what happened when you traveled here to Chitina."

That simple gesture showed he cared. Distracting a nervous patient was a familiar tactic. In some way he knew I was flustered and tried to help me relax. I lowered my eyes. His golden skin and the taut muscles of his chest through his half-open shirt beckoned to me. A strong urge to rest my head against him and bury myself in his arms entered my thoughts. I tore my gaze away.

I inhaled, cleared my throat, and said, "One morning, I walked to the back of my yard behind my house and saw a shiny circle. A mysterious force pulled me, and I fell in a bottomless hole. My chest was compressed so hard I fainted. I woke up on this world."

He listened to my explanation and pressed his lips on my palm once more before letting go of my hand. He waited for a moment and tilted his head. "It is possible you are a special Sheffrou. My people, the Chamranlinas, remind us often of old legends that describe how certain Sheffrous, called Ishk-ibu, possessed the capability to travel through space in gateways much like you described. They became key figures in our history, and some initiated major changes in Chamranlina society." He paused and leaned back on the wall behind him.

"The Ishkibu Sheffrous were the first to understand that Chamtali, our home world, was dying. A rogue planet located light-years away had produced a minor deviation of our planet's orbit and this simple change brought it closer to the sun. Over a short time of two hundred sequences, our planet became un-inhabitable. We searched for another world to sustain us. The Ishkibu were the ones who journeyed through gateways and guided us to this place we call Chitina. Without them we would have perished.

"Your presence here may be important, possibly vital. Per-haps you will play a significant role in our people's destiny. Because of this, Chamranlinas will always cherish and protect you."

I wanted to believe his fable, but it didn't ring true. He denied Chamranlinas had anything to do with my arrival here, yet he seemed to consider my presence as a good omen for his people.

I blurted out, "Your tale about those Sheffrous has nothing to do with me. I'm not a Chamranlina and I'm not convinced of your innocence. Perhaps your people tampered with something that caused my fall into the wormhole.

"Why should I go along with your plans? What is the pur-pose of this joining of the minds? You must understand all I want is to go back home. Nothing else."

He tilted his head backwards. His eyes grew bigger. His face and neck paled to a sickly alabaster color.

Emboldened by his reaction I stood upright on my knees with both hands clenched at my sides. "As for being a Sheffrou," I said, raising my voice, "I have no clue of what that is. All I know is I miss my family and my home, and I will find out what happened and go back with or without your help. Do you understand my words?"

I meant everything I said. I didn't want to let my unexplained attraction to him control me. My place was home with my children. The guilt for forgetting them in the last few days weighed on my mind.

Maashi sighed and bent his head down. He stared at his hands without uttering a word.

After a few minutes I couldn't stand the silence between us. I blurted out. "Well, don't you have anything to say?" I wanted to push him to reveal more, to tell me what he really knew.

He closed his eyes then opened them. "I know nothing more than what I have told you. I am very sorry."

I bit my lip. Was he telling the truth? Was this all? This meant my chances of going home were almost nonexistent. I wasn't ready to accept that.

"Yes," Maashi said, "that is all."

I sat back on my legs and stared at him, numb with his revelation, irritated by my outburst.

His blank face glistened under the pale light of the encounter room making him look sad and vulnerable.

He turned his head away, paused, then rose to leave.

"Wait," I swallowed, kept my eyes locked on him. "What about the meeting?"

"We do not have to proceed if you do not want to." Maashi's voice sounded grave, unrecognizable. His hands shook. "It can be done another time."

I hesitated. What if the Chamranlinas had nothing to do with my arrival on Chitina? If this were the case, there was no point in attacking Maashi. Instead, I should use him as an ally in my quest to return home. I should accept the meeting.

"Maashi," I said, "if this is important to you, I'll do it."

Maashi paused and looked at me. "You agree to the meeting?"

"Yes."

Maashi settled back on the rippling floor. His eyes gained some color, and a moment later, he said in a soft tone, "Let us start then."

Without saying a word, he undressed me, first my top, then my pants, then he waited until I removed my underwear.

I sat in silence, tense and ready to react if he hurt me.

Maashi held my face in his hands and his fingers slowly traced every feature. He repeated the same process over my scalp. Then he glided his fingers over my skin from the neck all the way down the back, the chest, breasts, and stomach. He observed and palpated each part of my body with care, finishing with the buttocks and legs. He looked at my genital area but didn't touch it.

I watched his every move. He proceeded in a thorough and rigorous manner as if he performed a medical evaluation. Admiration for the alien's detailed and complete examination gradually replaced my earlier apprehensions.

Maashi treated me with kindness and respect. I relaxed under his light probing and my fears dissipated.

After he completed his part of the meeting, he removed his clothes, keeping only a piece of clothing covering the area between his legs. He placed my hand on his upper arm signaling me to start.

I proceeded with my exam step by step, senses on alert, very much aware of his fragrant body. I pressed on his shoulders, which were well-developed, firm but supple like a competitive swimmer. A delicate teardrop pattern started on each shoulder and cascaded down his back creating two wide bands of silver that joined right above his buttocks. The skin on his back was warm, but thick and smooth, almost like rubber.

His oval-shaped face sported a prominent brow instead of eyebrows which gave him an alien expression. He had two big almond eyes shaded by long light-brown eyelashes on his upper eyelid. His nose was small and flat, but with two distinct nostrils. His chestnut hair was short, coarse, but soft and wavy and his body appeared to be hairless. He had round ears, positioned on each side of his head, reminding me of seal ears. I saw no unusual appendages on his neck or elsewhere.

His wide chest exhibited a striking gold design like a complex Chinese character in the upper middle section and his crescent-shaped breasts were well-formed with oval nipples. The pale golden skin on his chest felt soft as a kid glove. His arms reached well below his thighs, and he had wide hands equipped with three long slim fingers and a shorter thumb.

I was surprised to palpate a beating heart in his abdomen in the same vicinity where I would've expected to see the umbilicus. The lower pelvis and genital area were enclosed in a thick stretchy underwear. Maashi didn't offer to remove it, and I refrained from asking him to do so.

He had sculpted muscular legs with wide feet and palmed toes. There were no fingernails and toenails, but the tops of his fingers and toes were hard, and the pad underneath pleasantly soft. The overall impression was of a tall, perfectly proportioned body which oozed strength and power, but also elegance and nobility.

I backed away and slipped my clothes on. My curiosity wasn't satisfied, however. I needed to confirm something. "Maashi," I said, "you're a male, right?"

He gave me a quizzical look then smiled and said, "I am Sheffrou. We, Chamranlinas, have three genders: male, female, and Sheffrou."

"Oh." I stared at the diamond pattern on the wall. I couldn't recall any species on Earth which possessed three genders as adults except insects. Bees had a queen, males and drones.

Maashi didn't seem concerned by my reaction.

"I am aware most species have only two genders, so I understand that for you, this is unusual."

"So," I asked, "are you both male and female?"

"I am a male. Sheffrous are generally male, but in rare circumstances may be female. They have special attributes and behave differently."

"Why did you say earlier I was a Sheffrou?"

"You appear to have Sheffrou qualities."

I winced in disbelief.

"Do not worry yourself with this. It is not important right now."

Maashi pulled me close and kissed my palms. I cringed. He reached for my mouth and emitted soothing clicking sounds which had an immediate calming effect on me. He pressed his lips against mine and I tasted his saliva. Pleasure oozed in me and the aroma of warm caramel invaded my mind.

Within seconds I flew to a wonderful and safe place. Light as a feather, I floated over a vast blue ocean, rocked by gentle waves. I closed my eyes and the calming illusion erased all my apprehensions. Maashi held me for the longest time, clicking non-stop, and I melted in his embrace. I descended step by step in a deep slumber.

# Chapter 5

I gritted my teeth and stared at the empty lounge-chair across from where I was resting. Maashi would walk in my quarters any minute now because he came to visit every morning about this time, and I didn't want him to notice anything was amiss.

"Come on Tamara," I ordered my body, "sit up." What would have been, in normal circumstances, a simple process was an almost insurmountable task this morning. My legs were stiff, my bones ached, and my queasy stomach growled. With my sleeve I wiped the sweat beading on my temples.

I heard the familiar swoosh of the door and Maashi appeared. He strolled in wearing a simple blue shirt with khaki pants and sash. "Good morning Tamara," he said in a casual tone.

"Good morning," I said, avoiding eye contact.

Maashi sat on the lounge-chair opposite mine, leaned back on a giant size gold cushion, and positioned his long legs in front of him. "How are you today?" he said.

"I'm a little tired," I said, "I think I'll just stay here and rest for a while." I put my arm around my abdomen to suppress a sudden sharp cramp and stared at his open-toed sandals a couple of feet away from me. My husband had always refused to wear casual footwear like that.

Maashi bent his head down and spread his hands on his knees. "You're tense," he said, concentrating his gaze on his fingers, "your stomach is making noises. Do you need to eat?"

"I would like a fruit," I said, ignoring the nausea.

Maashi provided three by pressing controls on the floor.

If I stayed here long enough, I might learn how to do that.

"Thanks." I took the fruits, one light orange and fragrant, the other two, firm and lime green. "I'll eat them later. I want to relax and write on my pad." I picked up the device ignoring the tearing pain below my right knee and pretended to position myself to write.

He turned his head the other way as if having to watch me eat was offensive and said, "I'll leave and let you eat in private."

"That's fine" I said, relieved to see he wasn't planning to stay, "I'll see you later."

"Yes, later." He stretched in his feline way, stood in one swift movement, and left.

Good. Just in time. A stabbing cramp folded my weak frame in two. I clenched my teeth, took deep breaths, and waited for the searing pain to pass. I pushed with both hands on the couch to get upright. I wobbled over to the water room around twenty steps away. After several bouts of diarrhea, I walked back towards the receiving room only to turn around and head for the restroom as fast as I could to throw up. I vomited once more, and my legs buckled under me.

I sat, exhausted, on the hard granite floor. The vomiting and diarrhea had subsided. I removed my pants and top and sent the soiled clothes to the recycling chute. I had learned the first day that all you needed to do to get a new identical set of clothing was press a control button on the wall.

I put a new top on and examined my right leg. The cuts on the leg looked superficial except one which appeared angry and red. The whole leg throbbed from the knee to the heel. I hoped that ingestion of contaminated food caused my current gastro-intestinal problems and not the infected cut. I cleansed it and wrapped it in a small piece of cloth but in this alien environment, any infection might produce unexpected symptoms and spread throughout the body in a short time.

I didn't want Maashi to know what I had done. As far as I knew my escapade in the tunnels last night had gone unnoticed. I had planned it since our arrival to this place. Had it not been for my unfortunate fall around a slippery turn and a subsequent gash on my leg, I might still be out there. I knew it was foolhardy to leave and search for a way back by myself, but I had to do something. I was determined to go home. It wasn't in my nature to sit and wait for things to happen. After all, what proof did I have that those aliens were really searching for the wormhole?

With a heavy heart after an exhausting trek, I had to abandon my search. Angry tears had flooded my eyes and wet my cheeks. With just a little luck I could have reached the place where I had arrived in this world and found that damned gateway.

The vomiting resumed with a vengeance. Afterwards, I sat on the floor, weak and disheveled. My shirt, damp with sweat, clung to my skin. My hair smelled of spoiled milk. The bitter taste on my tongue lingered even though I rinsed my mouth several times. The room danced before me. I hated to feel helpless, and I knew I needed intravenous fluids and potassium. My condition was worsening. I couldn't keep anything down.

I closed my eyes and struggled to my feet. With small steps I went back to the receiving room. I wanted to rest and sleep, but the cramps were merciless and the pain intolerable. I surrendered and pressed the controls on the floor to call Maashi. After a few seconds I pressed again.

I saw Maashi's long legs amble in the room. My vision blurred, and gray clouds filled my thoughts.

"I'm sick," I mumbled, "I need your help."

I crumpled backward and sensed, rather than felt, his arms lifting me with care.

Later, I came to. I was lying on a smooth rubbery surface. The smell of wild clover tickled my nostrils. As a child I used to play and roll with my brother in its fragrant green carpet when we visited my grandparents' cottage in the country. My fingers tapped on the rubbery surface and to my surprise, it moved. I blinked and looked up. I was resting on Maashi, my head on his chest. I licked my lips with my tongue and resisted the sudden urge to kiss his skin.

His alien eyes were the color of warm amber. His voice was grave and concerned. "Are you feeling better?"

I felt as if I had awakened after a long restful sleep. I moved my limbs one by one. "Yes," I said.

He sat up and held me close. "I am pleased you're better."

"What's going on with me?" I said, noticing for the first time how Maashi's chest didn't expand much with each breath. "My stomach feels bloated."

"You were unwell," Maashi explained, "we had to put an onumdum in your abdomen."

"A what?" I let out a mean burp and covered my mouth.

"Something to provide you with fluids and readjust your electrolytes at the cellular level."

My mind flashed with alarm.

What did he do?

I said, "How did you put it in? Is it a kind of device?"

"We made a small opening here," he pointed to a half-inch below my navel, "and inserted it in. It will grow and adjust to the size of your abdomen."

My brain was still foggy although I felt good, and it took a minute to process what he said. I looked down at my stomach and didn't see any cut. "What is it? You said it'll grow. Is it alive?"

"Yes."

A cold chill went up my spine and I slipped away out of Maashi's arms.

"Is it still in there?"

Maashi nodded, "Yes."

"Are you going to remove it?"

"We need not remove it." He folded his arms on his chest. "Your body will gradually dissolve the onumdum."

Good! I didn't like having some strange live thing in my stomach. "How long will that take?"

"As long as needed."

"What exactly is an onumdum?"

Maashi responded in an even tone but his eyes were shiny and larger than usual. Did he think my misfortune was funny? "It's a unicellular organism with a thin membranous body containing a large amount of what you call electrolytes."

I had a creature in my body. "How does it know what to do? When you say dissolve, do you mean I will kill the thing?"

"It will remain in your abdomen as a much smaller entity and grow as needed to protect you against further bowel problems."

I coughed to hide my uneasiness. What a remarkable little creature. Using a live organism to treat a medical condition was not unheard of, as with leeches, but some patients were quite uncomfortable with this approach. I guessed I was part of the latter group. I grimaced. "How big was it when you put it in?"

"Big enough to expand and coat your entire abdominal cavity with its membrane."

"Oh." I swallowed and suppressed a burp. I was grateful for the clover smell. "Thank you for treating me."

Maashi's expression softened. "Thank the onumdum."

I nodded. "What about the wild clover smell?"

"We inserted a small onumdum in your mouth to make the bitterness disappear."

Another one. "Where is it now?"

He bent his head sideways and chuckled. "Most likely you swallowed it and it will settle somewhere in your gut."

"Right."

Maashi leaned way back on the couch and crossed his arms. Perhaps he found all this amusing.

"As for your leg," he said, in a more serious tone, "it's almost healed."

I pulled my pants up and sure enough the larger cut was barely noticeable. The others had disappeared. I opened my mouth to say ask him how they had healed in such a short time but Maashi added, "I must leave now. You may eat fruit. Keep the meal light." He pressed a control again and a large tray of colorful fruit appeared.

I stared at the tray loaded with food. It reminded me of my relatives on Earth. In my family a lot of food equaled a lot of love.

I watched him get up without saying a word.

The door opened when he approached it and I saw a guard standing outside.

Maashi turned his head and said, "The tunnels are dangerous. The guard is here to protect you. No more wandering in the tunnels without supervision." He shot me a sideway glance and left.

# Chapter 6

When I was a teenager, I used to think I had been born in the wrong century. I watched sci-fi shows on television and my greatest wish was to travel in space and live in the future. Now my reality was all I wished for and none of it was what I had envisioned.

Weeks had gone by without any information about the wormhole. My hopes for a swift return to Earth faded with each passing day. I avoided thinking about my former life because I was crushed with sadness when I did. Memories of special occasions spent with my children, like birthdays and Mother's Day brought tears to my eyes. If I didn't return soon, I would miss my son David's engagement scheduled for July this year, and this fact alone hurt terribly. I had not attended his graduation ceremony after college because of work and poor planning on my part, and I still harbored tremendous guilt about it.

I spent hours working on the little pad Maashi gave me. I wrote any tidbit of information he passed along about the search for the wormhole but apart from retracing my steps to the exact location where I appeared; the Chamranlinas had found no evidence of a gateway to my world.

To keep my spirits up, I jotted down all I could remember about my family, my house, and everything I loved about Earth. I drew animals, plants, and places. I had to laugh at a few ridiculous-looking sketches, but this was a simple and effective way to hang on to my world and my sanity.

Maashi stepped in my quarters one morning just as I woke up.

"How are you today, little one?" he said.

He liked to call me that. I had lost weight, about twenty pounds, since my arrival on Chitina. My stomach was a lot flatter and my legs thinner. "I'm okay," I said, even though I was irritated and teary-eyed and struggled to keep my composure in his presence. "Any news about the wormhole?"

"We haven't found any clues about its location. The team is widening the search area."

I sighed, sat up, and rubbed my eyes.

"I've made some plans," he said, "today we'll go to a different section for a swim. My men will accompany us."

Swimming? Where? I hadn't seen any water at all. Aloud I said, "Why do you always need your men?"

"Sheffrous need men to protect them against attacks by our enemies. They work together as a team and accompany me wherever I go."

The enemies again. "Are you at war?" I asked.

With his eyes half-closed, Maashi paused before answering, as if considering this for the first time. "Yes, I guess you could call it war."

"Who are they? What do they want?"

"They're aliens from another world. We call them the Krakoran, it means the Untouchable." Maashi's brow darkened, his eyes became small slits, and to my astonishment, he hissed his displeasure.

His reaction was so intense I didn't press the subject further. I sensed there was a much bigger story, one he wasn't ready to divulge.

Maashi stared into nothingness for a few seconds as if lost in thought then said, "Come, Tamara. Now is a good time to go. There is a vast cave with deep water not far from this section. It's a popular gathering place. You do know how to swim, don't you?"

I frowned and said, "I do. But I'm not a good swimmer." My fingers rubbed the back of my neck where the hair was standing on ends. "I think I'll just stay here." On Earth, I would've jumped at the opportunity to do something different, but I was on Chitina and swimming with an alien wasn't a tempting activity.

Maashi was undeterred. "Don't worry Tamara. I'll make sure you're safe. The exercise will be good for you."

Not convinced, I tried another excuse. "I need a bathing suit. I definitely can't go swimming without one." I folded my arms across my chest.

Maashi turned around and pressed on a few colored buttons on the wall. A two-piece garment appeared on the couch beside me. It was a gorgeous turquoise two-piece suit with a gold border. The top was like a fitted T-shirt, and the bottom was a boxer short. It looked exactly my size.

"Tamara, go and change your clothing. I'll come and pick you up later."

I was so annoyed by the fact that I would have to go swimming after all, I blurted out, "Exactly when is later? You guys can be so confusing. You don't eat at regular hours, and you seem to sleep very little. As a matter of fact, I haven't seen *you* eat at all. You have to understand the lack of a regular schedule is difficult to deal with." I stood and took one step toward him. "I don't function well if I don't maintain a routine, especially if I don't get enough sleep." I stopped to catch my breath. I hadn't realized until now how strongly I missed my Earth habits.

Maashi's eyes widened. "Chamranlinas deal with time differently," he said, "we live underground in caves and tunnels, so keeping time has become inconsequential. Our daytime is set by the sun, but we don't have a specific time to eat, sleep or do activities." He added, "Forgive me for not noticing this is important for you. I'll make sure you have access to food when you need it, and that you're able to sleep as long as you find it necessary."

A Chamranlina walked in wearing a gray outfit with an olive-green sash. I had seen him before when I first arrived and occasionally when he stood guard in Maashi's quarters. He had a crew cut and a long bony face. "This is Lado," Maashi said. "He is my chowli, my companion. He's also my feeder and my guardian."

His personal guard and his own personal chef. Nice. I wondered if Maashi ate the same food I ate or if he was served a different type of food. I sighed. What wouldn't I give to have a steak dinner with a loaded baked potato and chocolate cake for dessert after days and days of puddings!

Lado stood at least a foot taller than Maashi with probing dark brown eyes. His hands were larger and wider than any other I had ever seen. He took my hand with two fingers. "It is a pleasure," he said, and bent down and kissed my palm.

Such a formal greeting, like one you would expect from an official representative. I answered with a simple "Hello."

"If you require assistance and I'm not available," Maashi said, "ask for Lado. I must leave now. I'll be back later." He added, with a small grin, "In about two Earth hours."

We had a discussion a few days before about how the Chamranlinas measured time. After studying my watch, which had been recuperated from the surface, they understood how we measured time. They explained to me that their day, or one rotation of their planet, was the equivalent of 26 hours with 66 minutes per hour if calculated in my time.

True to his word, Maashi was back two hours later. He brought someone new with him.

"Tamara, this is my friend Choban. He's a Sheffrou like me. He'll come and swim with us." Maashi stood close to this new Chamranlina, keeping an arm around his waist.

Choban had honey-colored eyes and a kind expression. He was the same height as Maashi, but thinner. He moved slowly and gracefully as he came closer to greet me. "It is a pleasure to see you. Maashi told me much about you."

"How do you do?" I answered.

His leathery face was much more wrinkled than Maashi's. His hair was streaked with gold and silver strands. I wondered if this was a sign of aging like us humans.

"Shall we go?" Maashi picked me up, and we left, all three of us followed by Lado, with the other guards staying close behind.

On our way to the pool Maashi said, "Your living quarters are adjacent to mine, both in the innermost section of the Central Compound to ensure our safety. Other sections located closer to the perimeter open into big caves, some with deep pools and swift underwater currents. The pool where we will swim today is large with a shallow end suitable for you."

"Sir," Lado said, "we should travel under the central dome through the greenhouse. It is a safer route."

Maashi agreed. "I haven't been there in several weeks. It should be a pleasant stroll."

The tunnel soon opened wide into a large area covered by a translucent dome about four stories high. The warm humid air overwhelmed our senses as we stepped in. Maashi set me down to walk beside him on the trail covered with flat pebbles. I had the impression of being in a giant tropical garden. Intoxicating perfumes mixed with the odor of the rich soil. Trees heavily laden with fruit mingled with flowering shrubs and other plants grew in hydroponic containers. There were many paths crisscrossing through and numerous workers, some watering and tending the plants, others collected dead leaves and wilted flowers and put them in big containers, possibly compost bins.

"This is where you grow your food." I said, observing the workers with interest. Each one wore a sash with several colors, with brown as the dominant one.

"Yes," said Maashi, "we have six domes like this one. They were designed and constructed two hundred sequences ago by our ancestors and since then we have been growing many varieties of plants for our enjoyment and our consumption."

"I see you recycle the organic matter in those bins. . . " I stopped mid-sentence. One of the workers, his face streaked with dark green and orange markings, stepped in Maashi's path. He shot us a hateful stare and yelled, "No more Sheffrous. Give us back our right to mate." He hissed loudly and spat on the ground in front of Maashi, missing his foot by an inch.

The worker's eyes thinned to black slits and he tilted his head backward to spit again.

Lado immediately positioned himself between the worker and Maashi. The worker fired a series of loud clicks. Lado barked harsh clicks and blocked his way.

Maashi kept his distance and ignored the worker's posturing. He said in an even tone, "Let's continue through this way." He marched on, chose another path parallel to the first one and everyone followed. Maashi's brow darkened and his eyes thinned. He didn't utter another word all the way to the pool.

It seemed Maashi had alien enemies and some among his own people.

The guards retreated closer to the Sheffrou and we continued our route through the dome. Even though we traveled without any further incident, I sensed Maashi's displeasure. He kept a brisk pace and stared straight ahead without uttering another word until we reached our destination.

After walking along several wide halls, the path connected us to a tunnel which soon turned sharply to the left. We arrived in a spacious open area in front of an Olympic-size pool. I looked up at the five-story high ceiling and the sharp rugged walls. I remembered the scent of wet soil from our recent trek from the mines to the compound, but this time the odor of fresh spring water dominated. A thundering roar which reminded me of rapids, or a waterfall resonated from the far left.

Large white globes about three feet in diameter lighted the cave. They floated freely in mid-air and produced a soft glow reminiscent of moonlight and made the tea-colored water sparkle as if sprinkled with glitter.

The water was shallow and clear close to the edge but swiftly changed to dark cocoa. The hair on the back of my neck stood on ends. I was used to pools where you could see the bottom even in the deep end. I felt uneasy and kept at least two yards between me and the edge.

There were several Chamranlinas present. A few wore something reminiscent of boxer shorts, but most wore nothing at all. Like Maashi, they were hairless, except for the hair on their heads. There were no females. The males appeared to have genitals like human males but bigger.

Right away we were greeted by a friendly and affectionate crowd. The Chamranlinas hugged both Sheffrous affectionately. They kissed their shoulders and their necks, all the while clicking loudly and glancing curiously at me. Some of them tried to come and touch me, but the guards emitted sharp clicks and prevented any contact.

Maashi removed his shirt and pants keeping his rubberlike underwear on. "Tamara, I will go for a quick swim. Choban will stay with you."

Before I could say anything, he slipped in the water, and dove in about thirty feet away. Lado followed right behind. Several other Chamranlinas ran and rapidly jumped in unison in the dark water. The teardrop patterns on their backs shone and created a silver streak under the pale light. Maashi swam effortlessly, gathering impressive speed with the agility of a dolphin. He quickly distanced the other swimmers. I admired his ability to remain submerged for minutes at a time then breach above the surface and plunge deep without any apparent effort. These aliens possessed the agility and grace of beings that had evolved in a watery environment. As I stood motionless, a soft musical voice beside me said, "Tamara, would you like to go in?"

"I'm not a good swimmer Choban," I said with a nervous chuckle, "I think I'll stay right here for now. What is that loud rumbling I hear coming from over there?" I said and pointed to the other end of the immense pool.

"That is the Gorganna gorge. This pool drops sharply into a narrow tunnel that joins it to another large pool a hundred feet deeper. Young Chamranlinas often dare each other to dive in the waterfall. In fact, only experienced swimmers can negotiate it without injury."

Maashi swam back toward us. He called to me, "Come, Tamara. Come with me in the water."

I shook my head. "I don't know," I said warily, "Are there any fish? I'm not sure I should go."

"Come, it's safe here. There are no fish." he said.

Close to the edge, the water was tempting. "Maybe I can swim right here in the shallow part."

"Yes, swim right here. It'll be fine for you."

Why not try?

"Okay, then. I'm coming." I entered slowly. The sudden coolness gave me goose bumps. I swam a few yards, staying in an area no more than four feet deep. I gradually relaxed and began to enjoy myself. "This is not bad, not bad at all."

Choban removed his clothes, kept his underwear like Maashi, and joined us in the water. He crossed to the other side of the pool in just a few long strokes. A moment later he was right back beside me.

"I am pleased to see you like the water," Choban said in his melodic voice.

"This is a really big pool," I said, "It takes some getting used to, but I admit I like it." I turned my head to look at him, and realized he possessed a second eyelid which automatically closed underwater. I exclaimed, "You have a second eyelid, like a crocodile."

Choban erupted in laughter, and the high-pitched sound echoed all over the pool. He floated toward me and said mockingly, "I am not sure what a crocodile is, but the way you said it did not sound very flattering."

I couldn't help but laugh as well.

Maashi chuckled, "At last, you look much better." He swam away and said, "Enjoy yourself. I'll be back later."

"Tamara, did Maashi tell you we come from another realm called Chamtali?"

"Yes. He said you had to leave that planet."

"Chamtali was our mother world. Although it was not as large as Chitina, vast bodies of water covered a third of its surface. The land bloomed year-round with luxuriant plants and fragrant flowers, and hundreds of species of animals lived there." He paused. "Chamranlinas used to spend a lot of time underwater over there, and that is why we developed certain adaptations like the second eyelid and palmed toes. In fact, to this day, all Chamranlinas love to swim and are perfectly at ease in the water."

"Earth has oceans that cover more than seventy percent of the surface," I said.

Choban continued his wishful reminiscing. "It was a most enchanting world. I have seen pictures of Chamtali and heard many stories from the old ones who heard them from others who had actually seen it."

The Chamranlinas had also traveled here. What were the odds of that happening?

"Choban, why did the worker in the greenhouse spit at Maashi that way?"

"Maashi is part of the elite. He is Sheffrou and is entitled to privileges not conferred to other classes of Chamranlinas like the Multicolors. Some of them are envious and use every opportunity to show their loathing."

"All the workers wore brown sashes mixed with other colors. Were they all Multicolors?"

"Yes, Tamara. Workers associated with the domes or general maintenance are all Multis."

"So," I said, "this means there are more of them than single color?"

Choban smiled. "The Unicolors are called Pure Colors and they form less than one tenth of the total population."

I stepped out of the water and stood shivering on the edge of the pool. Choban also came out. A fine mist formed all around him and within seconds he was completely dry.

"Impressive," I said, "How do you do that?"

"It is a simple process. We raise our body temperature and the water evaporates."

A new group of Chamranlinas, shorter and thinner but much noisier, entered the pool area. They pushed and shoved each other and laughed merrily as they played with a large shimmering ball that changed color every time someone touched it.

Some of them dove in the water, and soon it was a fantastic game of water-polo. The ball flew high in the air only to be caught and immediately launched back again. A few then swam across the pool in a flash of dazzling silver and gold to catch the ball.

"I love a game of chututu," Choban said. "Come this way. Let us get closer." Choban walked in their direction toward the deeper end of the pool and I followed right behind.

The ball flew over Choban's head, missing him by an inch. "Did you see that?" He erupted in a high-pitched laughter and waved his hand at the players. One of them ran out of the pool to retrieve the ball and the game continued in earnest.

The ball bounced back and forth over the water. I watched them play and sighed. I thought of my kids, David, Allison, and Jonathan, kicking and bouncing a soccer ball high in the air over a green field. They would run with such energy that their faces glowed with excitement. Where were they now?

My hands were turning blue, and I shook hard. "Choban, I want to leave now. Can you call Maashi?"

"Yes, sweet one. I will call him for you."

From the corner of my eye I saw a bright object coming right at me. I quickly ducked avoiding a direct hit but lost my balance and fell headfirst in the water.

I gasped, shocked by the icy cold of the deep end. Instinctively, I looked up, kicked my feet and started swimming toward the light but the current pulled me. When I reached the surface, I checked my position. I had drifted a few yards away from the edge. I gulped some air and swam towards Choban, but a strong undertow sucked me under. I started paddling furiously against it. I pushed as hard as I could, but the current pulled me deeper and deeper.

The light above faded with every stroke while I struggled to suppress the urge to breathe. My movements became sluggish. The cold water paralyzed my muscles. My legs cramped. My arms felt like lead.

I struggled with all my energy but soon darkness surrounded me. I was seized with fear when I realized fighting the current was useless. I opened my mouth to scream and swallowed large mouthfuls of water. Everything turned black. My mind raced, and precious memories flashed before my eyes: laughing and dancing with my children, holding hands with my husband, walking alone on the soft white sand of the beach.

Long arms grabbed me and brought me back to the light. I clung to my rescuer and held on with great effort to the little oxygen left in my lungs. At last my head was out of the water and I gulped life-giving air. I spat and choked and cried at the same time.

Maashi swam slowly to the edge of the pool then pulled out of the water, holding me securely against his chest. He made soft sounds and said, "You're safe, Tamara. You're safe."

I shook hard both from the fear and the cold water. My teeth were clattering. A crowd of Chamranlinas gathered around wide-eyed. They surrounded us, waved their arms up and down and clicked wildly.

I glanced at them and crossed my arms in front of my chest. "Maashi, what's wrong with them?" I said between bouts of coughing. "Why are they behaving this way?"

Choban answered. "The young ones have just now figured out you are female. They have never seen a female up close before."

"What do you mean?" I had just finished my question when one of them slid his hand and reached between my legs. I cried out, shoved his hand away, and closed my legs tightly moving out of his reach.

Maashi clicked at the others and held me protectively against him. "They mean no harm, Tamara," he said. "Don't be alarmed."

The guards approached and positioned themselves between the three of us and the young Chamranlinas and fired warning clicks.

Maashi took a small piece of material the size of a credit card from one of the guards. It rapidly expanded into a warm fuzzy bath size towel, and he covered me with it. He signaled to Choban and said, "We must go back."

I let out a sigh of relief. I was glad to leave. I certainly wasn't coming back to this dreadful place any time soon.

We arrived in Maashi's quarters, and he ushered me right away into the encounter room. "Please remove your wet clothes," he said. "I'll get you some dry ones."

I removed my bathing suit and wrapped myself in the towel. Maashi put his arms around my waist and pulled me close to his warm body. A light aroma floated around him like a delicate perfume. He kissed my neck, pressing his cheek against mine.

I gently pushed him away. "Maashi," I reminded him, "you were going to get me dry clothes."

"Yes, Tamara, I will." He took my head in his hands and let his fingers run through my hair. "You have such different hair. I have never seen any quite like it. It's long, shiny, and quite an unusual color." He gently massaged my scalp and his warm fingers glided through my hair and dried it as he said this.

"It's called auburn. The color is called auburn," I whispered. I closed my eyes, unable to resist the gentle touch of his fingers. It was such a wonderful sensation. Safe and warm, I hesitated to move, fearful of disturbing this tranquil moment.

His mouth brushed gently against my lips, once, twice. I remained still, mesmerized, waiting. He pressed his mouth over mine and all the while continued to caress my head. A sweet wave of pleasure rushed over me. The smooth taste of caramel overwhelmed my senses.

I floated, light as air, delicate as a translucent soap bubble. The sensation was so extraordinarily delicious that I was swept away in pure bliss. Then the bubble burst and dissolved in a million tiny pieces and my whole being melted from the exquisite sensation.

I rested unmoving in Maashi's arms, savoring the wave of pleasure. Maashi released me, but I was still under his spell. Calm, lightheaded, I released any lingering tension from my body.

Maashi said gently, "You are precious, little one."

I inhaled a slow deep breath. My head clear at last I said. "Maashi, what did Choban mean when he said the young Chamranlinas had never seen a female up close before?"

"Only a few females or Fanellas, as we call them, remain. The males outnumber them 1,000 to 1. They live together in four closely guarded compounds. These youngsters had probably never seen a female at all."

"That's strange," I yawned, suddenly overcome with a strong urge to sleep. The pressure of the day slipped away, and I couldn't keep my eyes open. "By the way, Maashi, Chamranlina is a long word. Can I just say Chami instead?"

Maashi chuckled, "It is acceptable if it's easier for you."

"Good." I opened my eyes for a second. "Maashi," I whispered.

"Yes, Tamara."

"Thank you for saving my life."

Maashi caressed my cheek. "I'm terribly sorry," he said, "about what happened at the pool. The waterfall creates an undertow which can exert a strong downward pull. Chamranlinas can easily overcome the current but this is impossible for you. I'll be more vigilant next time and that won't happen again."

He gave me a final sweet kiss on the forehead. I thought about the young Chamis and how they had never seen a female up close. My daughter would have thought that was very strange.

# Chapter 7

I woke up with a start. Diffuse light emanated from the lower part of the walls and bathed my receiving room in a quiet glow. A guard standing at the door was staring at me.

I looked down and shrieked. I was totally naked. How did this happen?

I grabbed the towel lying in a heap beside the bed, flew off the couch, and ran down the hall.

I fumbled to get in the water room, closed the door behind me and set the lock. My heart pounded in my chest.

Focus. Take a deep breath.

I listened and didn't hear footsteps. Good.

Hot with anger, minutes passed before I calmed my nerves. I stood there and contemplated my next move. In my haste to get away from the guard's inquisitive stare, I forgot I could summon a set of clothes by pressing a simple control button on the wall.

My level of frustration had increased since my arrival on Chitina four weeks ago. Step by step, I adapted to their customs, but the Chamis couldn't understand mine. Modesty, an important distinctive feature of human culture, didn't exist in the Chami world. Also, a regular schedule wasn't a priority. Worst of all, the lack of progress in the search for the wormhole didn't appear to trouble Maashi. Today, I would demand answers.

A slight knock on the door startled me. It opened a few inches, and I heard a familiar voice.

"Tamara," Maashi said, "Go in your receiving room. I'll be waiting there."

I peered through the small opening. "This door locks from the inside. How did you open it?"

"I can unlock any closed space by touching it with my palm."

I muttered to myself. That alien would have been a successful magician on Earth.

I tied the fuzzy towel with a secure knot, stepped out, scanned the hall to make sure there was no one else, and trotted to my bedroom.

Maashi sat a few feet away from the bed on a couch overflowing with gold cushions, a couch that didn't exist before I walked in. With his back leaning against a plush pillow, arms folded in front of him, he waited.

Irritated, I pointed to the couch. "How do you make furniture appear like that?"

The corners of his mouth stretched in a little smile. "All basic items have been selected and scanned by the computer and any one requested will materialize within seconds."

I raised my eyebrows. "You must show me how to do that."

"In due time."

I tightened the towel around my waist. "How did you know I was in the water room?"

"I asked the guard."

"Am I under surveillance?"

"Yes, for your safety."

I changed the subject. "Anything new about the wormhole?"

"The search has been unsuccessful so far."

"Has anyone traveled through a wormhole before?"

"We never saw an alien appear on Chitina the way you did."

I frowned. "Do the guards understand what it looks like?"

"I have given them the appropriate information. If the gateway is still there, they'll find it."

I sat on the opposite couch and sighed.

"Come, Tamara."

The command annoyed me. He sat with one arm outstretched, expecting me.

I dillydallied toward him, intimidated by my state of undress. "I should get dressed. I can't walk in the nude like that."

"In a moment."

"Maashi," I glared at him. "I'm not in the mood for games."

He had something planned and it was obvious he was accustomed to having his own way. That reminded me of my husband Nate and how stubborn and abrasive he could be.

I stepped closer, folded my arms against my chest, and sat on his right.

"How are you today Tamara?" he said in a low soothing voice.

"I'm not happy this morning," I answered. "I don't like to have my privacy invaded this way."

"You have made this clear." He leaned down to my level and kissed my shoulder.

My heart fluttered. I nudged him away. How could his presence stir me so?

Maashi rested his palm on my lower back and brushed my neck with moist lips. I shuddered. A delightful prickling sensation spread in between my legs to my lower abdomen.

My mind reeled with bewilderment. Nate's hands used to be the ones caressing my skin and only his demanding lips searched for mine. I shuddered as I recalled our first years together. We were so happy and carefree. What happened to us? Why did we drift apart?

I inhaled Maashi's pungent scent and wild wishes raced in my usual sensible mind. I imagined the alien touching me, kissing me everywhere. I wanted to feel him inside me.

Shocking. Ridiculous.

I shuddered and fought to dispel the disturbing thoughts.

His brow darkened, and he observed me with questioning eyes as if searching for answers in my own. With his left hand he reached under my chin and tilted my head.

"Look at me, little one. Don't be frightened." He added in a whisper, "I sense your needs. I know you haven't been pleasured in a long time."

Torn between fear and lust, my will to resist faded with every second. Hunger from deep within grew and threatened to take control. I sat limp in his hands, powerless against his fragrant embrace, the power of his presence.

Maashi bent over and with his smooth tongue licked my lips. As if hypnotized by an invisible force, I couldn't refuse him. Our lips parted, and his luscious tongue glided in and caressed mine. Weak with desire, I melted in a warm puddle. He backed away, leaving me breathless and wanting.

He put his arm around my shoulders, hugged me close. I whimpered like a child. My cheeks burned, and my insides shook. My mouth, so dry a few minutes ago, salivated at the thought of his touch.

For a short instant, I pushed his arm away with my hands.

"Hush, sweet one," he said.

Helpless, I abandoned all resistance.

Maashi pressed his lips on my forehead and his amber gaze drowned into mine. His fingers traced my eyebrows, cheeks, and jaw. He bent over and his lips brushed my cheeks, teasing me once, twice then he slid his tongue in my mouth.

I tasted his sweetness and my head spun. My feet lost contact with the ground. I moaned in delight.

He retreated a few inches and spoke in a voice soft as silk, "I see a wide blue sky with puffy white clouds, tall green plants, pink, and lavender flowers."

"Earth," I whispered. He bowed down and kissed me again, a long gentle kiss.

A warm creamy caramel taste lingered in my mouth. I put my hand on his chest to steady myself.

"I see," he paused, "a vast expanse of water shimmering under a gold sun. Like a great breathing beast, it sways back and forth on a long shore covered with sand."

His words brought a smile. "The ocean."

"Yes," he whispered. He raised his head and gazed into nothingness with wide clear eyes. "Four centuries ago, on Chamtali, our mother planet, we had an ocean such as this. The old ones still remember the tales of times past. A Chamranlina could swim for days in water so deep he never reached the bottom. On land, opulent perfumes from a multitude of exotic plants floated in the air under a pale lavender sky." He stopped. His voice was unrecognizable, filled with immense sadness. "The Chamtali we knew then is gone, scorched beyond recognition and covered with dust and ash. Colossal volcanic eruptions all over the surface destroyed it." He looked away. "Every Chamranlina grieves for his homeland."

He gazed at me and his brow softened. "Earth seems to be a wondrous place."

"It is." The thought of Earth filled my heart with joy. The desire so intense moments ago dissipated.

Maashi took my hand in his and said, "We are doing everything to find the gateway to your world. If it still exists, we will find it."

I nodded. I wanted to put my trust in him but part of me still doubted.

My stomach, silent until now, growled.

Maashi chuckled. "Would you like something to eat?"

"Yes," I said, "I also need to get dressed."

"Later."

I raised my arms to protest.

"First," he said, "you must eat." With just a few pushes on concealed buttons on the floor, several jars of pudding and a spoon materialized at my feet. I recognized them, the yellow which tasted lemony, the mango one, and my favorite, the tangerine.

I picked up the spoon and proceeded to eat.

He worked on a virtual screen by moving color coded diagrams from one area to another with the swipe of a single finger. He didn't glance in my direction until I was finished with the meal.

I ate until my hunger subsided. I was relieved for now from my wild desires. I drank a bottle of water with an oval opening and asked, "What are you doing?"

"My task consists of reviewing pertinent information on Chamranlinas I'll meet in the next few weeks."

Using my spoon, I pointed at the diagrams. "What are these colors for?"

"We call them speaking codes, like the ones you write on your little pad."

I nodded. "You mean like some kind of alphabet but based on color."

"Yes."

I chose another jar with a pink mixture containing pieces of fruit in it. I tasted it and savored its tartness. Nice change from the sweet puddings I had every day.

When I finished eating, he removed his shirt, and said, "Come with me. I want to show you a special place where I relax with my companions."

Both frustrated and intrigued, I followed his steps.

Maashi led me down the hallway through several doors. We arrived in an oval room dominated by a large pool surrounded by blue walls with undulating mosaics of waves and sea creatures. The water looked pristine, and I could see the bottom from yards away. Lights under the surface illuminated the pool with a soft white glow, creating the illusion of a blue lagoon in a tropical paradise.

He commanded, "Come swim with me."

Still naked under my towel, and apprehensive following my recent experience at the Gorganna gorge, I stopped in my tracks and my body turned to stone.

He ignored my qualms. "The current is gentle here. There's no danger." He lifted me and went in.

"Maashi," I said and gritted my teeth, "put me down." But contrary to my expectations, the water felt warm and the current nonexistent. After one powerful stroke, he set me free.

I turned and started back to the edge of the pool. Within seconds, the towel got completely soaked, clung to me like a second skin, and to my dismay, rapidly disintegrated, leaving me stark naked. I paddled away, hoping to keep some distance between us, but to no avail.

"Come," Maashi said. He took my arm and floated sideways with slow leg movements. He swam away, and the water glided over and under me. I gasped at the heavenly sensation. Despite or because of my jittery nerves, I started to giggle. We completed one full run and came right where we started.

"I am pleased to see you're enjoying the water." He reached over to a small shelf behind him and pressed it until a tall silver jar appeared.

Wary of a new scheme, I said, "What's that?"

Without answering, Maashi opened it, poured a white creamy substance and, still holding me with one hand, applied it on my face and forehead.

"Hey! What are you doing?" I lifted my arms up to remove it. As soon as I raised them, he put cream on my breasts and on my abdomen, spreading it as if applying sunscreen. It made my skin tingle, and I protested. "Maashi, stop. Stop it."

"This is good for your skin."

Before I knew it, he spread the lotion everywhere then raised me up high to lather my buttocks and lower limbs without forgetting a quick application between my thighs.

"Maashi," I yelled, "Why don't you listen?" I squirmed and wiggled to free myself. My skin became ultrasensitive, and the more I moved, the more it tingled. He rubbed and massaged my back and generated intense pleasure. I panted and screamed.

He stopped and held me close to his chest. "There, there, Tamara. Relax. Breathe."

The sensation subsided, and I dropped like a rag doll in his arms. He spread kisses all over my face. I moaned. My limbs refused to obey even though I fought to move them.

Maashi didn't appear concerned. He continued to arouse me with his hands reaching every inch of my body. With no means to refuse his relentless caresses, I became more and more aroused.

I sealed my eyes shut. Soft whimpers escaped my lips. I felt hot and dizzy, and my breathing deepened. Soon the familiar rush overpowered me. I climaxed and cried out and the high-pitched sounds echoed all over the pool.

Maashi cradled me and I rested on his soft chest.

Overwhelmed, embarrassed and angry, I lowered my head and waited until the intensity of my reaction lessened. I had never experienced this kind of wild outburst before.

He whispered in my ear, "Tamara, your cries and the passion you experienced are normal. I am Sheffrou. I exude pheromones which can increase your pleasure a thousand-fold."

He added, "Do not be troubled. These are my private quarters. No one can hear us or come in without my permission."

Speechless, I kept my eyes closed. A sense of calm and peace had replaced my frustration and fear, but I had crossed an invisible barrier. I never thought this extraordinary level of pleasure could occur on a different world, with a non-human.

I saw his shoulders relax, and he inhaled several times. An intense sweet aroma filled the air as he whispered in my ear, "Everything is okay, Chumpi."

"What did you say?" I asked, my voice barely audible.

"You are Chumpi." Maashi paused, as if relishing the word. "It means sweet one."

He had extinguished the fire in me. I nestled close in a semi-comatose state. He stepped out of the water and carried me to the bedroom. I tried to remain awake but in vain. He patted me dry, covered me with a fluffy throw, and laid down beside me. I drifted away in utter contentment.

# Chapter 8

Hours later, I woke up in my bedroom shocked by what happened at Maashi's pool. The alien had invaded my mind and sensed my most private thoughts and desires. I tried to quell my agitation. In a certain way, I could explain my attraction to Maashi; his charisma and gentle lovemaking combined with a sensual body made him hard to resist, but experiencing this level of pleasure, of total ecstasy was a new phenomenon. He had fulfilled my wildest dreams.

I had been in love years ago with my husband Nate but had never experienced this intensity of desire. Trepidation and fear rose in my heart. What if the Chamranlinas found the wormhole? What would happen between Nate and I if I went back home?

I thought of my children. I imagined them on the beach; Jonathan and David, surfing together in friendly competition, Allison, under the bright sun with her oversized pink hat, laughing at the seagulls. What if I never saw them again? What if I didn't go home? I was torn between wanting to return to my world and my hunger for Maashi. I had tasted the forbidden fruit and ached for more. With my fingers I wiped the hot tears that filled my eyes.

I heard something stirring behind me. I turned and saw Maashi sitting on a couch a few feet away, with oval eyes watching. He said, "How are you feeling Tamara?"

I turned my head away and sat up covered with the fluffy throw. This was too much. I suppressed a scream.

"Are you angry with me?" He came and sat beside me.

How should I answer that? I said between gritted teeth, "I don't know where to begin."

"Tamara," he said, "did you consider our intimate meeting unacceptable?" He paused.

"What you did was very upsetting," I said, raising my voice.

Maashi spread his hands in front of him. "Forgive me if I hurt you. My only goal was to pleasure you."

I fought to find an adequate answer before I lost all countenance. "If you think that because I felt . . ." I stopped, searching for the right word, but only one came to mind. "pleasure, what you did was okay, then you are mistaken."

"Tamara," he said in a gentle tone, "pleasure is a vital thing. Without it your life would soon become unbearable. You would lose your life energy and wither away."

I was overwrought with anguish. Did he believe that intense pleasure was a suitable remedy for my homesickness and feelings of loneliness? Did he think he could seduce me and then ignore how this tore me apart? I was desperate to return home to my children but returning home meant I would have to be apart from him and face my disintegrating relationship with my husband.

"There are many things more important in life than pleasure," I said and glared at him.

Maashi stated in a calm voice. "Life without pleasure is meaningless. What could be more important?"

"Well, in my world, pleasure isn't what's most important." I took a deep breath to clarify my thoughts and added, "On Earth, the will to survive is the driving force in humans and in all living creatures."

"I don't understand," Maashi said. "Are you under attack? Do you have enemies?"

"Yes," I answered. The conversation was taking an unexpected turn. "We have enemies. Nature can be harsh and destructive. For example, extremes of cold and heat, lack of water or flooding can cause havoc in our lives. Other humans can be deadly. Different countries fight against other countries, people killing each other."

"Kill?" Maashi straightened his shoulders. "Humans kill each other?"

"Yes," I said, "Humans kill other humans. They torture others and do all kinds of horrible things."

"Why do humans kill and torture others?" His face and neck had become ghostly pale, so much so that his color contrasted with the ivory markings on his upper chest.

"They kill each other for many reasons." I saw how upset he was and wanted to explain my statement. "There are more humans and fewer resources. The planet is already overpopulated; we are over seven billion and our numbers continue to increase."

"This is incomprehensible." Maashi blinked. "How can there be so many humans?" His eyes searched mine. "Are there many females on Earth?"

"Females make up fifty percent of the population, so I'd say, more than three billion."

Maashi bolted from his place as if struck by lightning. "I can't believe your words." He paced the length of the room, turned to face me, and raised his head high, "This can't be true. How can a weak and vulnerable species like yours be so prolific?"

His comments, delivered with so much emotion, shocked me. The Chamranlinas seemed to be intelligent, strong and technologically advanced, but Maashi's reaction indicated he was deeply troubled by this information. Was it because humans were so numerous, because they committed murder, or another reason?

"Humans must have special qualities that enable them to survive. Are there other species on your world who threaten humans?" He sat on a couch across from me and spread his hands on his knees.

"We have to deal with many species," I answered, "from the microscopic to the extremely large, some of which are harmful, even lethal."

He bent his head sideways. His eyes darkened. "Please define *deal*."

I sighed. This would be difficult. I needed to explain human behavior without making it sound as though we were mindless killers. "Humans are aggressive and can become violent. They will hunt any species that poses a serious threat until the threat is eliminated or their population reduced in such a way as to become insignificant."

Maashi stared at me. His eyes formed a thin line. "Humans hunt other species?"

I sensed his displeasure, his brow appeared much darker, his eyes had decreased to thin slits, so I explained with care. "Yes. Some humans hunt, a few raise livestock, others farm and grow crops. All humans strive to make a living. Earth has an incredible amount of natural resources, but everyone works hard to succeed."

"If I understand correctly, humans form the dominant species on your world?"

"Yes. With the help of technology, we've adapted to many living conditions and thrive in a variety of environments. In the last century, we have developed treatments against most infectious diseases that used to be deadly. We have made tremendous progress against other diseases like cancer and we are experiencing a population explosion. There are now serious concerns about overpopulation, depletion of natural resources, and pollution of the environment, not to mention global weather changes on our planet."

Maashi shook his head and said, "Your world differs completely from ours." He paused and stared at his empty hands. "We are facing tremendous obstacles just to keep our population stable. We have few females and most males are sterile. Although we are a peaceful race, we are under constant threat of attack by enemies who hunt us for their pleasure. Our numbers decrease every sequence, what you call a year.

"Even mating has become a difficult and complicated process and it is often unsuccessful." Those were his last words. His voice broke and he stared into nothingness. His face grew pale and his eyes shone with tears. He looked away, rose, dragged his tall frame across the room, and left.

I sat there stunned. Maashi had never looked so distraught. Something was very wrong with the Chamis.

# Chapter 9

Days later, Maashi's sector buzzed with activity. The Chamis increased the intensity of the light throughout the section and remodeled the receiving rooms by adjusting their length and width to create new spacious areas. Furniture appeared out of thin air, single or double lounge-chairs with an abundance of cushions representing the color theme of the day. The guards brought in oversized banners, posted them along the walls, added small crescent-shaped tables, and created a new decor. The Chamis clicked non-stop and burst out laughing for no apparent reason. In this bubbly, exuberant mood, they touched, kissed, and hugged each other even more.

Unfamiliar faces visited and appraised the transformed quarters with lengthy streams of clicks. Newcomers mobbed Maashi; they patted him, rubbed his back, or kissed his shoulders and his neck. Maashi hugged them back and kissed their cheeks.

A group of smaller and slender individuals, wearing a light green, turquoise, purple or pink sash, invaded the main receiving room. High-spirited and energetic, they laughed, played, and teased each other non-stop.

Intrigued by their unicolor sashes and their boundless exuberance. I asked Maashi, "Who are they?"

Maashi's eyes brightened, "They are immature Pure Colors from a sector to the north, no older than thirty sequences therefore not having reached adulthood. The ones wearing a turquoise sash have the potential to become Sheffrou. All of them will require a skilled mentor to reach full maturity."

With a small grin he added, "This is the first time they have received an invitation to attend the events preceding the Great Eclipse celebration, and they are overjoyed to be part of the festivities. It's also an opportunity for them to mingle and find a mature sawisha willing to serve as a mentor."

My interest was piqued. "A celebration? What are you celebrating?"

"Once every sequence or year, our two moons align in front of the sun and this event plunges Chitina in total darkness for hours. We call this the Great Eclipse and it is the first day of the season of renewal. According to tradition, we emphasize this celestial occurrence by holding competitions between the compounds: wrestling, swimming, and shoshan races. Those competitions promote a sense of unity and solidarity among the Pure Colors and the Multicolors. Indeed, the Chamranlinas can't wait to attend the most elaborate and meaningful gathering of the whole sequence."

"Spring. The new year. I love that." I observed the young Chamis. They stood apart from the adults and steered clear of the Sawishas and Maashi in particular. "Those Chamis didn't greet you and kiss your shoulders like the others."

Maashi's brow softened. "They are inquisitive and hover close but don't dare touch me. I intimidate them. Being here with the Pure Colors is an exhilarating experience for them."

"Are they intimidated because you're a Sheffrou?" I smiled. "By the way, I love your outfit today, such a striking attire:

an ivory shirt with gold embroidery and impeccable dove gray trousers with a wide royal blue sash."

Maashi chuckled. "I am considered an important Sheffrou Tamara, part of the elite as all the Sawishas, the Pure Colors. You will see them at the shoshan race."

"What kind of race? When is it?"

"We have several important events scheduled in the next few weeks," Maashi said. "The first one is the shoshan race. Let me show you a picture of the animals." Maashi sat on a couch close by and signaled me to sit beside him. He flicked his fingers and a virtual computer appeared and hovered a foot in front of us. "Shoshans are swift and agile quadrupeds. Only the Sawishas and the Sheffrous may ride them. Look."

The 3D picture showed an animal that resembled an antelope, but bigger and taller, with a full mane and a tail. It was a beautiful caramel color, had a splash of cream across its belly and a wide chocolate line decorated its flank. Its head was long and narrow with large oval eyes.

"These stunning creatures," Maashi explained, "possess a wild temperament but respond well to an experienced trainer. They race in great events, and today's race is the most challenging competition of the sequence."

"I agree sir," said Lado who strolled in the room carrying two tall glasses. "Everyone is pleased to see you are taking part in the final race." In contrast to his usual dull clothes, he wore an elegant outfit: tight black pants and a light green shirt with leathery belts crisscrossing his chest.

I turned to Maashi. "Are you a jockey?"

"Yes," Lado said, "Sheffrou Maashi is a korbi." He handed a glass to each of us. "The Sheffrou will ride with the Sawishas. The Council chose him to represent the Central Compound."

"Congratulations," I said.

Maashi's back stiffened. "They should have chosen someone other than me," he said. "I haven't trained at all these last few months. I hope I won't disappoint them."

"It is a great honor to be chosen as korbi sir," Lado stated. He raised his head high and straightened his shoulders, "a chance to prove you have regained your strength and your skills."

Maashi didn't reply.

I frowned. "Were you sick?"

"I was recuperating from an unfortunate event," Maashi said without any further explanation.

"I wish you the best of luck then. I hope you win," I said. "Cheers. To your success." We brought our glasses close together without touching and I took a sip of the sweet nectar.

"Tamara," Maashi gave back his glass to Lado and rubbed his left shoulder in a circular motion, "the race is just a friendly competition. Winning is a minor achievement."

I tilted my head sideways and chuckled. "Everybody says that, but the winner is the one people remember."

"I would be grateful to finish the race in good standing, in the first five," said Maashi.

He nodded at Lado and said, "Come, it's time to go."

"Now?" I asked.

"Yes," said Maashi, "the competition will start soon."

He clicked at his guards, picked me up, and we left, accompanied by several other Chamis. We followed two long corridors and arrived at our designated area: an oval room with several metallic doors wide enough for six Chamis to walk through at the same time. The guards scanned the place and then stepped aside, letting us board the huge elevators.

The ride took several minutes, and I felt lighter as we rose. I looked at Maashi. "Are we going to the surface?" I asked.

"Yes, Tamara."

"How do these elevators work? Are they electric?"

"We control their movement with anti-gravity. A grid inserted through the walls of the elevators controls the gravity of the elevator and its occupants. We can control the speed of the ascent and stop at any level."

"You mean there are Chamis living underground on different levels?"

"Yes. The higher levels permit easy access to the surface while the lower levels are safer."

"What level do we live on?"

"We live on one of the lower levels because I am Sheffrou."

After weeks enclosed in caves and tunnels, I emerged in the wide-open space and stared in astonishment at the world above ground. Much bigger than Earth's, their sun hung high in the sky and bathed the landscape in its orange glow. The air was hot and dry and smelled of burned toast. The warm breeze whistled in my ears and tousled my hair.

"Look above Tamara," said Maashi. He pointed with his arm. "The sister moons, Ara and Kori, are advancing towards each other as we near the date of the eclipse."

Ara's crescent was slightly smaller than our moon on Earth whereas Kori was a large globe sitting below its sister. Both cast a pale glow in the indigo sky and stood closer than the last time I had seen them over five weeks ago.

The uneven ground was covered with reddish soil and was just as flat and barren as I remembered it: no vegetation, no signs of life, and no water. I ached to go back home. I wondered how far I was from the site where I first arrived. Was the wormhole still there?

We came to an enclosure that reminded me of a racetrack, but much wider. I could envision the movie *Ben-Hur* with the chariot race and the gorgeous teams of horses. The track, about three hundred feet wide, stretched as far as I could see. It was oval-shaped but like an asymmetrical ellipse, since one end was narrower than the other. I realized that as the riders reached full speed, a lot of skill and finesse would be required to negotiate the tight turn on the dry dirt strewn with pebbles.

Thousands of brightly attired Chamis, draped in long gowns and wide pants flowing in the breeze had gathered for the racing event. Their continuous clicking filled the air with a distinct clatter like a giant flock of nesting birds. They stood or sat on padded chairs, positioned on semicircular cornices on one side of the track.

At both ends of the seating area I noticed twenty tall panels, each a different color with an intricate design composed of five characters placed vertically, not unlike Chinese characters. The middle one was always a circle with a smaller sign inside.

"I counted twenty banners Maashi. Do they each represent a compound?"

Maashi glanced at them and said, "The banners bear the official names of each team. There are fourteen compounds, but larger ones have more than one team. The third banner corresponds to the Central Compound which I represent."

"What about the sign in the middle? What does it mean?"

"The circle represents the pledge that binds the competitors and members of the teams. They have sworn to behave honorably in every circumstance related to the races."

Maashi transferred me to Lado's arms and clicked several times. He said, "I must go now. Stay with Lado. He will keep you safe and will find a good location to observe the competitions." He caressed my head and turned to leave.

"Hey, Maashi," I called out, "break a leg," I grinned. "It means good luck."

Maashi chuckled, "I'll see you later."

Lado held me and climbed the wide stairs up to the fifth level. He walked behind the seats until he found what he was looking for: a perfect place to watch the riders. We could see the whole racetrack and miles of arid landscape beyond that. I shielded my eyes and noticed large clear domes that shone under the orange sun. I pointed at them. "What are those out there?"

Lado glanced in the same direction and said, "Those are the Fanella, the female compounds. The Fanellas live under the protection of these domes built by our ancestors. The structures collect and concentrate the sun's rays and the energy produced is transmitted underground to the different sectors."

"I thought Maashi said all Chamis live underground."

"The Sheffrou meant the males. The Fanellas live above ground during the day and seek protection in the caves at night." He turned and pointed to a chair on his left. "You must sit. The races will begin soon."

I sat on the edge of the wide chair beside him with legs dangling and carefully observed the crowd. Unless I was mistaken, all the spectators were male.

"Where are the females Lado?"

"They do not attend the races. The Council of Elders have deemed it unsafe for them to stay on the surface for such a long period."

"I see." The Elders decided every important matter, and in each case, security seemed to be the deciding factor. I wondered what the Fanellas thought of the Elders' decisions. Were they submissive or did they openly question their unilateral decisions?

"Lado," I said, "tell me more about this race."

"Every sequence," he said, "the korbis are chosen among the Pure Colors and the Sheffrous. They ride the shoshans from our mother world. The day before the races, each rider draws a color code that corresponds to a specific animal.

"We brought the shoshan more than two hundred sequences ago from Chamtali, our mother world. Chamranlinas had to leave Chamtali when it became inhospitable to life." Lado's face changed, his eyes got bigger, his long face became unreadable. "We had the horrendous task of choosing which species to save and bring with us. We could not part with these magnificent creatures."

□"Why did you come to this world?"

□"We had to find a suitable planet, one that was inhabitable and could offer us shelter from our enemies." In a somber tone he added, "Aye, even here on Chitina, the Krakoran still threaten our people."

□The enemies again. "And the Sawishas? Who are they?"

□Before he could answer, the thundering sound of drums announced the start of the races. A strong odor of wet fur filled the air, and I saw them at last: twenty shoshans and their korbis. The proud riders dressed in vibrant colors mounted bareback the restless animals. With long narrow heads and fierce-looking black eyes, the tall beasts snarled, bit, and kicked each other but obeyed the jockeys' commands. Riders and mounts positioned themselves at one end of the track and waited.

"The master of ceremonies introduces the contestants to the crowd before each race," Lado said. "There will be four races. Then he will announce the winner, the one with the best time."

The crowd soon hushed. Each korbi advanced and saluted when his name was called by lifting one arm up high. The shoshans pranced, snorted, and tried to kick each other.

A long steady drum roll followed. The riders took their positions. The shoshans, nostrils flared, ears pointed forward and grunting, waited for a signal from their korbis. A second drum roll and all bolted ahead from the starting line. Much faster than thoroughbreds they reached incredible speeds in the straightaway. I watched in awe as the flurry of white and gold manes contrasted with the bold colors of the jockeys. The spectators shouted, clicked and waved at the korbis. They stood and whistled, and thumped their feet with great force, and this propelled the beasts even faster.

"How many times do they run around the track?" I shouted above the foot thumping and the pounding of the hooves, my eyes riveted on the animals who flew by and deftly negotiated the tight turns.

Lado answered without losing sight of the riders. "They have to complete three full turns around the enclosure."

I observed the jockeys with great interest. They rode bareback with no reins and controlled the mounts with their own bodies. The shoshans' gait was almost identical to a horse's gallop but covered much more ground in one stride. They were as competitive as their jockeys and fought each other to take the lead. The animals pumped their tails up and down as they ran and when the speed increased so did the swishing of the tail.

I became part of the widespread fever and stomped my feet wildly as the Chamis did, but I didn't spot Maashi until the fourth race. He wore a red shirt with blue sleeves. When he first appeared, he scanned the crowd, saw me, and waved. I raised my hand and yelled as loud as I could, "Good Luck!"

A flood of memories swept over me; Allison and David chasing each other in our backyard, Jonathan, my youngest son, trotting behind them as fast as his little legs could let him. The three squealed with delight and scattered in the yard with my brother Matt in close pursuit. His laughter echoed in the breeze as he growled with arms outstretched pretending to be a bear. My husband Nate circled my waist with his arms, and I heard his deep male voice. "Happy birthday Tamara."

The images vanished as quickly as they had appeared. Tears blurred my vision, and a big lump filled my throat. My family was so far away now, most likely sad and bewildered, unable to understand what happened the day I disappeared while I was here on another world far away from them, enjoying a shoshan race.

I blinked my tears away and collected myself as the fourth race started. Maashi was in good position as he passed in front of us in the first turn. The second time around, I smiled and admired his riding skills. He leaned over the shoshan and urged him on, his head buried in the golden mane. I yelled my encouragement. "Go, Maashi. Go. Go!" Immersed in the race, Lado stomped his feet in sync with the crowd.

A Chami with a tanned leathery face, wearing a flowing mint colored shirt and a purple sash, clicked loudly behind us. Even though I didn't understand what he was saying, I could see his eyes were riveted on me. He approached, grabbed my hands, and attempted to pull me into his arms. He bent his head to kiss me. I struggled to pull away and cried out in their language. "No. No. Let me go."

The crowd cheered and stomped with such enthusiasm Lado didn't hear my screams. He looked on as Maashi sped by. Then he turned and saw me fighting off the purple Chami. He stood, hissed a warning, and the Purple released me and backed away.

I turned toward the track, but it was too late. The race was over. I had missed the end.

"What happened, Lado? Who won?"

"The Sheffrou looked up to find you, got distracted and fell off his mount. He ran as fast as he could and jumped back on his shoshan. The crowd thumped hard to encourage him, but even with his best efforts, he finished second."

"Damn." I slammed my fist on the back of the seat in front of me. The fine dust that had settled on its surface after the races lifted and floated, then scattered in the breeze. "That's too bad," I said, "I would've loved it if he had won. I hope he won't be mad at me." I wiped the powdery dust away from my forehead and eyebrows and rubbed my neck.

"The Sheffrou would never be mad at you," said Lado, his eyes tiny dark slits.

The final winner was a Chami wearing a deep blue jacket. I observed him with interest from where I stood. A foot taller than Maashi, he roared with laughter and slapped Maashi's back. At first Maashi looked disgruntled, then erupted in laughter and soon both gave each other a congratulatory hug.

I didn't care about the races anymore. The sun hovered low on the horizon. I was thirsty and tired. "Do you have anything to drink?" I asked Lado.

"I have this." He gave me a tall cup filled with a yellow liquid.

I took a sip, and it was awfully bitter. I wrinkled my nose and gave the cup back to him.

"Do you not like it?" asked Lado.

I shook my head. "No. I don't."

Lado took the cup back and said with a disapproving look, "Only Sheffrous do not appreciate this drink."

I ignored his comment. Maashi would be back soon and I wanted more answers. "Lado, earlier you mentioned Sawishas. What makes them so special?"

"The Sawishas are the Pure Colors, the Purples, the Greens, the Reds, the Pinks, etc. and the Blues, also called Sheffrous. Only the Sawishas and Sheffrous are fertile. They form the elite of Chamranlina society."

"I don't understand. What do you mean?"

"Fertile," Lado answered in an even tone, "means they can produce offspring."

Right then Maashi appeared with a torn shirt and pants covered with reddish soil. He picked me up, and I noticed a fresh cut on his left wrist. He greeted Lado with loud clicks and kissed me. "Are you thirsty?" He asked. "Would you like something to drink?"

"Water is fine, but first let me look at your wrist. You have a bad cut."

Maashi waved at a guard who brought a tall glass of water.

"Maashi, you're hurt." I said and gulped the refreshing liquid, "You should get this cleaned or it might get infected."

Maashi glanced at the cut and said, "It's nothing. I'll take care of it later."

The gentle breeze we enjoyed earlier had dissipated. The air hung heavy, ominous. Maashi raised his head and looked up at the sky. The two moons, Ara and Kori, were rising fast, the bigger one still trying to catch the smaller one. "It's time to leave now. The sun will set soon, and we won't be safe anymore."

"Why not? What happens when the sun goes down?"

"The breeze is nonexistent," said Maashi, "and the air density changes. This makes it much easier for the Krakoran to scan the surface of the planet with long parallel sweeps. As soon as they find the Chamis they are hunting for, they seize and transport them away."

"Who are they looking for?"

Maashi hissed.

Lado answered in his stead. "The enemies target Fanellas and Sheffrous."

We boarded the elevator again and traveled back to our quarters. Maashi got lots of hugs and kisses from the excited Chamis assembled to congratulate him. They shot curious stares in my direction.

The last one who came to hug and kiss Maashi was the winner of the races, the tall Chami. With a great booming laugh, he clicked at Maashi and held him in his arms for the longest time. He wore a royal blue sash like the one Maashi wore the day we had our meeting. The Chamis came to him, kissed his shoulders and neck, and patted his back the way they did with Maashi. The two were alike. But what kind of Chamis were they? All I knew was that they were called Sheffrous, they were part of Chami society's elite, and they were fertile.

Everyone left except the tall one. I heard Maashi call him Tom Tom. He kissed Maashi's neck, then his chest. Maashi closed his eyes, inhaled, and put his hand over the other's shoulder.

I felt strangely disturbed to see them together. Maashi glanced towards me and called, "Tamara," and pointed at a door. "Go to the other room. You can sleep there for a few hours."

Under normal circumstances, I would've taken offense to his cavalier dismissal, but I was weary from the day's activities and ready to get rest. Also, I sensed he was eager to spend time alone with the winner of the races, Tom Tom.

I grabbed the blanket he offered and hurried out. I laid on a couch filled with large comfortable cushions and fell asleep.

My stomach woke me up a few hours later. It growled and cramped without cease, protesting the lack of food. I sat up and recalled the events of the day. The races had been exciting, but the trip to the surface was a stark reminder we had made no progress in the search for the wormhole. Was there another way to find it?

The door opened and Tom Tom entered.

Up close his physique was impressive. More muscular than Maashi, he looked calm, self-assured to the point of arrogance. He beckoned me. "Come," he said.

I hesitated. I only came when Maashi called.

Waiting no further, Tom Tom covered the ground between us in two strides, and picked me up in his arms. I felt as a dwarf held by a giant. He gently tilted my head by putting two fingers under my chin.

"Maashi was right. You are a sweetheart," he declared.

His seductive style surprised me. His skin was a rich golden color and his warm body smelled like freshly cut wood. "Hey, put me down." I said without too much conviction.

Tom Tom looked at me up close and said, "I am Maashi's friend. Do not be frightened." His eyes were darker than Maashi's. They had a joyful, playful expression as if he was laughing, even though he stood there with a slight frown. "How old are you?" he said. His masculine voice was rich with an unusual musicality.

Only then did I realize he spoke in English. "I am forty-four Earth years old."

"Is this old?"

This Chami was different. "Still young."

He gave me an odd sideway look and then chuckled. "Tell me about your world."

How could I describe Earth? "Earth is a beautiful planet filled with plants and animals. Seventy-five percent of its surface is covered with water. We have a yellow sun, and Earth is the third planet from the sun."

"So, your species lives in the water?"

"No, humans live on dry land."

His eyes were laughing, "Is this how you call yourself, humans?"

"Yes, human or humans for plural."

Tom Tom bent his head to kiss me and I turned away. I wouldn't avoid his advances for long. Where were you, Maashi?

He said, "The Sheffrou said you were not comfortable with kisses. He told me you have never mated with any other male besides your mate. Is this true?"

Why did he ask that? A warm sensation spread on my cheeks. "Yes," I said, "it's true."

Tom Tom exclaimed, "No wonder you shy away from kisses. You do not even mate with other males of your own species." He resumed his questioning: "Are there other intelligent species on Earth?"

"Yes," I said, relieved to change the subject. "There are many species on Earth but none we can really communicate with."

"What do you mean?" he said with his eyes growing bigger.

"Well, for example, shoshans are a species but you can't talk to them." I hoped my simple explanation was satisfactory.

"I understand," he said. "Have humans been in contact with alien species from other worlds?"

"Our world has made no contact with aliens, and we can't travel in space yet. Some humans don't even believe that other intelligent alien species exist," I said. I was curious to find out how he would respond to that.

The big Sheffrou roared with laughter. He put his hand in the middle of his stomach and laughed so hard his whole body was shaking. After a few minutes he calmed down. Only his eyes appeared to be laughing.

That Sheffrou had a unique style, different from any other Chami I had met.

With a smile, he said, "Did *you* believe that other alien species existed?"

"Yes."

"What was your reaction when you first saw Chamranlinas?"

My heart skipped as I recalled how terrified I was the first time I met the miners.

"She fainted," answered Maashi, who strolled in the room. "That's what the miners said." He extended his arms, retrieved me, and kissed my cheeks. Such a relief to see him. Maashi was here and none too soon.

"She is Sheffrou," he said, as if this explained everything.

# Chapter 10

B ack in Maashi's quarters, my stomach cramps sent an urgent message.

"Maashi, I'm starving. I need food." I said as I sat on a plush couch and pulled one of many solid blue cushions against me. "Why haven't you shown me yet how to get some myself?"

"I didn't teach you because certain fruits and nuts can be harmful. However, I will instruct Lado to teach you how to summon a few simple choices."

He pressed a few buttons on the wall, and a section opened, bringing forth a tray overflowing with tougui, tempting tangerine fruits that resembled a blend of pear and apple, a choice of sweet puddings, and unusual pear-shaped nuts speckled with light brown spots.

Maashi settled on a couch across from me and rested his long legs. "The chorila nuts," he said, "have a satisfying bold taste but you must eat only the speckled ones. The others may contain worms."

"Thanks for letting me know." I separated the nuts and discarded the dull brown ones in an empty pudding container. I gulped everything else without saying a word. After I was full, I got up, put the tray in the recycle holder, and trotted back to my spot. I sat, grabbed a rectangular fuchsia cushion, and rested my elbow on it. I traced the gold thread running along its border with my finger. On impulse I asked Maashi a question I had been wanting to ask for some time. "Why don't you ever eat with me?"

He stared at his hands and said, "I eat very little and only food which doesn't require chewing because it's complicated for me."

"I've seen the others eat. Why is it different for you?"

"My tongue is much longer than the other Chamranlinas, so eating is a difficult process. I eat in private with Lado."

"Why is that?"

Maashi made a grunting sound. "Little one," he said, "this subject isn't a subject open for discussion. However, you are a stranger," he paused, "and ignorant of our customs so I will give you more details." He crossed his legs and spread his fingers on his thighs. "As a Sheffrou, I use my tongue to establish a connection in meetings with Sawishas, but my tongue is also a key component in the mating process with the Fanellas, the females."

"Is that why Sheffrous are important? They mate with the females."

"Sheffrous are the only Chamranlinas capable of producing female offspring."

"I see." I shifted in a more upright position on the couch. "What about the Sawishas?"

Maashi's eyes grew wider. "You have a lot of questions to-day."

"Yes. I want to learn more about your society."

"An acceptable pursuit." Maashi stated. "The Sawishas, or Pure Colors, with tongues of one color are the other fertile Chamranlinas. They father only male offspring."

"Are the females Pure Colors?"

"All the Fanellas possess a light pink tongue, lighter than yours."

"What color is your tongue?"

"Sheffrous have blue tongues."

I turned over on my back, rested my head, and gazed at the solid cream ceiling. "On a sunny day on Earth, the sky is blue with puffy white clouds." I sighed. "Is your tongue the same color as your blue sash?"

"Yes," he said, "Our sash represents our color. It's unacceptable to show one's tongue in public."

I picked a strand of my hair which now reached below my shoulders and twirled it in my fingers. "You often mention mating. I'm sure you've figured out how this works for us humans, but I would like you to explain how it works for Chamis."

A wave of clicks broke the air and I turned and saw Maashi smile. "I hope you are not expecting a demonstration. My size precludes any possible mating with you and it's completely forbidden for Chamranlinas to mate with other species."

"I didn't mention anything about a demonstration." I shook my head and chuckled.

Maashi reclined on his blue pillow and bright amber shone in his eyes. "However, since it is a legitimate question let me answer as truthfully and thoroughly as I can.

"Mature females ovulate once every sequence and they remain fertile for seven to ten days. Since there is no contact between the chosen Pure Color and the female before the actual mating, there is a certain amount of time devoted to what I will refer to as courtship.

"A period of hide-and-seek lasting as little as an hour or as much as several hours occurs. The couple is under close surveillance by the Gray Feeders in a specific area under one of the

Fanella domes. The female is lighter and faster than the male and will run away from him. The male will need to give chase until she tires or simply stops running. Please take note that the couple have 24 hours to perform the mating and must copulate three times for the female to conceive."

"You're kidding."

"My comments are true. On more than one occasion, I have been the unfortunate male running behind a reluctant female until the time for mating had almost completely elapsed. It has been said that this chase is a means for the female to assess the endurance and the virility of the male."

Speechless, I stared at him in disbelief.

"When the female is ready, she remains still, but her suitor must stay on guard. If he is too eager to approach her, she may become aggressive and attack or scream at which point the Gray Feeders will intervene and forcefully remove the male."

"Has this ever happened to you?"

"I am grateful to all the females who showed kindness and accepted me. I do recall an incident that happened many sequences ago." Maashi shook his head to one side and tapped his fingers on his knees. "The only reason I will mention this is because I know you will appreciate the humor of my misfortune."

"Oh?"

"At the time, I was a young Sheffrou with more bravado than brains and had not mastered the expertise needed to pursue a female without getting caught in her crafty tricks. That mischievous female didn't hesitate to set a trap to get rid of an inexperienced Sheffrou to be paired with another contender. She bounded ahead of me and easily leaped over a thicket in which lay concealed a noola-noola bush. This plant is treasured by the females who enjoy its tasty fruit, but one must never come close to it in the months preceding the blossoms. The females, usually naked, take care to avoid the plant because it is covered with small hairy barbs which secrete a thick, gooey, and irritating substance along climbers which will entrap any unsuspecting creature that wanders too close."

"Oh no. The plant caught you."

Maashi grinned. "To my dismay and embarrassment, I didn't notice the noola-noola and plunged in the bush behind the female. The creepers quickly encircled my body and immobilized me. The Gray Feeders came to my rescue and carefully extricated me from the plant's clutches under the mocking eyes of the Fanella. The intense skin irritation caused by the secretions cut short any further mating. I vowed to be more careful in the future."

"I guess this ruse happened before to other Pure Colors."

"Yes, but I endured months of teasing by the Sawishas including my former mentor who failed to understand the humor of the situation."

"We all go through something like that at some point," I said with a chuckle. "In the Emergency Room, one can be faced with cases which will bewilder the most astute doctor. I had a patient once who came late in the evening with sudden onset of abdominal pain and cramps and we found her full-term pregnancy only after she had an ultrasound." I wrinkled my nose at the memory of the incident. I really missed the diagnosis that time. "So, what happens after the female lets you catch up?"

"The male removes his clothes and lays down on his back in a safe place, over leaves or a soft bed of groundcover plants. The couple touch in the same manner as a meeting like the one we had when you first arrived on Chitina. After that the male will feed the female and they will kiss and lick each other until she opens her legs wide to demonstrate she is ready, and the male will introduce his tongue inside her and lick her thoroughly. Then he will penetrate her and flood her with his pleasure. This must be accomplished at least three times to ensure a pregnancy. An experienced male will show patience and gentleness, so the female only feels pleasure during the actual copulation."

"What happens if the couple doesn't complete the process in 24 hours?"

"The Council of Elders chooses three candidates every sequence. If the first male fails, then there is a rest period of two hours then the process starts again with the second chosen one. This hasn't occurred often since the first choice is always a Sheffrou to produce female offspring, and Sheffrous complete the mating in almost all cases."

I turned on my back, stretched, and rested an elbow on a firm pillow beside me. "You've called me Sheffrou several times now. Why do you keep calling me that?"

Maashi paused before answering. "I have observed characteristic Sheffrou traits in you."

"What do you mean?"

"For example," he paused, "Sheffrous are shy and sensitive, but also strong and resilient. They show empathy for others, especially for the weak and vulnerable, and excel in the art of healing, which you call medicine. Most important, they need constant attention and physical pleasure otherwise they lose their charissa, or *joie de vivre*, and become detached from reality."

I waved high up with my right hand and said, "Stop. You're mistaken. I'm just an ordinary human."

"I disagree, Tamara. You're a physician. You possess tremendous strength and determination and have adapted to a new environment even though you're sensitive and you are separated from your loved ones."

"A lot of humans would've done the same. What makes me so different?"

Maashi tilted his head and stared at me with dark eyes. "You traveled through a gateway. Only Sheffrous travel this way."

"That's why." I exclaimed. "You think I'm a Sheffrou because I stumbled into that wormhole. The other characteristics you referred to don't count that much."

I sat up. I took a deep breath to contain my irritation at the mention of the wormhole. "Maashi," I said, "do you think I'll ever get back home?"

Maashi spread his fingers on his knees. "I don't know, Tamara. We're still searching for signs of the gateway. So far we have found very few clues." He added in a low voice, "Sheffrous rarely go back where they originated."

This new information, disclosed without warning, struck like a blow. I sat still, in shock, unable to say anything. My heart thumped hard. My ears went deaf.

I'll never see my children again.

Maashi stood and came beside me. He held me close and kissed my forehead. "I'm sorry," he said.

A tear rolled down my cheek then several more until my face got all wet. I wiped them off with the back of my hand. "I can't," I said, "I can't accept the thought I may never see my family again."

Maashi hugged me and kissed my hair. "Don't cry, shapinka, precious one. We will continue the search."

# Chapter 11

Several days passed without any visit from Maashi. Alone in my quarters, a heavy silence filled the room. Only the tapping of my fingers on my pad or my own steps when I paced my quarters echoed on the empty walls.

Sadness overcame me. I missed the booming laughter of my boys, Allison's giggling, even the annoying sound of Nate's snoring. Time stretched on without a visitor or a guard checking to see if I was still alive. To keep my mind busy, I wrote on my little pad anecdotes and fond memories of my former life on Earth and composed a series of letters to my daughter. This lifted my spirits and gave me strength and hope.

In the afternoons, I spent hours lying on my couch staring at the ceiling; Maashi had changed its color to a pure blue like the sky on Earth and added some puffy white clouds when he understood it enhanced my mood. Surrounded by plush pink cushions, my mind wandered back to my childhood in upstate New York. How I loved winter; the first snowflakes of the season, snowball fights with the neighborhood kids, and ice skating with my favorite aunt. How carefree my life was back in those days.

I thought of each of my children. Before our move to the south four years ago, their childhood had been like mine, growing up in a small northern town, enjoying the same simple pleasures I had known.

My oldest son, David, serious, ambitious, had completed his first year at the Medical University of Charleston. At twenty-two, he was among the youngest in his class. A friend had introduced him to Jessica, an energetic ash-blond girl from Maryland with remarkable violet eyes who studied pharmacy at the same university. They fell in love, spent all their free time together, and planned to get engaged in July this year. Now, I feared I wouldn't return home by then.

My daughter Allison was thrilled to be a freshman at the prestigious College of Charleston. She had a bubbly, engaging personality and her excellent work ethic helped her succeed in everything she tried. My youngest son Jonathan, a music enthusiast, junior in high school and avid surfer, planned to be a professional football trainer.

Thinking about them upset me so much my mind took a spin and my vision blurred for a few minutes. I closed my eyes and inhaled deeply.

I envisioned my family during our vacation at the beach last summer. There were a few tense moments between Nate and my son David. My husband's overbearing personality often caused strife between the two but overall, we had a wonderful time. The kids surfed, swam, and loved every minute spent in the ocean. They would dive under the big waves and ride them all the way to the shore. They would tease and chase each other until one of them would trip and crash in the sand.

At the end of the week, my husband's usual cynicism had morphed into a more positive outlook. One morning, a wide grin had replaced his habitual sour expression. "This is a great vacation," he had said, "I'm glad the kids are enjoying them-

selves. We haven't spent time together like this in a long while."
My chest tightened as I remembered his words. How little did
he know that this vacation would be our last one together.

Everything seemed so long ago, so far away, in another
world. It felt as though I dreamed it all. Deep and painful longing cut into me like a blade. I brushed the tears on my face
and dried my eyes trying in vain to contain my sorrow. Crying
wouldn't bring my family back.

I accessed my pad and asked the device to show me the
tunnels surrounding the compound. A whole map of tunnels
appeared on the screen. Show me the point of arrival I asked,
not sure how it would respond. The device blinked for a few
seconds then it underlined a clear path connecting one tunnel
to the surface. I saved the information and hugged the pad in
my arms. If I traveled on the surface to survey the area myself, I
might find clues the Chamis never thought of. It was a remote
possibility, but I didn't want to dismiss any option.

The lights in the room dimmed as they did every day in early evening. A chime went off, signaling Maashi's arrival. The
two-paneled door slid apart, and he stepped in dressed in formal
attire with cream shirt and dark blue trousers, and a royal blue
sash tied at the waist.

"How are you, Tamara?" He bent down and kissed my
forehead.

"Okay, I guess." I stretched my limbs one by one and set my
pad on an ottoman. "I haven't seen you in a while. It gets lonely
here without you."

"I had to travel out of the sector for a few days." He sat beside me. "Tonight, we shall go to Lantillica Sher. It's a place to eat, drink, and renew with old acquaintances. It will be an excellent distraction for you."

"Sounds good," I said and yawned. I glanced at his left arm. The cut he had sustained at the races was gone. "You heal fast. I can't see anything, not even a scar."

"I am Sheffrou Tamara. Small cuts disappear quickly." He straightened his shoulders. "You can prepare yourself now. I'll be back in a few minutes." He stood and left.

I rose and strolled to the water room. A quick shower was all I needed. I came out wearing my usual khaki shirt and pants. Clothes were so boring here: always the same bland mono-chrome outfits. Only the sashes were different.

As soon as I was ready, Maashi stepped in accompanied by Lado who wore tight black pants, a khaki shirt, and a short olive sash. He nodded in my direction.

We left at a brisk pace and soon arrived at our destination. The Lantillica was much larger than I expected and, with its ebony granite walls and high ceiling, reminded me of an elegant restaurant.

Lights originated from the base of the walls and filled the room with warm hues of ochre, rust and gold. Hundreds of clear diamond-shaped pieces of quartz hung in clusters from the ceiling. A gentle breeze rocked the clear pieces, and they swayed, chimed, and created flickers of light that danced on the tables.

Impressive glass sculptures stood in each corner of the din-ing area. One reminded me of red and orange flames leaping in the air. Another represented clear bubbles rising ten feet high from a large container filled with crystals. Still another portrayed tall vivid green and purple plants swaying under an imaginary breeze.

"The sculptures," Maashi said, "represent the basic elements of fire, water and air, and the plants symbolize the life created by the harmony of the elements.

"The sculptures are beautiful."

"Rare Yellows created them," Lado said, "they are renowned for their artistic abilities."

Small groups of Chamranlinas sat on thick couches arranged in pairs around low stone tables. The mood was relaxed and peaceful and everyone communicated with soft clicks.

We chose a table, and I sat close to Maashi. Lado offered a lumi to everyone, a sweet drink served in a long slim glass like a champagne flute. The glass was opaque with an oval opening. Maashi applied it against his mouth then modestly dipped his tongue to savor the fruity flavor.

Lado and the three other Chamis joining us this evening were eager to show me how to eat the chati, a local delicacy. They were soft edible creatures that lived encased in a firm shell same as mollusks. The Chamranlinas set the bivalve creatures on a smooth hot surface in the center of the table. The heat immobilized and rendered them more palatable but, most important, the Chamis believed the creatures wouldn't feel pain when ingested. I watched as they swallowed them whole and it reminded me of my love of oysters.

Lado showed me how to open the shells and I ingested the soft and salty creature.

"Tasty," I said. "I like them."

"I am pleased to see you're enjoying the food tonight," Maashi said.

"It's a welcome change from the puddings. Why don't we get chati more often?"

"They are in season now," Lado said, "but they are available only for a short period every sequence."

"That's too bad."

"Do not be sad," Lado added. "In a few weeks the lichi will grow in the deep pools, and we will eat them. It is also something we enjoy."

"Are they creatures like these?"

"They are more like plants. We make delicious soups with them and some puddings."

"More puddings." I chocked on my chati.

Maashi patted me on the back. "Don't eat too many at once."

An unfamiliar Chami strolled towards us with a confident stride. He was about the same height as Maashi but more muscular. He wore a beautiful sky-blue sash and a lighter powder blue shirt. His brow wasn't as prominent as the other Chamis and this gave him gentler facial features. The newcomer clicked at Maashi, then at the others. He glanced at me with a friendly expression.

Maashi gave his glass to Lado, stood to greet him, and circled his arm around his waist. The Chami spoke to Maashi in their language, punctuated with clicking sounds. They both embraced and kissed deeply. The others stood and kissed his neck, and he kissed their cheeks. Then Maashi sat down close to the new Chami while the others settled around the table.

"Tamara," said Maashi, "this is Shonava Dasho Fontina. He is a physician and a close friend. We have known each other for many sequences."

"It is a pleasure to see you," Dasho said in a mellow voice, small wrinkles fanning around his golden eyes.

"How do you do, sir?" I said.

The new Chami laughed. "Please, call me Dasho."

"I'm impressed. Only one kiss and you understand and speak English."

"We can communicate," Maashi explained, "with kisses much faster and with more accuracy than with speech."

Dasho kept his eyes on me. "Maashi tells me you are also a physician. I would love to exchange words with you." He turned towards Maashi, "We can get together later."

"Of course." Maashi tilted his head sideways in agreement.

"You have been here for a few weeks now," Dasho said, "and I am sure that trying to understand us and our culture has been a challenge."

I chuckled. "That would be an understatement. Every day, simple things surprise me. Without the good fortune of meeting Maashi," I glanced at him. "I wouldn't have survived."

Dasho said, "Maashi was the perfect person to assist you in adjusting to our world."

Right then someone clicked and came from across the room. "Excuse me," Maashi said, "I will be back in a moment." He stood up and walked over to that Chami and several others sprung to their feet to hug and kiss him.

Lado offered a glass of lumi to Dasho.

"I see you're wearing a blue sash," I said, "so you must be a Sheffrou. Why is yours a lighter blue?"

He responded with an easy grin. "There are three kinds of Sheffrous designated by the numbers 4, 6, and 8." He took a sip of his drink. "I am part of the most common group, the Sheffrou 4, and most of us are physicians. Sheffrous 6 wear a dark blue sash and possess tremendous physical and mental strength. They administer justice. Sheffrous 8 wear a royal blue sash and are trained in the art of seduction and pleasure. Maashi is part of this latter group. Any of them may be chosen to mate with the Fanellas."

My eyes grew wide. "Ah, the females. I haven't seen any."

"You will see them," Lado said, "at the Great Eclipse Celebration."

I stared at Dasho. "Is my understanding correct? The females do not choose their mates."

Dasho's face softened. "The Council of Elders decides which males will be given the privilege of mating with seven Fanellas, the ones most likely to conceive. The Elders will announce their choices at the celebration."

I considered this for a moment. "Neither party can choose. Love doesn't matter."

Dasho bent his head sideways and looked at me. "Mating is extremely important. It cannot be left to random choice."

"The Council of Elders decides everything," I grumbled, set my glass down, and folded my arms on my chest. "May I ask if you have ever been chosen?"

"I had the honor of being chosen for mating, but not often. I am certainly not a successful Sheffrou like Maashi. He is one of the few Sheffrous who were able to impregnate all seven females in two successive sequences. This level of success had not been seen for over sixty sequences, if my memory is accurate."

"Sir," Lado said, "you have considerable experience and an excellent mating record, and your memory is accurate. It was Sheffrou Shanadou who was the last one who accomplished this feat."

Dasho lowered his head in respect and all the others at our table did the same. "Unfortunately," he said, "after his two successive sequences, on his way back to his quarters after the Great Eclipse Celebration of the following sequence, he suffered a ferocious attack by the Krakoran and was killed."

"Wow. That must have been quite a blow to the Chamran-linas. How did this happen?"

Lado explained. "His party was ambushed by two Krakoran and all the guards and all his chowlis except his first chowli were killed. His first chowli was never the same after that."

Dasho nodded. "A sad ending for such a powerful Shef-frou." He took a long sip.

"Wait," I grabbed my glass, "you talk about Sheffrous, what about the other males, the Sawishas, do they also mate?"

"The Elders," Lado said, "have only picked Sheffrous in the last fifty sequences."

"Fifty sequences. Why?"

Dasho tilted his head toward me. "They produce female offspring and have been more successful than the Sawishas with the younger Fanellas who are the most fertile but also the most challenging."

"Why is it difficult to mate with them?"

"They are easily frightened," said Lado, "by the powerful males and fear the mating because each time it is painful for them."

"No wonder they fear mating."

"The truth is," Dasho said, "experienced Sheffrous and Sawishas can significantly lessen the pain and make sure the Fanellas feel pleasure."

"Maashi mentioned the females could conceive for seven to ten days at a time. How many times during a sequence does the female become fertile?" Infertility had always been a fascinating subject for me.

"The Fanellas are fertile only once every sequence," said Dasho.

"A sequence or a year," Lado said, "is 712 days and our days, as you should know, have 26 hours."

Why haven't I asked that before? They reproduce slowly, one baby every two Earth years if everything goes as planned. I took a sip of my drink and thought of the pandas on Earth who have a similar mating pattern and are an endangered species. "Do you think they'll choose Maashi this year?"

"I do not know." Dasho said. He pressed the lumi to his lips and swallowed, set the glass on the table, and rubbed his hands. "There are a few suitable candidates. The Sawishas are putting a lot of pressure on the Council because they want some of their group to be among the first chosen. Maashi is an excellent contender but he will face stiff competition, and some say he is not ready."

"Shonava Maashi has a few weeks to prepare," said Lado. The others sitting with us, silent during our exchange, clicked briefly and nodded sideways in agreement.

Dasho asked Lado, "Has Maashi found a first chowli yet?"

Lado stared straight ahead and said, "Not yet. Although I am encouraging him to do so as much as I can, the Sheffrou has been busy with Tamara these last weeks."

"I see." Dasho took his glass, rubbed it between his hands, and sipped.

I gulped a chati and said, "I've been eating only fruits, puddings and nuts. Don't you have other sources of nourishment? How can you stay healthy and fit with a diet so limited in protein?"

Dasho's brow became more pronounced and his eyes narrowed. "Are you not aware we also use sunlight as a source of energy?"

"Sunlight? Like a plant uses light?"

"Yes, sunlight is our main source of energy," said one Chami sitting across from me. The three sitting on the other side of the table kept their eyes were riveted on us. "Each day we go on the surface and we expose our body to the sun's rays for as many hours as we can."

I remembered the light, see-through clothing the miners wore. "The ability to derive energy directly from the sun is awesome," I said. "Do the Sheffrous also go on the surface?"

Maashi came at that moment and sat down as Dasho was about to answer. He produced loud clicks, and Dasho clicked back at him. Then Dasho said in English so I could understand, "Maashi, Tamara is a physician. She will understand."

Maashi's eyes darkened a deep amber.

I glanced at both. "What will I understand?"

"Sheffrous and Sawishas do not feed the same way," Dasho said and paused, as if waiting for Maashi to object.

Lado explained matter-of-factly, "The other male Chamranlinas breastfeed them."

I raised my eyebrows, looked towards Maashi, and said, "You haven't told me that."

Maashi looked away then said, "In your mind I saw that females breastfeed only young offspring. I did not feel comfortable to disclose that we, Pure Colors, are fed by our chowlis and other males. It's forbidden for us to go to the surface because of the risk of attack by our enemies."

"We had to improvise," Lado said, "and encourage a practice that was common a long time ago."

"Why can't you use ultra-violet lamps or something like that? On Earth we use machines called tanning beds that imitate the sun's rays."

"We tried," Dasho said, "but the orange sun is the most efficient energy source for us, and we could not replicate its spectrum in its entirety with artificial lighting."

The Chami sitting across from me said, "We have to be exposed to the sun's rays to extract the maximum energy."

Their society reminded me of a beehive where the worker bees collect pollen and bring it back to the hive. In their case, the Multicolors were the ones taking the risk of attack to reduce the risk for the fertile individuals. I wondered if that meant there were many more of the infertile Chamis than the fertile Pure Colors.

"What about the females? Do they also use the sun for energy?"

"Unfortunately," Dasho said, "the Fanellas live secluded for their own protection under large domes. They can use the sun's rays, but most are fed by sterile male Chamranlinas called the Gray Feeders.

"What?" I sat straight up and shot a questioning look at Maashi. "It sounds like they're prisoners."

Dasho stared at me speechless, his glass held in mid-air. Maashi stared in mid-air.

"The constant threat of the Krakoran or Untouchable," Lado said, emphasizing the word Krakoran, "has forced us to take drastic measures to protect them. The Fanellas are free to go about as they please within the limits of their compounds, but they cannot leave unless they obtain a special authorization from the Elders. In recent years the attacks have increased, and Sheffrous and Fanellas remain as vulnerable as ever."

I frowned after hearing his last sentence. "Why do you call them Untouchable, and why do they attack Sheffrous and females?"

Dasho's brow paled. He glanced over at Maashi, who lowered his head and sighed. He had never discussed this with me. It was obvious this was something difficult for him. Dasho said in an even tone, "We can address that subject when we are in a more private location."

Maashi clicked and stood up, "I shall leave now, Tamara. Eat as much as you want and enjoy the rest of the evening with Lado. I will see you tomorrow."

Dasho stood. "It was a pleasure to chat with you. We can get together later."

"It was a pleasure also," I said, "Good night. Stay safe."

Dasho bent down, took my hand, and pressed his lips on my palm, "Good night shapinka."

The information about the Untouchable and the desperate situation of the Chamis, especially the females, troubled me. I had lost all interest in spending the evening in the Lantillica. I bid goodnight to everyone and left accompanied by a guard. I didn't want to be alone in my quarters tonight and settled instead in Maashi's quarters.

I lay down on one of the soft couches, surrounding myself with thick cushions. The encounter room door was ajar, and I overheard Dasho's mellow voice.

"I love your royal blue and gold choice of colors, Maashi," he sounded pleased. "This English language is much simpler and so much less emotional than ours. I would like to use it for a while just to pronounce the words out loud. Do you mind?"

"I don't mind if it pleases you," Maashi said.

I heard kissing then Dasho's concerned voice. "What's wrong, chumpi? Are you fearful of deep contact even after all this time?"

Maashi said in a low voice, "I apologize for my behavior. Holding back a kiss is an insult and I do not wish to insult you my friend." He sighed. "I still find deep contact daunting."

What an awkward position. I worried leaving would reveal my presence, and I wanted to learn more about Dasho. Luckily, they were still speaking in English.

"Maashi, you should not be ashamed. Everyone knows what happens when you are a prisoner of these monsters. No one will hold you responsible for any wrongdoing."

What? Maashi was a prisoner?

"You are a kind person Dasho, but I did many despicable things, horrible things that even I cannot forgive. I can never share this with anyone." Maashi's voice broke.

I held my breath.

"Look at me," Dasho said. "Listen to me chumpi. You survived. That is what everyone sees. That is the only thing that counts. You must put everything else aside. Forgive yourself and discard those terrible memories."

"I survived but at what cost," Maashi cried out. "All my chowlis died. Several guards died, and a few more suffered serious injuries when I was rescued."

My chest tightened. I could hear the pain in his voice.

"They have not died in vain since you are alive today. To honor them and for your sake, you must recover and be a successful Sheffrou once again. I know it is a long and arduous process." Dasho paused. "Maashi, you must remain strong. I have seen many Sheffrous come back from darkness only to remain shadows of their former selves forever. Believe in yourself and you will find your charissa."

"I don't know if I will find the strength to be who I was before the kidnapping." Maashi's voice faltered.

My heart went out to him and to all the others who had suffered.

"Maashi, you are a Pure Color, a Sheffrou 8. You will always endure shame and sadness because of what happened, but the pain will decrease with time. Do not shy away from deep contact because it is the one thing which will heal you."

They clicked and kissed.

Maashi pleaded, "Be patient with me."

Someone stirred. Dasho said, "My friend, you are so thin, do you not eat every day?"

There was a moment of silence. "I eat often enough with Lado. The Elders have assigned him as temporary chowli for me."

"An assigned chowli is not like one you have bonded with. You must find new chowlis. You know well that for a Sheffrou 8 such as you, one companion is not enough to feed you and satisfy your needs."

What needs? Exactly what was a chowli supposed to do? Were they required to swear allegiance and defend the Sheffrou until death? What did the chowlis get in return for their loyalty? Wealth? Power? Something else I wasn't aware of? Was Maashi unwilling or unprepared to complete the daunting task of finding someone willing to risk his life for him after the sad fate of the other chowlis?

I strained to hear more, and there was only silence. I held my breath so I wouldn't reveal my presence.

"I know you are in pain, my friend, but you must eat every day." Dasho sounded upset.

"I'll try to follow your advice and I'll let Lado feed me regularly."

"With the Great Eclipse events," Dasho said, "you will have ample opportunities to meet new males and perhaps your search for a chowli will be successful. In the meantime, the little human female can help you find your charissa, your balance." He paused. "I saw how you were holding her. She can satisfy your need for affection. As for your other needs, there are plenty of males out there. Do not hold back, Maashi."

The mattress rippled then the encounter room went silent

I lowered my head. My heart was thumping in my chest. I understood now why Maashi never disclosed his kidnapping, the loss of his faithful companions, and the time spent as a prisoner of the Krakoran. It must have been a horrific experience of abuse and torture, an experience he would never want to share with anyone, and certainly not with me, an alien female. Thinking of his ordeal overwhelmed my mind and tears stung my eyes. Why was the world so cruel?

I slept and dreamed dark dreams for several hours until footsteps startled me awake. Maashi had just walked out of the encounter room and stared at me in surprise. "How long have you been here?" His voice cut the air like a blade.

I swallowed hard. "Since last night. I didn't want to sleep in my quarters."

He glanced back at the door. "Did you hear us?"

I hesitated. "Yes, but I wasn't trying to spy on you." I paused. "I heard about the kidnapping. I had no idea."

His eyes paled. His face hardened, and he clenched his fists. He took a few steps away from me, turned, and stood facing the wall. He rested his head against it and his breathing deepened.

"Maashi," I whispered, "I apologize for listening to your conversation. I'm sorry if I upset you." My hands shook. "I'll go now, back to my quarters." I stood up quickly and started towards the door.

In two strides he was at my side. I gasped.

He kneeled beside me, took me in his arms and hugged me. He traced the contour of my face with his long slender fingers and kissed my forehead, then my temple, and put his cheek against mine.

"Don't be alarmed, little one. I'm not angry with you."

"I understand now why you never talked about the Untouchable."

"The kidnapping doesn't concern you. I'm the one who has to bear the shame." He bent his head down.

"Maashi," I raised my head to look in his eyes, "if you had to live that ordeal all over again, would you do anything different?"

He hissed his displeasure. "I had to do what I did to spare the others. Otherwise, they would have suffered even more." He closed his eyes.

"You did what you had to. You had no choice."

He opened his eyes. They were glistening with tears.

"Everything you did was out of compassion for the others. You need to show the same compassion to yourself. Once you forgive yourself, your spirit will be free. Your life will have meaning again. You'll finally be able to move on." I touched his cheek and kissed it.

He rested his cheek on mine. "I hope with all my heart it'll be so."

# Chapter 12

Maashi took me this morning to his private pool with the crystalline water, the one I loved. Today, globes floating high above inundated the surface with a light so bright you felt like you were under a glorious summer sun. The white marble floor and the blue walls speckled with turquoise and gold mosaics created a peaceful and relaxing atmosphere.

Maashi smiled as we entered in the lukewarm water. With just a few strokes he swam the entire length of the pool then eased back close with an amused look on his face. His long slender body hovered on one side, dove under me, and reappeared on the other side. I chuckled at his antics.

"Come, Tamara." He took my hands in his and led me around the pool.

"The water is so nice here," I said. "Such a pleasant change from the cold underground pools." I wore my turquoise bathing suit, and he wore his steel color chemcha. I was at ease in his presence. What a contrast to the day we met when fear overpowered my senses.

"Come," he repeated. He pulled me close and observed my face, his amber eyes looking deep into mine. I sensed the slow movement of his legs as we treaded in the calm water. There was such strength but such gentleness in him.

"I love when you are in my arms," he said. He bent his head and kissed my cheek just below my ear.

He held me against him and stepped out of the water, sat down on the edge of the pool and settled me on his knee. He traced the contour of my face with his middle finger then tilted my chin up. Bending his head, he pressed his moist lips on mine. I caressed his face. His skin was smooth as silk.

He clicked soft clicks and purred. His lovely aroma filled the air like a mist. His tongue licked my lips and glided inside creating a delicious sensation. I touched his tongue with mine and he pulled it back. His eyes laughed and he plopped kisses all over my face.

I squirmed and giggled, "Stop. You're tickling me."

He reached a console on the floor. He pressed two buttons and a tall glass filled with a white liquid appeared beside us.

"Here, gentle one," he said, "drink this," and handed me the glass.

I brought my lips to the rim and tasted it. Sweeter than milk with a hint of vanilla, it was delicious. I took a sip and then drank more. The drink was filling, satisfying.

He looked at me and smiled. It was a charming smile. This was the first time he smiled and showed his tiny teeth. He squeezed me and rubbed his cheek against mine.

Happy to be in his arms, I hid all thoughts of home far away in my mind. Refusing to think about Earth considerably improved my mood. I was free of worries for the first time in a long while.

"I love the taste," I said.

"Enjoy your drink. We call it choun. Before mating, it is customary to feed the Fanella." His brow softened, and he clicked a few times as if he recalled special moments spent with the females.

"You give them a glass of choun?"

Maashi laughed and the clear bright sound carried over the pool and echoed on the walls. "No, Tamara," he said, bobbing his head to one side, "We have to establish an intimate connection with the female, so we breastfeed her."

"Oh."

He grinned. "I thought you would prefer to drink the choun with a glass."

I chuckled and put my empty glass down.

He reached behind me and pulled up the top of my two-piece bathing suit and removed it. He placed his hand on my stomach and rubbed it my slow circular movements. His fingers glided over my skin, and I shivered with delight. Then he held my breasts and caressed them, feeling their roundness, touching their firmness. His mouth traveled across my chest, leaving a trail of kisses. I put both arms around his neck and surrendered to his touch. My skin tingled as pleasure spread through my body.

I looked around, and whispered, "Do the guards ever come here? What about Lado, does he have a key?"

Maashi's eyes shone. "Little one," he said, "no one is allowed in my private quarters without my permission, especially when I have a guest."

He leaned back and held me, so I lay flat over his bare chest.

"Oh," I cried out, "this feels so nice."

"The females love to lie down over the males this way," he said, "they find great pleasure in rubbing their skin over my skin."

Maashi pulled me up higher. "They also enjoy this." He licked my breasts with his long silky blue tongue as his hands massaged my scalp. What an exquisite feeling.

He turned to his left keeping me in his arms. His warm body radiated energy like an aura. He lifted his right leg and applied light pressure on my leg and lower body. Then he rocked me back and forth. Sheltered in his tender embrace as if wrapped in a cocoon, I wanted this sensation to last forever.

He slid his hand in between my legs and massaged me until I throbbed. My heart pounded and jumped from beat to beat. I moaned, engulfed in his loving arms. Maashi purred and clicked and a warm feeling rushed through me until I climaxed with cries that echoed across the pool.

Maashi covered me in a protective embrace. "It is a delight to hear your pleasure. You cry out like a young Sheffrou."

While I recovered my senses, he lay on his back and closed his eyes. His breathing deepened and his body relaxed. I was amazed to see him climax in a private and contained fashion right beside me.

A faint but definite blue glow surrounded us. A powerful aroma of orange and raspberry pound cake, like the ones Nate used to bake, filled the air. The aroma was so strong it brought back vivid memories of my house, my husband baking in the kitchen, my young children eating pound cake with vanilla ice cream. The unexpected vision filled my mind and my heart broke with longing. My eyes watered, and I cried out.

Maashi cooed. "Don't be alarmed little one. There is nothing to fear."

"I try so hard," I said and blotted my tears, "not to think about Earth but I keep remembering things about my home and it hurts so much. How can I chase those thoughts away?"

Maashi held me close. "Chumpi, sweet one," he said, "you should cherish memories of your home world. They're part of you. Even though they may bring forth pain, they belong to you and constitute a crucial part of your life experience."

He was right. I was afraid to forget a lot of fond memories of Earth and instead of chasing them away, I should hold on to them.

"I can't stand this unending wait Maashi. When will I go home?"

"I don't know."

"Isn't there anything else you can do?"

Maashi tilted his head and said, "A message was transmitted to all our fleet. They should alert us of any information concerning your species. It will take time before we know if they found something meaningful."

I sighed and let my head drop on his chest. Spaceships and space travel. Humans on Earth only went back and forth to the space station.

I lifted my head. "Why do you smell like pound cake?" Against him, the scent was so powerful I could almost taste the cake.

Maashi stiffened, and searched in my eyes, "Do you like the way I smell?"

"You smell wonderful." His exhilarating aroma made my head spin.

His amber eyes grew wide. "The aroma is part of a phenomenon called holoma. This happens when Sheffrous mature. They glow a purplish-blue color and exude pheromones when they feel pleasure. It is most important in mating. It entices the Fanellas to come to us and they become aroused by the aroma and the bluish glow of our bodies."

"Your odor attracts the females like perfume?"

He smiled, "Yes. And, like our Fanellas, you are aroused by my holoma. It's different for the males. They possess a stronger sense of taste. When a male greets a Sheffrou, custom dictates to kiss his shoulder and his neck. This is to show respect but also enables the male to taste the Sheffrou." He smiled. "The holoma taste and smell varies for each individual. I'm relieved to see that you enjoy mine because it would have been terrible for me if you didn't like it."

"Who wouldn't like it? You have a great aroma."

Maashi's eyes narrowed to small slits. "The Untouchable cannot stand it. They have a strong sense of smell and they hate it."

I considered this for a moment. Did this mean what I thought it meant?

As if reading my thoughts, Maashi said, eyes glowing with joy, "The Untouchable don't kidnap mature Sheffrous because of their bad smell. I will soon attain maturity. That's why you can smell my holoma."

"That's fantastic."

He chuckled, "It is." He whispered in my ear, "Are you happy, little one?"

"Yes, I am," I snuggled closer.

"I'll come to pleasure you more often if this makes you happy."

"You can pleasure me any time you wish." Was he happy? I rested on him, my mind at ease. Aloud, I said, "What do I taste like, for you?"

Maashi grinned. "You taste sweet and tart, like a fresh fruit not fully ripened."

He sat up and held me on his lap. "Tamara," he said, "the swimming competitions will be held in the Western Compound where Sheffrou Tomisho lives. He has asked me to join him for the last few weeks before the Great Eclipse Celebration."

Without thinking I blurted out, "Can I come with you?"

Maashi's brow darkened, he took a deep breath. "I have to go for a few days to another sector," he said, "to work with the men. I could come back here afterwards to plan our trip." He seemed to ponder this for a moment. "Yes," he said, "you can accompany me."

"Fabulous."

Only later did I realize this was a bad idea because I would be traveling further away from the area of the wormhole.

Maashi appeared absorbed in his own thoughts. "Yes." He smiled. "We'll see Tom Tom again."

# Chapter 13

Tomisho Sannalachan, or Tom Tom, as Maashi called him, was the Sheffrou 8 in charge of the large but distant Western Compound. I understood now that each compound was under the direction of several Sawishas and at least one Sheffrou 6 or 8, and the Multicolors oversaw maintenance and the daily functioning of each compound. Local security depended on the skills of the proud Silver Guards and security of the whole colony was controlled by the Black Guards.

Our trek through the wide underground tunnels was swift and without incident. Contrary to the dark narrow tunnels of my first trip almost two months ago when I came to the main compound, these tunnels were wide, bright and comfortably warm. The guards didn't terrify me anymore and being held in Maashi's arms proved a pleasant experience.

I hoped traveling further away from my place of arrival wouldn't compromise my chances of returning home. I couldn't verify if the Chamis had continued their search for the wormhole. Although I trusted Maashi, the upcoming competitions, his new friend Tomisho, and the various events before the celebration all required his attention. I sensed finding the wormhole wasn't a priority for him right now.

I followed Maashi everywhere unless he was invited to a private audience by a sawisha. Then I had to stay in our assigned quarters with Lado.

The younger Chamis, curious and friendly, often attempted to touch me. The mature Sawishas observed me for a few minutes, clicked, and then ignored me. I hadn't expected such a lack of interest.

"Why don't the Chamis show any reaction when they see me?" I asked Maashi one morning as we made our way back to our spacious quarters in a wide and bright tunnel with Lado. "They've never seen humans, yet they don't appear shocked or troubled by my presence at your side."

"Chamranlinas have been in contact with several alien species," Maashi said. "Only the Krakoran are enemies. The other species are either friendly or indifferent. Also, you are small and female, and you look the same as a Loloyan."

"A what?"

Lado, standing just a few feet away, explained. "A Loloyan. They are aliens almost the same size as you."

"They are the dominant species on planet Koronos." Maashi added. He caressed my head, picked up a strand of hair and let it slide between his fingers. "They have the same facial expressions as you and communicate by clicking the way we do. Their planet was devastated by floods in recent sequences, and many were orphaned. Chamranlinas have adopted a large number that would have perished. You'll see them at the Great Eclipse Celebration."

"So, the Chamis have been in contact with other aliens but have never seen humans?"

"No," said Maashi, "not humans."

"I see."

"Tamara," Maashi said, "We have received a promising report from the search team. They found a circle like the one you described and they're trying to determine if it's a functional gateway."

My heart skipped several beats. "When will you know?"

"The investigation will last a few days." He put his hand on my shoulder. "I'll let you know when it's completed."

I nodded.

Dizzy with the implications of this finding, I followed the group with my head in the clouds.

The dominant color throughout the vast Western Compound was a striking royal blue. A large gold engraving like a coat of arms with a secondary solid color on the portal of each section identified the sawisha in charge. In this compound, Shonava Shitan Garavella, an Emerald Green, controlled all affairs of state with a firm hand. Lado had mentioned he possessed a long experience and complemented well Shonava Tomisho' exuberance and often spur of the moment decisions. A smaller engraving could be seen every twenty feet on the granite walls of the receiving rooms. The two colors formed a wide band that ran along the left wall of the entire section. Bold and prominent in the large areas, they became subdued and thinner in the secondary hallways and private quarters.

I was stunned by the overall affluence. Thick rippling mattresses, usually present only in encounter rooms, covered the floors throughout the sector. The halls were adorned with intricate carvings and sculptures, and I saw multiple fountains with fern-like plants illuminated by white globes.

We reached our new quarters. Wall sconces provided abundant lighting throughout. Small oval tables were scattered about in the receiving room amid plush couches overflowing with diamond-shaped cushions of deep red, green and gold. The dark teal walls splashed with exuberant gold swirls contrasted with the cream carpet which rippled with each step. We settled in our luxurious accommodations and the rooms soon filled with Chamis eager to greet and meet the new Sheffrou.

I took Lado aside and asked him, "Why are the surroundings so lavish, much more than those in Maashi's compound?"

"There are many mature Sawishas here including Shonava Shitan. They are worthy of respect."

"What did they do to earn respect?"

Lado looked at me sideways and clicked a few times.

"What?"

"Do you not understand?"

I blurted out, "Don't patronize me."

"Aye. There is no need to raise your voice at me."

"I didn't raise my voice. You're the one who's clicking."

Lado turned his head. Although busy with his guests, Maashi had set angry eyes on him. "Forgive me," Lado said, "I should not have clicked at you this way."

"This may be simple to you," I said, "but it's complicated for me."

He proceeded to explain in a low voice. "Only mature Pure Colors can succeed and produce offspring. Official recognition, wealth and power are awarded to those who are successful."

"I haven't seen any children."

"The offspring are raised with the Fanellas until they reach the age of twenty sequences then they join the Multicolors until they become adults around forty sequences old."

"This means the fathers don't spend time with them. Don't they get a chance to know their own children?""

Lado's brow darkened, he looked at me as if exasperated by my ignorance. "The offspring belong to all."

"I see." I pursed my lips. The whole population took responsibility for them like certain communes on Earth. "I understand Maashi was successful," I cleared my throat, "at mating so why aren't his quarters as elaborately furnished as these?"

"Shonava Maashi was kidnapped by the Krakoran one sequence ago and months passed with no news of his condition. We feared he had been killed and access to his quarters was denied to everyone except his closest friends." He paused. "When the Sheffrou came back, he deemed the luxury of his quarters unacceptable after the extreme conditions he experienced during his capture and he requested more simple surroundings."

Lado, his mouth set in a tight line, his eyes half-closed, added, "Sheffrou Maashi will have to prove he can mate and produce offspring before he can recover his status and power. Until then he will be treated with the same level of respect as any other Pure Color."

Maashi had to prove his fertility to regain his status. A sobering thought.

"Did the Elders select another Sheffrou to replace him as head of the Central Compound during his absence?"

"No. There were no other Sheffrous who could fulfill the required functions."

"Why not? Surely other Sheffrous would've accepted his post."

Lado bellowed, "there are no other." He glared at me and bent down. With a voice so low only I could hear, he said, "The other candidates are young and lack experience and training. They have not even completed the Draharma trials."

I stopped there. I had no idea what the Draharma trials were, but I decided not to press the matter further.

>———‹‹‹ ● ›››———‹

The next morning, Tomisho came in Maashi's quarters wearing an enigmatic smile I immediately dubbed his Cheshire cat smile. He strolled in the receiving room with a confident swagger and made a beeline towards Maashi who stood to greet him. The tall Sheffrou, sporting a khaki-colored shirt made of a thin material which showed off his sculpted physique in the early morning light, bear-hugged Maashi and kissed his neck. He kept his gaze locked on him and clicked several times. A few moments later he acknowledged my presence. In two long strides he was at my side and lifted me up in his arms. He kissed both my cheeks and applied a soft wet kiss on my mouth. I blushed.

With twinkling dark eyes, he said, "Good morning, sweetheart."

"Morning," I said, struggling to recover my cool.

"I explained to Shonava Maashi that swimming is the most popular activity in the Western Compound. We have the best whitewater runs on Chitina." He added, turning toward Maashi, "I have a favorite one I want you to try. You will love it."

Maashi's shoulders stiffened. "I've been told this run is dangerous," he paused, "I have just recovered from injuries and I don't want to take any risks."

Was he referring to injuries inflicted by the Untouchable? What were they? I hadn't seen any scars on his body.

Tomisho laughed and set me on the ground. "I promise you will be safe. My chowlis, the twin brothers Bako and Roro, will accompany us, and they are the best swimmers in the whole compound. Come with me."

"I'll think about it."

Tomisho insisted, "The deep pools hold crystal clear water, and the scenery is magnificent. Underwater lights are positioned strategically to show the sharp turns. It is not as dangerous as you think. Come. You will enjoy the run."

Maashi's brow darkened. "Very well," he said. "I'll go."

His hesitation was odd. He loved swimming. Why was he holding back?

We started off in the steep tunnels with Tomisho leading. The sound of rushing water echoed from afar. I followed as best as I could in the ascending terrain which twisted and turned as it mimicked the path of the underground river. Along the way, a crowd of happy Chamis greeted us and kissed Sheffrou Tomisho's shoulders. The word spread that he had a high-ranking guest with him. Their clicks increased in pitch and intensity and curious stares followed my steps.

Maashi and I strode several paces behind the main group and he slowed his pace to give me a chance to keep up.

"Why is everybody so excited to see you?" I said.

"Tom Tom has been the only Sheffrou in this compound in the last few sequences," Maashi whispered.

"He seems to be a popular guy."

Soon we arrived in a cave the size of a large conference hall with a deep natural pool which overflowed at one end. The water cascaded downward ten feet then progressed further, gaining speed as it narrowed into an underground river.

Lights located on the edge of the pool made the entire surface of the water shimmer. The burgundy red and the gold of the granite walls flickered and shone with bright bouncing rays. Oval containers filled with golden flowering plants and a variety of deep green shrubs added a colorful touch. On the right of the large pool, there was a smaller one only a few feet deep.

"Flowers," I exclaimed. "Can I touch them?"

"Yes," Maashi said, "you may."

I inhaled their sweet aroma, and my heart overflowed with longing. I wished I was back home. "They smell like honeysuckle. Where did they come from?"

"We brought them from Chamtali," Maashi said, "our mother world. When we left, we took numerous species of plants and animals with us." Maashi extended his long middle finger and touched the delicate petals of a lone pink flower. "Unfortunately, we had to abandon many behind. Sheffrou Tomisho made a special request to have a few brought here so that everyone could enjoy them."

Other Chamis who came to see the new Sheffrou soon surrounded us. They emitted high-pitched clicks and mobbed Maashi. Patient and polite as always, he let them get close and kiss him.

"Everyone, it is time for our swim," Tomisho said in a pleasant voice. He removed his clothing keeping his chemcha, so did Maashi, and nodded at his chowlis who did the same. Then, he addressed the crowd, "You can greet our new guest later."

The eager Chamis stepped aside and let the group pass and walk to the edge of the water.

"I will go first," Tomisho said. "Shonava, you can follow me. Bako and Roro will protect your flanks and shield you from the sharp rocks."

Maashi turned towards me. "You can wait here for me with Lado or swim over there in the smaller secondary pool, but I must warn you, the water is freezing."

I grinned. "You know I can't stand cold water. I'll just wait here for you. Good luck."

Tomisho dove first in the fast current, then Bako, Maashi and Roro. They were out of sight in seconds. I sat nearby to wait for their return. Lado stayed in the vicinity to watch over me but every few minutes, Chamis came over to talk to him and hug him.

I settled on a large flat boulder some distance away and three Chamis walked over, sat beside me, and clicked softly. At first, I smiled, then tried ignoring them, but they inched closer and I was worried they would attempt to kiss me, so I called out to Lado, "Please make them go away."

Lado clicked, said a few words I didn't understand, and they moved to his side. He didn't seem to mind being kissed, hugged, and petted by the three Chamis. I sighed. I would never get used to such generous displays of affection by strangers.

As I sat there, Maashi's news about the wormhole came back to mind. What if the Chamis had found the gateway? I might go back to Earth soon. Instead of being overjoyed by this information I was ill at ease, disquieted by the possibility. I worried every day about what would happen if I didn't get back home and now, I worried about going back.

I watched several swimmers jump in and disappear at the other end of the pool. I couldn't understand Maashi's refusal to accompany Tomisho over the rapids. Why was he so hesitant? Was the run so perilous he was afraid or was he avoiding something else?

Minutes later he reappeared, accompanied by Tomisho and his chowlis. They were laughing and clicking. Tomisho stood with one arm circling Maashi's waist.

As soon as they got within talking distance, I asked Maashi, "How was the run?"

"It was a definite challenge," Maashi answered, his eyes wide, "but quite exhilarating, and the scenery is wonderful. I'm impressed by your skills." He glanced at Bako and Roro. "Thank you," he said, "and you also Tom Tom."

Tomisho laughed, and the sound boomed in the wide-open space of the cave. "You are very kind," he said. "I agree this is a great run. We swam the current at break-neck speed, but the rapids cover such a distance that the descent lasted for several minutes." He grinned in Maashi's direction. "You are a gifted swimmer. We should do this every day."

Maashi chuckled. "I agree, but I need to get in better shape. You will have to direct me to your training facility."

Tomisho squeezed Maashi's waist. "We have an excellent gym and our wrestling team has won many tournaments. You will be able to find skilled partners." He added with a mocking glint in his eyes, "We are aiming for high scores at the Great Eclipse competitions. But first," Tomisho gave him an affectionate hug and kissed his neck, "The two of us need to have a proper meeting."

I may have imagined it, but I was sure Maashi's back stiffened.

"Forgive me, Tom Tom, but I had planned a quick swim with Tamara."

I held my tongue.

Tomisho shot a glance towards me and said, "I will call on you later then." He bowed without insisting further.

"Thank you again for the superb run." Maashi gave him a peck on the shoulders and we strolled to the smaller pool. We didn't stay long because the water was so cold. Then Maashi, Lado, and I went back to the quarters we shared.

I walked straight to the water room to enjoy a hot shower and get ready for a quiet evening. Showers were a grand affair here. Water sprayed from above and every side in short squirts, long blasts, or pulsating bursts. Once I adjusted the temperature (the Chamis took their showers with cold water), my muscles relaxed, and I closed my eyes with contentment.

I still had the impression Maashi was avoiding something, a specific thing related to Tomisho. After the shower, I was in the process of drying myself when I heard the chime announcing a visitor. Bako and Roro had invited Lado to join them for the evening, and I knew Maashi was alone in the receiving room working on his virtual screen.

I heard some clicks.

"I was expecting your visit," Maashi said. "Speak in English. Tamara is here."

There was a moment of silence. Then Tomisho's strong voice resonated in the room. "Shonava Maashi, I am honored by your presence. I have been waiting for this meeting ever since I saw you at the Fall Celebration." A few clicks then he lowered his voice. "I am delighted to hold you in my arms. Your reputation as a powerful Sheffrou and your success with the Fanellas has traveled far beyond the borders of your compound."

"You are very kind," said Maashi. "I'm the one honored to be your guest."

I heard kissing and then Tomisho added in a much softer tone, "Shapinka, your thoughts are hidden. Why do you shy away?"

There was a pause. Maashi said, "Forgive me. Be patient. I haven't been held by a Pure Sheffrou such as you in a long time."

"I am aware of your kidnapping shonava." Tomisho spoke in a soothing voice. "I know what these monsters do and how it takes months to heal the injuries they inflict. You should not be fearful of our meeting. I will treat you with gentleness and respect."

"I'm looking forward to our meeting," Maashi said, "but you shouldn't expect much."

"I know you feel vulnerable, but I sense great strength and purpose in you. You must believe me. I would never hurt you." Tomisho added. "I only hope to be your friend."

"Thank you for your compliments but ----"

"Shapinka, let me hug you and kiss you. Do not hold back. In my arms you will find affection, unflinching support and boundless energy. Let me help you find your charissa, your sense of well-being. With time, the proud Sheffrou everyone knew and admired will return."

"Please release me, I can't tolerate your embrace."

"Shonava, you are trembling."

"Let me go," Maashi said, and in a much stronger tone, "now." □

"Do not fear me Shonava. I just wish to keep you in my arms. I won't restrain you in any way."

"Tom Tom, I----"

"I swear I will not hurt you," Tomisho whispered. "You're so beautiful chumpi. Your skin is soft like a Fanella. Let me lick your face and kiss your lips."

"Tomisho, this is not the time or place."

"Shonava," Tomisho pleaded, "I want to become your friend. When darkness invades your thoughts and despair threatens your soul, summon me. I will come, hold you in my arms, and provide reassurance and strength. Trust me. You are not alone. Together we can overcome your fears."

"Forgive me. I'm not ready." Maashi said.

A long silence followed.

"With time," said Maashi in a shaky voice, "I hope I will heal, but for now I'm just grateful to be alive."

What was Maashi not ready for? The sadness in his voice was too much to bear and I couldn't listen to them anymore. I cleared my throat, stepped in the hall adjacent to the receiving room, and said to no one in particular, "I will go to my quarters now and get some sleep."

I glanced in their direction and couldn't help staring. The two sat half-naked, facing each other on opposite sides of a lounge chair. They were holding each other, and Tomisho was caressing Maashi's back. He kissed Maashi's right palm and both, oblivious to their surroundings, gazed in each other's eyes.

I tried to leave without making a sound but, distracted, I tripped on my towel. I recovered before I fell and clenched my teeth. I peaked at them hoping they didn't notice. My jaw dropped when I saw Tomisho lovingly licking Maashi's neck with a long royal blue tongue. I stood mesmerized, too shocked to move.

A moment later, Tomisho licked Maashi's lips, nudging him to open his mouth. Maashi closed his eyes and, enticed by continuous clicks from Tomisho, extended his own lustrous blue tongue. It was at least ten inches long and speckled with minute gold flecks along both sides. Soon after, the two linked their tongues together and let them glide back and forth over each other.

Tomisho put his arms protectively around Maashi, engulfing him with his body. Maashi leaned on Tomisho's shoulder, and his skin paled and glowed a lovely blue. A wonderful aroma filled the room.

The two were totally engaged in each other, and I envied the special way they connected. Witnessing their intimate encounter was a stark reminder I was the alien in their world, and today I had intruded in their private meeting. I sighed and retreated to my own quarters close by, convinced they didn't notice or care.

I was eating breakfast the next day in the elegant surroundings of the receiving room when Maashi came to join me. Dressed in a cream shirt and dove gray pants with a royal blue sash, he sat on a nearby couch covered with light blue cushions and stretched his long legs.

The previous evening was fresh in my mind. The bond between Maashi and me was so fragile compared to the intense connection developing between him and Tomisho.

To understand what I saw, I quizzed Maashi. "How was your meeting with Tomisho? Or," I said in a mocking tone, "should I call it an encounter?"

Maashi's amber eyes widened. He said, "Good morning, Tamara."

"Good morning," I said. I stirred a pudding with my scooper and waited for his answer.

Maashi looked at his hands. "There are things that aren't meant for your eyes, little one," he sighed. "But, since you were there, I can tell you we had a meeting and shared our private thoughts."

I finished my pudding, attacked another one then blurted, "I didn't realize both of you could stretch your tongues out like that."

Maashi emitted a volley of clicks. "Tamara," he said, "I wasn't prepared for such deep contact with Tom Tom, especially since you were present." He lowered his gaze. "I might remind you that you've seen my tongue before." He mumbled, "From now on, we shall be more discreet when you're in the vicinity."

I glanced at him from under my eyelashes. It was obvious the meeting wasn't planned and Maashi's response confirmed he was ill at ease.

"I am Sheffrou, Tamara, and certain things make me uncomfortable." Maashi turned his head away. "Tom Tom is young and bold, and your presence is inconsequential for him. He wanted much more than a simple meeting."

"Why is he intent on having such close contact with you?"

"He wishes to be my friend and he needs information."

"What does he need?"

"He wants me to share my experiences with the Fanellas. Soon the Elders will consider him a suitable candidate for mating. He is younger than me, eager to learn, and has had little contact with the females."

I twirled a cracker between my fingers. Mating, females, the two were a recurring theme. "Chamranlina mating appears to be complicated and fraught with failure. Why is that? I don't understand."

Maashi gazed at me and spread his fingers apart on his thighs. In a low voice he said, "When the timing is right, the two partners connect, and the mating occurs with harmony. This is how it should be. However, in the last ten sequences only a few Fanellas have ovulated." He paused. "This sequence, none of the mature Fanellas have ovulated."

I frowned. "Why?"

Maashi crossed his arms in front of him as if shielding himself from a dangerous spell. "Our physicians and scientists have been searching for the cause.

"First, they thought it had something to do with this new planet, Chitina. They studied the chemicals in the water, the atmosphere, and the mix of gases being released from the soil. They looked at the food, the choun, the sunlight, etc. Nothing could explain the phenomenon.

"Second, the Fanellas, as you're aware, live confined in compounds. We have modified their physical surroundings to mimic our home world but they're only an imitation." Maashi's voice weakened then he was silent. He crossed his legs.

I observed his face, his eyes pale and wide, his lips a thin line, and realized the females weren't the only ones who missed their world. Chamtali and all its wonders had been a tragic loss for the Chamis. The profound distress it caused lingered to this day and remained a sad collective memory transmitted through generations of Chamranlinas.

He continued. "Third, the continued attacks of the Krakoran have produced a high level of stress. Fanellas are vulnerable even with increased security and this alone accounts for the problems the more mature Fanellas face."

"What about the young females? You said they ovulate."

Maashi leaned back, observed me, and no words came out of his lips.

"Well?"

His eyes locked on mine. "Tamara," he said in an even tone, "Do you remember when you first arrived here?" He paused. "Do you recall the unspeakable terror you experienced when you first saw a Chamranlina or how disconcerted you were the first time my presence aroused you?"

I would never forget those moments and his comments sent a shiver of unease up my spine. Only now did I realize that each time, he knew exactly how I felt. Troubled by this finding, I reached for my glass of choun and took a sip. "Why are you reminding me of that?"

"Young Fanellas," he said, "are just as scared when they meet a Pure Color, Sawisha or Sheffrou, for the first time."

I was puzzled. "I don't understand. Are you saying they have no contact with male Chamranlinas before they reach adulthood?"

Maashi bent his head sideways. "They are surrounded by the Multicolor Feeders, but they never meet a Pure Color until it is time for stimulation."

"Stimulation?"

"Males must trigger the ovulation. The procedure is almost painless when done by experienced hands. However, young females fear the meeting and the stimulation and become agitated which leads to unnecessary pain."

I agreed. I recalled a few instances in the Emergency Room where we had to cancel a simple procedure on a young patient and reschedule it at another time under anesthesia because the fearful patient panicked. "I understand."

"Young Fanellas are physically mature but not emotionally ready to face ovulation and mating. This is the reason the Elders choose only experienced Sawishas or Sheffrous to mate with them."

Everything became clear. Maashi was experienced and knew how to approach a frightened female and what to do to lessen her fear.

"That's why you understood my feelings and knew how to approach me," I said. "How did you find out I was here on Chitina?"

"We have an excellent communication system. You saw me work on my virtual screen. It can transmit any new information to the compounds within minutes. As soon as the miners found you, a team developed a plan. They contacted me and I agreed to go see you. You were a type of alien we had never seen before. Establishing communication and gaining your trust was of the utmost importance."

"But Fanellas are not aliens."

"Yes, but they live separated from Sawishas and Sheffrous all their lives. And we only have 24 hours to mate with them."

"That's so short. Why not longer, a week at least?"

"Tamara," Maashi said, raising both arms, "the Fanellas ovulate within a few days of each other. It allows the males only one day per female, then they move on to the next one and this goes on for seven days. It has been done this way for hundreds of sequences."

They move from one female to the next like an assembly line in a factory. I swallowed hard and said in a loud indignant tone, "That's awful, Maashi. You're putting tremendous pressure on them. The process is inhumane." My heart went out to the females. They were young and inexperienced and had to perform the duty of procreation under pressure and time constraints.

Maashi admitted, "It's a difficult situation."

"To say the least." I grabbed another pudding and popped the cover in one forceful tap. "Maashi, you all need to reconsider the mating scenario and brainstorm the problem. You must try to see things from their point of view. You can't keep the females under a glass dome from birth and expect them to develop the social skills they'll need to fulfill the important duty that awaits them. Your whole premise makes no sense."

Maashi sprang up and paced the room opposite a wall decorated with a giant mosaic of creatures from the world of Chamtali.

"Hundreds of sequences ago," he said, "things were different. There were more Fanellas and more competition between the Pure Colors. The Fanellas could choose their partners, meet them, and spend more time together before mating. However, even in those days, not all males succeeded. Some males, under the influence of Ru Kish, the intense desire to mate, became extremely aggressive and terrible fights ensued. On rare occasions, that would lead to the death of a Pure Color.

"The Council of Elders debated at length on the best way to deal with the problem and decided to control the entire process. The Elders choose the males and only the chosen ones can mate. The decision of the council is irrevocable. No other Chamranlina has any say in the matter." He sighed.

"That doesn't sound much better."

"We have eliminated the competition between the Pure Colors, and therefore there is no more fighting. But recently, some Sawishas, Purples, Reds and even Greens, have voiced strong objections at the Council and refuse to abide by the rules because only Sheffrous have been chosen for several decades to increase the number of female offspring."

"That's not a fair solution. I wouldn't agree either. I was raised in a free society. By deciding with no possible recourse who can and cannot mate, the Elders are intensifying an already volatile situation. Eventually, the Chamis will revolt."

Maashi shook his head to one side to show his disapproval and sat on a couch. "Widespread aggression has never been the preferred solution for Chamranlinas. However, a little over sixty sequences ago, a group of rare fertile Multicolors called Ghouli Ghouli started a rebellion to protest the Elder's decisions. We lived through several sequences of chaos before calm was restored. Today, they argue that the mature Fanellas don't ovulate because only Sheffrous are chosen. They are demanding a more balanced choice between all fertile males."

"Do you think they're right?" I held my little scooper spoon in the air and pointed it at him. "Can the choice of males influence their ovulation?"

"Fanella physiology is complex." Maashi's brow darkened. "Does the choice of the male impact the ovulation? I can't say. There isn't enough information."

"I see." I swallowed a couple spoonfuls of the pudding. "Are you going to be chosen this year?"

"We will have to wait for the Council's decision."

"Dasho mentioned you've had excellent success with mating."

Maashi didn't answer right away. "That was before the kidnapping." Maashi's brow darkened. His back stiffened.

It was time to drop the subject.

I finished my pudding and started on a fruit. The fresh taste made my mouth water. "Why were you so hesitant to go swimming yesterday? I thought you loved swimming."

"I do." Maashi sighed.

"Why then?"

"It doesn't concern you." Maashi lowered his head.

"It's something important, isn't it?"

He looked away. "Tamara, I'm not sure you would understand why."

"I'm sure I can understand."

"You can't read my mind but sometimes you act as if you could." His mouth stretched in a thin smile and he shrugged his shoulders. "I was worried Tom Tom," he said, "would initiate deep contact with me during the run especially since his two chowlis were there."

"Why would he do that? Why is it important to have deep contact?"

"It generates exquisite pleasure for the all involved and can increase one's charissa."

Perplexed, I said, "Did you have deep contact last night?"

"Yes," Maashi sighed. "I wanted to avoid it because I'm not ready."

"Why not?"

"What happened when I was a captive of the enemy has left me emotionally vulnerable. I can tolerate this type of contact only if the other Chamranlina exercises great caution to avoid hurting me. I wasn't sure if I could trust Tom Tom particularly with his two chowlis present."

I swallowed a mouthful and searched in his eyes. "You don't trust him?"

He grumbled. "I would love to. But he's young and I know how difficult it is to resist the Pure Color instinct to dominate and take advantage of a weaker partner. I'm still recovering from the psychological trauma I suffered with the Krakoran." Maashi kept his eyes riveted on a cushion beside him adorned with gold embroidery. "To survive, I had to perform terrible things and now I trust no one. To this day, this lack of trust has hindered my progress and deep contact remains problematic. I struggle daily to sustain my saweya, my life energy."

Maashi extended his arm and traced with his long slender index the delicate pattern on the cushion. "Dasho and the other physicians think I have the capacity to heal." He sighed. "I see little progress."

I said in a soft voice, "Everything heals with time."

We sat in silence for a moment. I selected another fruit, a toughi, and pondered what he mentioned about Tomisho. "How much younger is Tomisho?"

"He is twenty-five sequences younger than me."

I added quickly. A sequence was roughly two Earth years. Tomisho was fifty years younger than Maashi. I blurted out, "Maashi, how old are you?"

"I have completed 129 sequences."

My jaw dropped. Over 255 years old. "Oh, I had no idea," was all I could say. Fear crept in me. "How long do Chamranlinas live?"

Maashi rose, came and sat close, and took me in his arms. "There is no reason to be alarmed little one. I'll live for many more sequences. Most Chamranlinas live up to 200 sequences."

I rested my head against his chest and said, "This is mind-boggling. What is the secret of your longevity?"

"Our cells have the power to regenerate almost indefinitely." Maashi kissed the top of my head.

I inhaled his sweet aroma and looked up at him. "What did Tomisho mean when he said he would help you find your charissa? Why did he say you were like a Fanella?"

Maashi chuckled and ran his index along the curve of my lower jaw. "So many questions." He paused as if considering his answer. "When a Sheffrou is hurt or emotionally distressed, he will not heal until he finds love and happiness, what we call charissa." His gaze was faraway when he added, "I'm still struggling to find my own happiness."

"How did the enemy hurt you so much?"

"The Untouchable can make you see the dark side of your soul." Maashi closed his eyes and stopped. His face became very pale, his breathing labored.

I was touched by the intensity of his pain. I put my arms around his neck and kissed his cheek.

He bent his head, held me very close, and rested his cheek against mine. After a moment, he moved and tilted my chin up with his hand. He kissed me, his smooth soft tongue filled my mouth and his saliva tasted as delightful and sweet as honey. I inhaled his sweet scent and closed my eyes, savoring every second of this wonderful sensation. I melted in his warm embrace and floated light as a feather in a vast blue expanse.

Maashi unfastened his shirt. Then he unfastened mine. He lay back and held me tightly over him, letting his velvet skin brush against mine. The smallest movement sent shivers of pleasure through me. I shuddered.

His chest relaxed as he inhaled and exhaled. A fragrant aroma saturated the air surrounding us. He rocked a few times with eyes closed tight. His skin glowed a perfect blue.

I stayed in his arms for the longest time. I was in heaven.

He never answered my second question. Why did Tomisho say he was like a Fanella?

# Chapter 14

My jaws ached this morning. On Earth, I used to grind my teeth at night when stress overwhelmed me. Work-related issues were often the source of the stress but this past year, arguments between my husband and I had been more frequent and more serious and disrupted my sleep.

As the children got older, we clashed more and more about finances and our life as a couple suffered. It dawned on me that it had all started after a forty-two-year-old colleague of mine passed away from cancer. This made me realize on a personal level how tenuous our lives really were. From that day forward, I was determined to live with zest and passion and stop planning for the distant future. Unfortunately, my husband didn't experience the same epiphany, and this is where our lives took different directions.

Maybe because I hadn't seen Maashi in the last few days, it happened here. How senseless my life on Chitina would be without him. I rubbed my gums and settled on the couch.

When Maashi was around, I forgot my home world. Without him, my mind rushed back to Earth. I missed my children. Now, alone and with a heavy heart, I thought of each of them.

I wouldn't attend David's official engagement party in July. He wanted to introduce his fiancée to the extended family and was planning a formal affair. With no news of my whereabouts, he might postpone or even cancel the event.

I missed Allison the most. She was sociable and outgoing but more fragile than her brothers. I hoped she found the strength to continue through these difficult times. As if to keep her close to my heart, I often wrote letters to her on my pad.

Quiet and introverted Jonathan threw himself in sports and music when life hit hard. Perhaps he was surfing at this very moment.

How about my husband? Did he miss me? Did he think I had been kidnapped, killed, or simply that I had left him?

I had been gone for over three months. I didn't cry as much anymore. My sadness had morphed into a strange feeling of loneliness mixed with dread which followed me throughout the day like a shadow. It lightened only when Maashi was present or at night when sleep took me.

I sighed. I should quiz Maashi about the wormhole. Did they find anything? He said they saw something once but there had been no more news. Sadly, there was nothing I could do. I had studied the network of tunnels until my brain ached and concluded searching by myself was too risky. However frustrating the situation was, I had to remain optimistic and hope the Chamis would find a clue.

The next few days passed quickly between swimming and spending time with Lado. He kept watch over me but there weren't any warm feelings between us. I sensed he wanted to be somewhere else or with someone else.

Curious young Chamis often surrounded us and asked about my home world? Could I describe the surface or the animals that lived there? I explained ecosystems and how connected and diversified they were. I showed them animal drawings I made on my pad and this elicited a torrent of questions. They were avid listeners, and I was amazed at how fast they mastered the English language. Their capacity to repeat my exact words and to remember every detail was phenomenal.

One morning, I was walking alone with Lado and I asked about the Chami society's inner workings.

"What kind of government do you have?"

"The council of Elders, composed of fourteen members, each one representing one compound is our governing entity."

"Are the council members elected?"

"Many sequences ago, older Chamranlinas renowned for their wisdom or their intellect chose members."

"This means you don't have formal elections."

Lado tilted his head to the left, a sign he couldn't understand my question. "There is no need for elections if all the mature Chamranlinas of a compound agree on a candidate."

"What if some individuals don't agree with their choice?"

"Their point of view will be considered, but the choice of the majority will prevail."

It seemed there was little room for flexibility or possibility of innovation if the older members made all the decisions. "What if a younger Chami wants to be a member of the council?"

"Young males are not interested in being members because it involves grave responsibilities."

"Young males? What about the females? How many are there on the council?"

Lado chuckled. "Females?"

I straightened my shoulders and asked. "What's so funny?"

"The Fanellas," Lado said, "choose three among them to be part of the council. They may voice their opinion on any subject but are not required to be present at the meetings or participate in discussions."

I frowned. "Observers with no real decision-making role." They were a minority and powerless.

Lado acknowledged my disapproving look. "Tamara, we have discussed and decided most important matters a long time ago. Our society is stable and organized. Chamranlinas find it most tiresome to argue at length on matters which have been agreed upon in the past." He waved his hands in front of him. "We live in peace among ourselves and few Chamranlinas are at odds with the current system. We decide matters with care and consideration and for the good of all concerned."

"I see."

Lado believed the system was in the best interest of the whole population but Maashi had mentioned that sixty sequences ago, their society dealt with a major rebellion. Why didn't he mention that?

The Chamis grew more excited and impatient as the celebration of the Great Eclipse approached. I had learned to recognize the young Sawishas. Over six feet tall and slender, they wore light color sashes: green, aqua, pink or rarely, purple. They flocked in groups of six to eight like long-legged birds and often took off together in one direction without warning.

That afternoon, I explored a large gathering room and a group of six young Pure Colors appeared out of nowhere and knocked me over. A loud hiss startled me. I looked up and saw Lado staring them down. They quickly dispersed in every direction but regrouped a little further.

"They are impossible," Lado growled. He took my hand and helped me up. "They should respect the colors you wear and who you represent. Their behavior is unacceptable: devising unpleasant tricks and trampling over people."

"What tricks are you talking about?" I said, readjusting my shirt and my sash.

He grumbled, "Silly things meant to annoy the adults. They will add something in your food to make it unappealing, cut a lock of your hair as a prize, steal your clothing or your sash, hide your footwear. Things of that nature."

I laughed. "They sound like pranksters. Our teenagers behave much the same way." I looked around the cave and said, "I thought Maashi would be here today. Do you know where he is?"

"He is swimming with Sheffrou Tomisho."

"Again?" It was my turn to grumble. "When will I see him?"

"Not today."

Tomisho followed Maashi like a puppy. He held him by the waist, kissed him non-stop, and jumped on the opportunity to be alone with him. Whether there were other Chamis in the room or they were by themselves didn't bother him. This tested my patience. My presence didn't seem to be of any consequence.

When Maashi wasn't with Tomisho, he was off swimming with a few Sawishas or gone to the training area. Lado must have hinted my annoyance because the next morning he invited me to accompany him.

Before we left, Maashi said, "Tamara, you can sit on the benches provided for the spectators and observe. Lado will stay with you and answer your questions."

I nodded. I looked up at him and said, "Is it a big gym? Do you use a lot of equipment?"

"We have equipment, but most athletes use a training partner." Maashi extended his arms. "Come." In one swift movement he picked me up, and we left with long swift strides, accompanied by Lado and two guards.

I enjoyed Maashi's arms, even if it was just for traveling. I admired at leisure the wide tunnels carved by mighty underground rivers. In these tunnels, stalactites hung from above and created impressive and menacing sculptures. I decided I preferred the smooth tunnels adjacent to Maashi's compound.

After a short while we arrived in a spacious room with brown granite walls veined in black and orange. Over thirty Chamis were present and several pairs worked together in the sparsely furnished gym. White globes three feet in diameter, placed high on the ceiling, provided the lighting. Maashi released me and said, "You can watch from over there."

I followed Lado and tapped with my feet on the thick mattress and watched the ripples run all over the floor. Lado pressed buttons on the wall and a sturdy couch equipped with a back rest appeared.

Lado sat and signaled me to sit at his side.

I glanced toward Maashi and saw two Chamis greet him, wearing dark brown bracelets with a thinner green band. He undressed and kept only his chemcha, his rubberlike underwear. Only a few others wore the same. I asked Lado why most Chamis were naked.

"Sawishas and Sheffrous," he answered, "are required to wear protection. Multicolors are not and prefer to train naked because it allows more freedom of movement."

Maashi had been paired with a fierce-looking Chami. Lado explained the red markings on his chest, called quatay, proclaimed his sawisha status.

Maashi and his partner stretched using each other's body instead of using any apparatus. A few wrestlers glanced in their direction then towards me but soon resumed their own activities.

A brawny sawisha with a barrel chest and impressive biceps discarded the weight he had lifted and observed them. Then he crossed his muscular arms, turned, exposing a large dark green quatay over his shoulders and upper torso. After a moment, he proceeded to lift basketball- size rocks and carry them back and forth across the room.

A group of Chamis lay flat on long work benches, did crunches or pushed on square weights positioned at the end of a metallic bar. Others rolled heavy round metallic objects from one end of the room to the other. There were few apparatuses and overall the room seemed large and bare.

Maashi and the red Chami stretched for twenty minutes and then stood and faced each other.

I asked Lado, "Are they going to train or fight?"

"The best training involves sparring,"

The red made the first move. He grabbed Maashi, held him, and tried to topple him. Maashi stood his ground but his face was taut as he struggled against the visibly stronger opponent.

The pair moved back and forth for a few minutes and the red clicked at Maashi. Then, as if showing a specific move, he seized Maashi and hurled him in the air like a projectile. Maashi landed on the rippling mattress, spun and rebounded on his feet. They repeated the same maneuver several times.

"Why is Maashi having so much trouble fighting that Chami?" I asked. "Isn't he in shape?"

"The Sheffrou has been paired with opponents of similar strength and experience for the past few days," Lado said. "Today the trainers decided he should spar with a new partner called Zari. He is one of the stronger wrestlers."

Maashi, after several tries, toppled the red who immediately rolled on the mattress and, in an instant, leaped back on his feet. Before Maashi reacted, he grabbed him by the neck and held him tighter and tighter.

I stood up and said, "Hey, he's choking him."

Lado hissed. "Tamara, sit and be quiet."

Maashi fought hard to send his opponent to the floor and succeeded. But when the red stood up, he picked up Maashi and threw him across the room.

I winced. "That looked painful," I said under my breath.

"The Sheffrou must learn to keep his body low so his opponent won't grab him by the waist and throw him. It is a basic wrestling rule and most Sheffrous experience difficulties mastering it."

On and on it continued until I couldn't watch any more. Instead, I scanned the room and saw the same barrel-chested sawisha standing motionless with eyes locked on Maashi.

"It is over Tamara," Lado said, "You can relax now. The sheffrou has done well. Zari is a champion and therefore a powerful opponent. He will take part in the upcoming wrestling tournament held a week before the Great Eclipse Celebration." He nodded to himself. "Sheffrou Maashi has only recently been allowed to train. He had to wait for his injuries to heal."

"The injuries inflicted by the enemy?"

Lado hissed. "Yes, the Krakoran."

I remembered Maashi stating he was looking for new chowlis. "Do you think Maashi will want this red Chami for chowli?"

"This Sawisha has dedicated his life to wrestling. He would not be interested."

The bout had lasted an hour, and I was exhausted. Maashi stayed on the mat after the last hard landing. An onlooker went to him and extended his hand to pull him upward. Maashi saluted his opponent, and they both clicked and kissed each other's necks. He looked at Lado, said something I didn't understand, and headed toward the exit with the Chami who helped him.

"Is Maashi leaving?" I asked.

"He will shower, get a massage, and join us later," Lado said.

"A massage from the one who helped him?"

"Yes. He has been taking care of him since his first day at the gym. Come. We must leave."

A sawisha, taller than Maashi, wearing a red chemcha, strolled in the gym accompanied by three Chamis wearing multicolor wrist bands. He bumped into Maashi who was on his way out. The red pretended nothing happened until he walked to a slender purple Chami then he bellowed in English. "Yes," he said, his back to Maashi, "It is a shame to see how our private gymnasium has become a haven for the ones unwelcome elsewhere." He paused as if waiting for a response. "I speak in the alien female's tongue as requested by Sheffrou Maashi. She has a simple mind and therefore it is a simple language. Now, everyone is familiar with it." He snorted and threw his head backwards.

Maashi turned, and said, "Sawisha, I see no reason for insults."

The red continued, ignoring Maashi, his dark eyes flashing his contempt. "I was told the Sheffrou spends his time with her. Instead he should train to improve his wrestling skills." He erupted in a roaring laugh.

Maashi raised his voice. "My skills are no concern of yours."

"You are right Sheffrou, I should commend you. You must be special to have survived five months at the hands of the Krakoran. No one has accomplished this feat except you. How did you do it?"

Maashi's eyes became dark slits. He took a few steps toward the red.

"You were... How shall I say?" The red sneered. "Most useful to them. Oh? What use do the Krakoran have of a Sheffrou?"

Maashi lashed out. "Hold your tongue Sawisha." He fisted his hands.

The red pretended he didn't see Maashi coming at him. He addressed the few Chamis who were listening. "Many say only a coward could have survived so long." His lips curled in an insolent smile, "I am not afraid to state aloud what I think. Coward." He circled around Maashi, extended his arms with palms open, and swayed his hips.

Maashi glared at him. "I survived because I used my wits, a quality your weak mind doesn't possess."

"Sheffrous are all cowards." He gestured at the growing crowd of onlookers gathering around them. "Ask any red or black." He inclined his head sideways with a knowing grin. "But things will change. If you think you will mate this sequence," his head was within inches of Maashi's face, "forget those pretty thoughts. I am not the only sawisha who disagrees with the Elders. Many others loathe Sheffrous and want changes."

"And what changes," said Maashi, straightening, "are you referring to?"

"We Sawishas, plan to challenge the laws that allow Sheffrous to mate. What we need are strong males with the courage to attack the Krakoran and get rid of them for good." He glanced around expecting the crowd's approval. "The Elders are old and weak. They make irresponsible, ridiculous decisions."

A few Chamis responded with clicks. The others ceased whatever they were doing and watched.

Maashi raised his head and said in a firm voice. "Insulting me is one thing. Defying the Elders is another thing. You will suffer the consequences."

"How wrong you are." The red laughed. "The Elders will not choose you and you will walk in shame for the next sequence."

Maashi hissed. "We will see."

"No one," the red's eyes glowed with anger, "no one should be chosen because of the size of their schloppies and especially not cowardly Sheffrous."

"That's enough." Maashi shoved him. "Be silent and I'll forget your insults."

The red bent his head and shoulders as if stepping backward but instead, threw himself forward and delivered a hard punch in Maashi's stomach.

I gasped. A punch in the stomach meant a blow to the heart.

Maashi reeled from the pain. He blinked and stepped sideways. He recovered in an instant and, lithe as a feline, he twisted his body in a complete turn and threw a punch of his own to the red's jaw.

I covered my hand with my mouth.

The red wiped his mouth with the back of his hand and shaken, sent a weak jab and missed his opponent's face by a hair.

Maashi hissed. "Stop this nonsense or you will taste my anger."

"Why stop now? I'm enjoying our exchange." His forced laugh sounded like a growl. He danced in front of Maashi staying out of range but close enough to punch him again and again.

I couldn't believe what I was seeing. "Why don't the guards intervene?" I whispered to Lado.

Lado stared at me. "The Sheffrou is not in any danger."

I insisted, "Somebody will get hurt."

"Be quiet," he said in a tone that admitted no rebuke.

Maashi received a few more punches each one harder than the last. His eyes were black, his jaw tight with anger. He hissed a warning. "Enough. Enough of this."

The Red growled. "Tired? What are you going to do? You cannot touch me. I am a much better fighter." He jumped backwards and quick as lightning struck Maashi's jaw. His head shot back, and his mouth twisted in pain. One more uppercut and a jab in the stomach and he fell to his knees.

"I bet you the Krakoran didn't hurt you like that." The red lifted his arms up high, stepped back and stared at the kneeling Maashi who spit foamy pink blood.

I felt Lado's hand squeezing my arm. "Do not move," he whispered.

Punches to the face, the neck, and the stomach rained on Maashi. I bit my lip and saw stars. This had to stop.

The red paused a second. When he threw the next punch, Maashi brought one foot forward and tripped him. Swift and agile the red bounced to his feet, caught Maashi's arm, and twisted it backwards. A loud crack resonated in the gymnasium.

The elated opponent lifted his head in victory. In a strained voice he said, "You will be the one to suffer the consequences."

The red released him. Maashi stared at him for a long moment, rose, turned, and lumbered out. A few Chamis followed. Everyone present, friend or foe, stood silent.

Lado hustled me out of the gym.

"Why didn't the guards do something?" I fisted my hands and stared at Lado. "The fight could have been prevented. No one needed to be injured."

Lado answered in his condescending tone. "The altercation was limited to two individuals. The guards will intervene only if the Pure Color is in imminent danger or if several Chamis attack at the same time."

He brought me back to our quarters, and I stayed alone in the receiving room. I paced back and forth between the long couches and threw across the room the few cushions which dared to lie in my way. Damn you Lado. You should have done something. And if I had been a guard, I would have stopped this nonsense.

Even though significant violence existed on Earth, I had never witnessed a fight with my own eyes. I hoped this was the last one I ever saw. As an Emergency Room physician, I often took care of patients involved in brawls. Gunshot wounds were rare but fistfights and attacks with other weapons were common. Now, Maashi was hurt and I couldn't see or contact him. Was he in pain? Did they give analgesics here? Will they put a cast or something similar on his arm and evaluate him for internal bleeding?

I splashed my face with cold water and stared at the mosaics on the wall. My anger dissipated, replaced with disgust. Grabbing two large cushions I plopped myself on a couch. I took my pad and wrote a long note to my daughter. I told her how much I loved her and how I missed her and her brothers.

Later that evening, Maashi came. He sat on the couch beside me. His oval eyes were large and pale, his back stiff. He wore subdued colors: khaki clothes and sash.

He bent his head sideways and looked at me.

I got up and sat beside him. "Show me your arm."

"It's fine Tamara. It will heal."

"Aren't you going to wear a cast to help the bone mend? Is everything else okay?"

"It's a simple fracture, I don't need a cast. There are no other significant injuries."

"It could've been worse." I grumbled.

Maashi bent forward. "You're upset," he said with a soothing voice.

I turned my head away.

"I had to get rest," he whispered. He took a long breath. "I needed time to think." He spread his hands over his knees. "My behavior wasn't acceptable. I should have controlled my anger."

I pursed my lips. "I don't like violence."

He put a hand on the side of my face. I looked in his eyes. He bent over and licked my lips with his sweet tongue until my heart fluttered and my head spun.

After a moment, he said in a gentle tone, "Tamara, I am Sheffrou and I must find new chowlis. I may choose one called Chustan. You saw him at the gym today."

I pulled away.

"Lado will leave soon. The Elders are sending him to another sector. I have to choose a chowli."

Lado stepped in right then with a cold, detached expression. He came over and kissed Maashi's right shoulder. He said in a voice devoid of emotion, "Sir, the Elders have summoned me to explain your singular behavior today with the red called Hamra. You know the rules. A high-ranking Pure Color cannot fight with a younger Sawisha because this lowers his status. I told them I will discuss the matter with you."

Maashi stared straight ahead and stated, "There is nothing to discuss."

"The Elders are concerned," Lado said, "You reacted with undue aggression and increased your risk of injury. This is unacceptable behavior for a Pure Color."

"The red suffered no long-term injury."

"Sir, with respect," Lado insisted, "your response was out of proportion to the insult."

"You," said Maashi cutting him off, "weren't the one insulted."

I nodded. My eyes moved from one to the other.

"I gave a full report to the Elders," Lado said, "and they agreed not to issue an official reprimand and to dismiss Hamra's complaint. However, you must find a first chowli as soon as possible."

Maashi stared at Lado. "You have mentioned that several times and I am well aware of the Elders' demands."

"Sir," Lado pressed on, "did you see an Emerald Green at the gym today? He is eager to have a meeting with you. He is an excellent choice for first chowli."

Maashi cut him. "I'm not ready to choose right now. I want to spend time with Tomisho."

"Sir, there are several good candidates in this compound. The Elders agreed to let you travel here for this specific purpose."

"What I do with my time supersedes the Elders' plans Lado," Maashi said.

"Sir, I must insist. Sheffrou Tomisho will not feed you and the little female will not satisfy your needs."

"What?" I asked.

Neither responded to my question.

Maashi straightened his back and said in a low voice, "That's enough, Lado."

"Shonava, it is my duty to notify the Elders of your intentions."

Maashi stared at him with dark eyes. "I won't tolerate any interference with my decisions."

"Sir, I must insist. You need to concentrate on finding a possible candidate for first chowli." Lado returned his gaze without flinching. "I will inform the council on your progress before I leave."

Maashi hissed. "Do what you must." His brow was black. He stood up, turned and left without another word.

Lado hissed and left through another door.

I sat there bewildered. I hated all this chowli stuff. Maashi was obviously not ready to choose.      Where did I fit in this picture? His life consisted of meetings with others. Between Sheffrous, Sawishas, and Chamis, what was I for him? Did he care for me at all? My eyes filled with angry tears. What did Lado mean when he said I couldn't satisfy Maashi's needs?

I couldn't deny it anymore. Maashi was becoming an important part of my life. One look from him and I felt weak with desire. One kiss and my heart melted. Without him my life had no meaning. In his arms I didn't even think of Earth and kept old memories stored far away because thinking of my family just increased my sadness and my guilt.

I growled and punched the closest pillow. I should never have gone to the back of the yard that day. Why did I let my curiosity get the best of me? Why didn't I think before I approached that shiny circle?

# Chapter 15

Ten days later, we attended a swimming competition. Maashi and Lado had reconciled and there was no mention of a finding a first chowli anymore.

The oval cave, the size of an auditorium, teemed with animated Chamis. The surface of the Olympic-size pool sparkled like a jewel under the yellow globes floating twenty feet above. Streaks of burnt ochre and burgundy warmed the dull brown granite of the walls. Alcoves created havens of tranquility where Chamis could meet undisturbed.

Young and old turned to watch when Sheffrou Maashi strolled in, accompanied by Lado and four uniformed guards. Maashi stood out among the crowd of Multicolors with his loose butter-cream shirt exposing his ivory quatay, royal-blue sash, and cobalt blue pants. He joined the other Pure Colors with a confident stride.

Maashi's personal guards wore their ceremonial attire: light gray pants with a fudge shirt decorated with a salmon tear-drop pattern. Their multicolor sash was their only distinguishing feature. Lado sported the same colors but displayed a wide chartreuse and olive-green sash. I wore my usual khaki shirt and pants with the added touch of a turquoise sash with a thin gold border.

At first Maashi held me in his arms, but soon, surrounded by so many Chamis eager to greet him, he had to put me down.

"Maashi," I said, looking up at him, "I can't see anything."

"I will lift you Tamara," Lado said.

I frowned but soon settled in Lado's arms and surveyed the crowd. This was my first time seeing so many individuals in one arena. Maashi appeared to be the only Sheffrou present. The young Chamis were shorter than Maashi, but some of the flamboyant Sawishas, wearing wide unicolor sashes reached well over eight feet. I realized I had underestimated Maashi's height. He was well over seven feet with the upper body and long legs of a swimmer unlike the heavy muscular look of some of the Pure Colors, the Greens, the Reds, and the Purples.

Numerous Chamis patted Maashi's back and kissed his right shoulder. They consisted of two different groups. The first were attentive and affectionate whereas the second group approached him with an arrogance bordering on impudence. They didn't hesitate to administer long and overbearing kisses. Twice Maashi turned his head away to break free of a lingering kiss. At one point, a guard stepped in and clicked at the offending sawisha until he released his hold.

In Lado's arms, I watched the scene with interest. "Maashi looks annoyed. What are these Sawishas doing?"

"Some of them hate Sheffrous," Lado said. "They will take every opportunity to assert their power over them and humiliate them. The guards must remain vigilant to protect them."

"They protect Sheffrous against kisses but not against blows." I shook my head in disbelief. "Why do Sawishas hate them?"

"The Elders choose only Sheffrous for mating," Lado said. "This causes animosity and ill feelings among the Pure Colors."

One sawisha caught my attention: a gaunt older male, with raven hair and ashen complexion. His long purple sash floated at his side and almost touched the floor. Dragging his right leg, he lumbered across the length of the cave toward Maashi. The crowd parted to let him through. Silence filled the room as young and old turned and stared as he passed.

The purple paused, raised his head, and glowered at the crowd as if daring them. The cruel gaze of his violet eyes sent a shiver of apprehension up my spine.

"Who is that?" I whispered.

Lado, with the odd pinched expression of someone exposed to a foul odor, said, "Master Kokin Cronobutin, former mentor of Shonava Maashi."

Kokin stopped right in front of Maashi and cupped the Sheffrou's face with his hands. First a few clicks then he delivered a cold, hard kiss. He stepped back and a sardonic smile curved the corners of his lips. "Your presence here among the elite is unexpected," he said, "One sequence has passed since your capture by the Krakoran. We can only imagine the atrocities you suffered as a prisoner of these abominable creatures. After your rescue many thought you would never regain your saweya and would be incapable of mating again." He clicked. "My chowlis have informed me you are still struggling with the incapacitating consequences of the kidnapping."

At the mention of his ordeal, Maashi straightened his shoulders and the color drained from his face. "Master Kokin," he said with contained anger in his voice, "My saweya is excellent and increases every day. I am told my progress has been remarkable."

"My best pupil reduced to a weakling." Kokin said, ignoring his response. He patted Maashi's back and bestowed a condescending smile, tilting his head so everyone could see. "Do not entertain any hope of mating this sequence. The Elders have passed a resolution to choose only candidates who will perform at the highest level. Even though you possess a satisfactory record," he sneered, "you still require more time to heal. If they chose you and you met," he paused, "difficulties. . . your failure would only lead to more distress."

"I assure you," Maashi's firm voice resonated in the vastness of the cave, "I am ready."

"Yes, yes," said Kokin in a false soothing tone. He turned, addressing the crowd, "As you all know, the Council has been choosing only Sheffrous for mating for more than half a century now. This has created an intolerable situation. We failed to accomplish our goal of attaining a hundred Fanellas and we have weakened our position against the enemy by not providing enough male offspring to replace the high number of losses sustained during their attacks. Yet, the Elders, in their immense wisdom," Kokin snarled, "are blindly pursuing the same course and choosing Sheffrous to replenish our population. We must put a stop to this madness. We, Sawishas, must unite and challenge their choices with our own. This is our time. We must be the ones who alter the fate of the Chamranlinas and prepare for a brighter future. We ---"

Disapproving rumbles coming from the back of the room prevented him from continuing. The throng glared with disapproving eyes and hissed at the unwelcome visitor. It soon became obvious that Maashi was a favorite.

Kokin whirled around, his ornate sash swirled at his side. His gaze assessed the crowd and he gestured in my direction with a long gnarled middle finger. "Why do you insult your peers," he huffed, "by letting that lowly creature take part in this elite gathering?"

Maashi's eyes became thin black slits. "Tamara is Sheffrou," he said in a loud voice making sure the whole assembly heard him, "she is Ishkibu and worthy of our respect and our protection. She accompanies me everywhere I go." He added, "I need not remind you sir, that I am free to choose my entourage."

Master Kokin nodded sideways in a blatant show of disapproval. "Sadly so." He stared up and down at him with an air of command as if appraising his physical condition. "Your right arm appears to be healed. I don't know about the more important body parts." He produced a loud grating sound meant as laughter. "I trust they're also working well and that is why the alien female remains at your side."

Maashi's eyes paled. His lips thinned but he didn't comment.

I stood there flabbergasted. Who was this Master Kokin who clearly wasn't on Maashi's side? How could this purple throw scathing remarks and insults with such impunity?

A giant green wearing an elaborate emerald and gold sash exploded with laughter. He stepped forward, placed a beefy hand on Kokin's shoulder, and bellowed with a voice that oozed confidence, "I must disagree with you Master Kokin. Shonava Maashi is among the favorites for mating this sequence. Is it not what every mentor wishes for their former pupil?"

Kokin's silvery brow changed to ebony black. "My wishes are no concern of yours Benshimu." Stronger than his appearance might suggest, he freed his shoulder from the green's grasp, drilled his eyes into mine, and declared in a resounding voice, "I am told Maashi wastes a lot of time with that unsightly alien instead of concentrating on his training."

Maashi hissed and took a step towards Kokin but Benshimu slid his impressive mass between the two. "Old age hasn't been kind to you Master Kokin," he said. "Challenging the Elders' authority is a foolhardy pursuit and way beyond your physical and mental capacities. I believe your mind has become feeble. This would explain your foul language and obvious lack of respect for the ones present here today. I urge you to leave."

The crowd erupted with high-pitched clicks.

Kokin's face blanched. His violet pupils shone with fury. "How dare you hurl insults at me?" He hissed and pointed a finger at the big green. "I will summon my guards to remove you and your insolent tongue---"

Maashi took a step forward and faced his old mentor. "There is no need to continue this conversation any further Master Kokin. You're not welcome here. Do not presume to join us in any gatherings." He signaled to his guards. "My men will escort you out."

Two of Maashi's guards moved forward and positioned themselves on each side of Kokin who without the presence of his own entourage had no other choice but to follow them. He scowled, gathered his sash as if afraid to dirty it by touching Maashi or Benshimu, and limped away accompanied by the guards.

Benshimu gurgled with laughter. He turned around and hugged Maashi, kissed his neck, and presed his lips on his right palm.

"Lado," I whispered, entranced by the green's charming ways, "Who is that guy?"

"He is Shonava Benshimu Hellowina, first lord of the Seventh Compound, the most populous one among the fourteen compounds." Lado said. "He is a powerful green fond of Sheffrou Maashi and has confided to me that he wants to meet him. I was told he openly praised the Sheffrou for his performance when he sparred with Zari." Lado added under his breath, "Shonava Benshimu would be an excellent first chowli."

Now I remembered. He was the one at the gym with the green quatay covering his shoulders and upper back who kept watching Maashi.

"What more can you tell me about the purple?"

"Master Kokin was Sheffrou Maashi's mentor when he was a young and impressionable Pure Color. To this day, rumors circulate about his training methods. Many sequences after he had completed his last mentoring, charges of cruelty were brought against the master. They were dropped after an internal investigation by the Silver Guards in charge of security. However, the council of Elders decided to ban forever the master from interacting with young Sawishas and Sheffrous."

Lado whirled around. "Come, it is time for the competitions. We must hurry." He grabbed me and bolted across the cave to the other side of the pool.

I turned back and strained to see Maashi, but the crowd had swallowed him. Held tight in Lado's arms, I shouted above the loud clicks of the Chamis. "Where are we going?"

"Down."

Lado took a tunnel that led us down one level. Here, the walls were transparent and allowed us to see underwater. The spectators clicked and elbowed each other to secure the best positions to watch the competitions. Lado set me down on the stone floor beside him.

The swimmers stood on the edge of the pool and leaned forward ready to dive. They wore wide, bright green and gold or red and gold bracelets on both wrists. Thousands of air bubbles filled the pool and rose to the surface when they all jumped in at the same time. They assumed their starting positions, the Reds alternating with the Greens. There was a sudden flash of bright light and the competition started. The swimmers darted in every direction over and under the water at formidable speeds, like dolphins performing underwater acrobatics. I just had time to spot one before he disappeared in a flash, leaving behind a long trail of bubbles. The Chamis clicked and shouted and stomped their feet in unison creating a loud clamor that resonated over and over.

All I could see were streaks of green, gold, and red dashing in and out of the light. Lado, captivated by the competitions, stomped on the hard ground in unison with the other Chamis. I stood there in silence beside him; more alone than I ever felt, trapped in this alien world, far from home, far from Earth. Longing burned inside my chest with such intensity it dulled my other senses. Darkness and shadows replaced the light. Sound and movement slowed and blurred into stillness.

I thought about the two Pure Colors, the purple full of contempt and hate, and the big green, stepping up to Maashi's defense, showering him with affection. There was something unsettling about the way he held Maashi's gaze and the tenderness he revealed when he kissed his palm. I wanted to be the sole beneficiary of Maashi's attention. What could I do against this kind of competition? Maashi was my partner and my lover, but was our relationship true or an illusion I had created in my mind?

I sighed. I wished I was back home with my family; my days filled with gatherings of friends and neighbors, surrounded by my children and my husband Nate content. We would celebrate birthdays and holidays together and no longer worry about Maashi and his world. Life would be perfect.

The next evening Maashi summoned me to his quarters. He was in a playful mood and wore colors I had never seen: a white shirt and light blue pants. He had placed a wide couch stuffed with royal blue cushions in the middle of his receiving room.

"I missed you, little one," he whispered in my ear. He hugged me, tickled my neck, and gave me a warm kiss. That's all I needed to melt in his arms.

I sat on his lap and admired the intense glow in his eyes. On impulse, I touched his cheek and felt the velvety skin. "Maashi," I whispered, "have you ever been in love?"

His lips parted, and he smiled. "In love?" He slid his middle finger along my jaw all the way to my chin.

"I mean, have you ever had a special Fanella, a soulmate?"

He paused before answering. "It is forbidden to develop an emotional attachment to a Fanella, Tamara." He turned his head away.

He either had a blank expression or avoided looking at me when he wanted to keep something private. I insisted. "Don't tell me you've never had someone special in your life."

Maashi stared at his lap. "There was someone once." He closed his eyes as if remembering sweeter times and inhaled deeply. After a moment he opened them and caressed my cheek. "We don't have couples here the way you do on your home world. It's impossible."

I frowned. I had just thought about Nate and I and how close our relationship was when we first met. "You read my mind." I shifted my position on the couch.

"Little one, do not consider my ability to see your thoughts as a threat." He gave my shoulder an affectionate pat.

"Can you turn this sixth sense on and off?"

Maashi took in a long breath then said, "The skill weakens when I'm deep in my own thoughts or overwhelmed by powerful emotions."

All this mind reading was disquieting. I couldn't decide if I should be concerned or grateful. His capacity to probe my mind gave him an enormous advantage and put me in a vulnerable position.

"Do all Chamis possess this sense?"

"Yes, we are all telepaths, but the trait is more developed in Pure Colors."

"What if someone wants to keep his thoughts private?"

"The individual must avoid concentrating on that particular thought."

"Ah," I said and shook my head from side to side. I recalled a mentor in medical school who had a knack for stating the obvious.

"There's something else I want to ask you."

Maashi caressed my hand and whispered, "I'm sure it can wait."

"Why did Lado say I couldn't satisfy your needs?"

"You should ignore Lado's comments. He should hold his tongue."

"Why did he mention that?" I was irked by the insinuation and wanted an explanation.

"Sheffrous," Maashi murmured, "have intense sexual needs, Tamara. That's what Lado was referring to. We can discuss this later." His brow lightened, and he added, "I have planned something special this evening." He motioned the guard out.

I frowned. "Why did you send the guard away?"

"We don't need the guard." He smiled and touched my cheek. He caught a runaway strand of auburn air and tucked it behind my ear. His fingers traced a line around my neck then slid lower, in between my breasts. He opened my shirt and placed a light kiss on my chest.

I erupted in a nervous giggle. "You're full of surprises. One minute you're kissing a sawisha or a chowli, the next one you're with me. I don't know what to think anymore."

"Tamara, I care about you."

"I believe you, but I don't know if you understand feelings and love."

He kissed my nose and eyelids. "Close your eyes."

I looked in his face and saw only kindness. I did as he asked.

He took my head in his hands, pressed his mouth against mine, and slid his tongue inside. I tasted his sweet saliva, let it swirl in my mouth then swallowed it. I drifted into a pleasant drowsiness and rested my head on his chest.

"Do not fear me. I would never hurt you shapinka," he said in a voice sweet like honey.

I smiled as if in a dream. He called me his precious one.

He removed my clothes and took off his shirt. He traced the contour of my breasts with his fingers, kissed my nipples, and licked them with the tip of his tongue.

"Oh, that tickles," I said. My head spun with his intoxicating aroma.

He continued to lick my breasts and massaged my stomach in gentle circular motions with skillful fingers. Then he placed his hands under me and lifted my pelvis upward. His long satiny blue tongue glided over my belly and the inner part of my thighs.

The pleasure was overpowering. My pelvis tilted back and forth. My legs opened wide, and I whispered, "Maashi, Maashi, come."

As if answering my call, he moved closer and his soft mouth nibbled in between my legs. I held my breath. He covered me with kisses and tasted my wetness. His luscious tongue touched deep within me. What an exquisite sensation. I shivered and moaned, and bright twinkles of light shone in front of my eyes. He withdrew then slid it back in several times, leaving me empty, hungry.

With his fingers he introduced a device that looked like an hourglass with rows of fine hairs. It purred and rotated, creating a strange vibration. I lay there powerless to escape its sweet torture.

I shook my head and mouthed my disapproval when he took my hands and tied them on the mattress above my head. But soon, a warm sensation progressed and spread in my pelvis and my body. Incredible pleasure reached everywhere, even the tip of my fingers and toes. I rocked, twisted, and moaned. I climaxed and my cries of bliss echoed throughout the room.

Maashi clicked and smiled then he rested beside me on his back, eyes closed, face expressionless. His chest rose with each deep breath he took.

A moment later, something sharp pricked my vagina. "Oh," I cried out. I tried to reach down but couldn't because my hands were secured. I screamed. "Maashi, something's hurting me."

His skin color changed to an intense blue.

"Maashi," I yelled. "Help. Help me."

Seemingly in a trance, he took a moment to react. He sat up and turned in my direction. "What's wrong?" He reached over and released my hands.

"Down in between my legs," I said and blinked my tears. Something wet and warm trickled and reached my buttocks.

He spread my legs and his eyes grew wide. He extended his arm to reach in.

"Don't hurt me," I warned.

"Do not move," he said, "I must pull out the device with care to avoid cutting you."

I stayed still, and he slowly removed it out and set it aside. He offered me a small cloth to wipe myself.

After he did so, he asked, "How are you feeling?"

"You said you wouldn't hurt me," I growled.

Maashi's eyes became colorless. "There is a cut," he said, "the length of your little finger, on the left side of the opening and a little further inside." He bent toward me and kissed my forehead. "Chumpi, believe me, I never meant this to happen."

The two-paneled door of the receiving room opened with a loud swoosh. A pair of guards burst in. They glanced at me and saw the blood. They clicked loudly.

"What's going on?" I said, alarmed by the sudden intrusion. I grabbed my clothes and slid them on.

Maashi clicked at the guards and his face paled to a dull ivory. "They heard your screams and they are concerned."

Two more guards came in. With harsh clicks they seized Maashi and forced him to stand.

"I need to leave with them," Maashi said, his voice a mere whisper. Even though he stood tall, his hands shook.

"Why? Where are they taking you?"

"I will send a message to Lado and Tomisho," he said as he was escorted out of the room.

A minute later, a new Chami came in wearing khaki clothing and a sky-blue sash.

"Good evening, Tamara," he said. "My name is Tanshila."

"Who are you? Where did they take Maashi?"

"The Sheffrou is in custody. I am a physician and the guards summoned me." He gave me a sympathetic look. "They say you have been injured. May I examine you?"

Hot with anger, I said, "No, you may not. I can take care of myself." I gave him a nasty stare. Intense pleasure followed by sharp pain, intruded upon by guards who then removed Maashi, tested my temper and it was all I could do to remain civil.

The physician crouched down, pressed a few buttons on a device, and a small jar and a packet of cream appeared. He said in a calm, reassuring voice, "You can apply this to ease the pain." He had just finished when Tomisho and Lado burst into the room.

Tomisho, his chest naked and wearing only a blue chemcha clicked at the physician. Tanshila answered back with deferential clicks.

"Tamara," Tomisho asked, "what happened?"

Meanwhile, Lado remained silent. With a blank face and pursed lips, he stood there as stiff as a board.

"I . . ." I flinched. What happened between Maashi and me should stay between us. I didn't want to describe details of our intimate encounter to Tomisho. Hot tears burned my eyes.

Tomisho put his arms around me. He kissed my forehead, my cheeks and my tears. "Everything will be all right shapinka."

I pushed his hands away and wiped my eyes. "Don't call me that."

Tomisho turned to the physician and said, "Thank you."

The physician stood and said, "Goodbye. Please call if you need me." He bowed and left. The remaining guards followed behind.

"Let us get you comfortable," Tomisho said, ignoring my rebuff. "First the cold pack should go in between your legs. Then we will cover you with a warm blanket." He did as he said and added a plush pillow under my head. Both materialized after he entered commands on the floor beside me.

I regained my composure and mumbled, "They took Maashi away. What will they do to him?"

"Maashi is under house arrest while what happened is being investigated," Tomisho said.

Lado spoke. "In Chamranlina society," he blurted out, "hurting a female, intentionally or not, is not tolerated under any circumstances."

"The guards came in right away as if they knew something happened," I said.

"All the rooms are monitored by minute sensors in the walls," Lado said. "The security system was developed to detect the Untouchable. It has become an integral part of our lives." He bent down, retrieved the dangerous oblong device with my blood still on it, and wrapped it in a small piece of material.

"We are so accustomed," Tomisho said, "to living under continuous surveillance, we never think about it. The only rooms not monitored are the encounter rooms."

Now I remembered. Maashi had mentioned that before.

"Lado can stay here with you tonight," Tomisho stated in his best reassuring tone. "Call me if you need anything. Just put your finger over here," he indicated a small brown square on the floor, "and a yellow button will appear. Press it to call me."

"I want to be alone." I hurt in more ways than I cared to admit. I felt violated. How could Maashi have been so careless? Why did I let him tie me down? Aloud, I added, "Lado should stay with Maashi."

"The Sheffrou cannot see anyone," Lado said, "not even his chowli. That is the rule. I will stay in the adjoining receiving room if this is agreeable to you."

I nodded.

"I will find out more about Maashi's situation and come to see you tomorrow," Tomisho said. "You should get some sleep."

They both left, and I laid back on the couch. I did a quick check on myself and the bleeding had stopped. Most likely a superficial cut.

My mind was clear now, and I assessed everything that happened. Maashi had smiled right after he used that little toy on me which indicated what followed wasn't anything either of us had anticipated. I frowned. I knew he had an intense effect on me but this time, my reaction had been different: I had lost control quickly as if I had drunk too much wine or been drugged.

Maashi, I realized, had the ability to read minds, impair one's judgment, and possessed an intense sex drive. All these attributes revealed a different, possibly dangerous being. Did that mean he could exert some type of control over Fanellas and other Chamis? Was this why some Sawishas hated him?

His friend Dasho had mentioned at the Lantillica that "Sheffrous 6 can cause pain." Did he mean with their kisses?

Was it the same with a Sheffrou 8 like Maashi? I needed his help to return home, but I didn't like this unsavory side. I shifted my weight on the couch to relieve the pressure on my pelvic area.

Maashi didn't mean to hurt me. I was sure of that. But what if circumstances were different? What if I had refused his advances or provoked his displeasure, what kind of reaction should I expect? I was under his protection but also subject to his whims. There was a delicate balance between the two and I needed to be cautious. This reminded me of situations in the Emergency Room when I took care of a difficult case, and every decision I made had the potential to provoke an unintended consequence and increase the severity of the patient's condition.

I readjusted the cool pack between my legs. Painful cramps stretched and pulled in my lower stomach. Why did Lado pressure Maashi to take that green as chowli? Why did Sheffrous need chowlis? Was it to control them? I turned on my side.

Where did I fit here? Perhaps Maashi thought of me as an exotic pet and he could play with me at will. Lado had mentioned some Chamis had adopted young Loloyan and considered them as pets. The thought gave me chills.

I refused to be treated like a toy or a pet. That left me with the role of mistress or lover. Maashi himself said there were no couples here. Thoughts of women in the shadows waiting to serve came to mind. A life lived not for its own purpose but for someone else's, a life of submission.

Would the occasional encounter with Maashi be enough to satisfy me? Intense, exquisite pleasure so brief it became almost insignificant, interspersed with prolonged periods of void. I couldn't imagine that kind of life. On Earth, I always had a specific purpose in mind: finish medical school, complete my residency, start a family, raise my children. I worked hard to reach my goals.

I readjusted my pillow and pounded on it. The best solution was to keep the search for the wormhole alive. I had to go home. My children were there, waiting for my return.

The cool gel pack was soothing, and my pain subsided, leaving only a feeling of numbness. I closed my eyes and fell asleep.

The next morning Lado came in with an impressive breakfast tray complete with toughi, my favorite fruit, a blend of apple and pear. He brought small sour green balls and bright orange prickly ones that had to be pulled apart to get to the tasty insides. There were the usual puddings, some with colorful dots, and a tall glass filled with choun.

"Good morning, Tamara. How are you feeling?"

"I'm much better." I sampled the food. "These green balls taste good."

Tomisho joined us a few minutes later wearing a powder blue shirt with khaki pants and a wide royal blue sash. He plopped his long frame right beside me, hugged me, and bent his head down to kiss me. I raised my hands up to block him and he retreated.

"How are you today?" he asked.

"Good." I took a sip of choun. "Have you heard anything about Maashi?"

"The Elders," Tomisho said, "have reached their decision. Maashi will be confined to a specific detention room for five days."

"Five days? Is this what you expected?"

"The Elders have shown leniency." Tomisho shook his head to one side.

"But?"

"I am not pleased." He shook his head again. "Maashi has been found negligent, and it is a huge disgrace for him." Tomisho clicked several times and slapped his hands down hard on his knees with a resounding clap.

I jumped in alarm and winced at the sudden sharp pain in my pelvis.

Tomisho and Lado nodded at each other as if they understood an important detail I couldn't grasp.

"He will be scorned by the other Chamranlinas," Lado said, "and the Pure Colors will be relentless. Your injury and the way it occurred during an intimate moment between you and him may jeopardize his chances of mating."

Tomisho drummed his fingers on his thighs.

"Maashi must be really upset." I said, "I don't understand how my injury happened." I looked up at Tomisho.

"He was not trying to hurt you," Tomisho stared straight ahead, his eyes half-closed.

I remembered what Maashi had confided about Tomisho and mating. "What about you? Does it change your chances of being chosen?" I asked.

Tomisho's eyes widened, and he tilted his head to observe me.

"What do you know about my chances?"

"Maashi told me you were younger than he is." I mentioned his age but omitted the detail about his immaturity so my comment wouldn't sound like an insult. "and that was why you weren't a candidate for mating."

Lado's eyes opened wide.

Tomisho burst in laughter. His whole body shook, and his dark chocolate eyes danced. He kept on laughing until he held his stomach with both hands. After a few minutes, he recovered and said, "You are very kind."

In a more sober tone he explained, "I am not a first choice because of my age, but because the Elders consider me too immature and therefore less likely to succeed. In our society, successful mating is vital and my chances of being selected are very low no matter who is the first choice."

"Oh," I said, "So, whether Maashi is chosen or not doesn't change anything for you."

Tomisho smiled. "No." He rubbed his knees with his hands. "My concern is Maashi was beginning to replenish his charissa." He glanced at me. "It means his balance, his sense of wellbeing. I am sure he blames himself for your injury and, although I have never heard of anything similar happening with this device, he has been shamed. This incident will have negative repercussions on him."

"What do you mean?"

"Sheffrous are sensitive beings, more so than other Chamranlinas. Our emotions have an important impact on our physical health. Maashi will be distressed by the whole incident and, with no food for five days, his strength and resolve will weaken."

"No food?"

"It is part of the punishment," Tomisho said. "Water is allowed. Nothing more." Tomisho drummed on his knees with his long fingers. "Enough about Maashi. You are the one who has been injured. Would you like to visit the compound with me? I will carry you in my arms."

Held in Tomisho's arms for the day? "I think I'll just stay here and rest."

Tomisho insisted. "How about we visit the gardens?"

My face lit up. I loved gardens. I had seen none here. On Earth, I used to love strolling in botanical gardens. I would pretend I was in another world . . . Then I thought about the Chamis we would meet and how they would stare at me and want to touch me all over. "Perhaps some other time."

"What is wrong? Are you still hurting?"

I swallowed hard. "I don't like the way the Chamis stare at me and touch me. It's very annoying."

Tomisho considered my answer for a moment. "You behave like a young Sheffrou. You shy away from touching and kissing." He stopped to find the right words. "Let me explain why the Chamis do this. I will give you an example I have found in your mind."

I slammed my glass of choun on the tray. "I don't want you to probe my mind. My thoughts are private."

"I did not intend to offend you," Tomisho said and bowed. "Forgive me if I did." There was no mistaking the tenderness in his eyes. "Please. Let me explain. Every Chamranlina here is elated to be near you. Each one wants to touch you, hold you, and kiss you. Some males have never been in contact with a female and you are the perfect imitation of a young Chamranlina female."

I drew a breath. Was I just another young female for Maashi? No. I was sure I wasn't.

Tomisho finished his explanation and turned towards Lado, who nodded and added, "What Sheffrou Tomisho says is true. I have witnessed it myself. It is different with you compared to the way Chamranlinas relate to Loloyan. That bond is like the bond between a master and his pet."

"I have also experienced this," said Tomisho. "Some days I want to hold you so much I cannot stand it."

I crossed my arms on my chest.

"I hope you do not mind my big hugs." He laughed with a shy look I would never have thought possible.

The last few days' events had shaken me but, most of all, I worried about Maashi. He could be hurt or sent away and the thought frightened me. Furthermore, it would be dreadful if something happened to him because this might compromise my chances of going home. My chest tightened, and I blinked tears.

"Do not cry, sweetheart," said Tomisho. "Do not let what happened upset you."

He reached for me and I let him hold me close against his chest. I inhaled his woodsy masculine aroma, and a deep sense of calm came over me. He caressed my hair and pressed his lips against mine. I closed my eyes. My soul lightened. I drifted away in a vast blue expanse of calm water where the air was pure and fragrant.

# Chapter 16

I sat in the middle of a perfect green lawn under a vivid blue sky. A flock of brown pelicans flew in formation high above. In front of me, a pine tree stood straight and tall, its branches motionless as though it was part of a huge canvas.

□The voluptuous smell of honeysuckle filled the air and its sweet and powerful aroma suffocated me. The green lawn and the sky spun round and round until I became dizzy. I opened my mouth to call, but no sound came out. I tried to breathe but could not inhale. I moved my arms but flailed like an injured bird.

□A soothing voice whispered. "Little one, don't panic. You are not in danger. Take a deep breath, hold it, release. Again. Again." Long fingers caressed the back of my neck. "Open your eyes. You're safe," said Maashi.

□After a moment, the spinning stopped, my vision cleared, and I focused on my surroundings. Where was I? My gaze settled on the wall facing me. Light green and blue sapphire waves danced on a shimmering, sandy-color background. My head was resting on Maashi's wide naked chest, and his light fingers were massaging my scalp.

□He bent his head down. His oval eyes glowed under long chestnut eyelashes, and I felt his light breath on my neck. He parted his lips and his tongue moved.

"Let me go. Get away from me." I clenched my teeth and jerked away from his grasp.

Maashi closed his mouth and swallowed. "Don't be frightened," he said, "I won't kiss you." He leaned his head back on the thick mattress of the lounge chair and sighed. He took the end of his blue sash and rolled it between his fingers. "I'm glad you're awake."

Awake? I considered his words. My body felt sore and my muscles were stiff as if I had been in the same position for a long time. I struggled to understand what happened. I got up and walked a few steps to sit in a different lounge chair.

"What happened to me?" I asked in a loud voice.

Maashi, his face pale and his cheeks hollow, said, "You have every reason to be angry."

I pursed my lips and eyed him wearily. "How long was I out?"

"Tomisho kissed you and you slept for two full days," Maashi's mouth stretched into a slight grin. "He kissed you to help you relax and overdid it. We're in the evening of the third day."

"No wonder I'm sore," I said. Maashi had mentioned Tomisho was immature. He was much more than that, he was dangerous.

Maashi rose and sat beside me on the chair. He kissed my neck with a passion I hadn't expected. "I'm very sorry you were hurt. Please forgive me." He caressed my cheeks and my forehead. His chest heaved with each breath he took.

Waves of pungent honeysuckle circled us. The walls started to spin.

"Maashi stop it. Your holoma is making me nauseous." I tried in vain to prevent the walls from dancing.

He relaxed his hold and slipped an arm over my shoulder to steady me. "Is this better?"

"No. Go back to your seat. You're too close."

He stood and moved back to his previous seat and the walls came into focus. I glanced around. The lounge chairs in this receiving room overflowed with powder blue and apple green pillows with gold borders. The thick carpet delineated the perfect oval of the chamber, cream in the center and darkening to a warm caramel at the base of the walls.

I cleared my throat and said, "Where are we?"

"We are in a guest receiving room. Shonava Benshimu intervened with the council on my behalf and I've been released in Tomisho's care. He brought you here so we could be together."

This reminded me of our recent incident. Anger rose in me and my temples throbbed. "Why did you tie my hands? I never agreed to something like that."

Maashi looked down. "I wanted to create a pleasurable experience, a memory you could cherish. Restraining young Sheffrous during sexual stimulation increases their pleasure."

I shot him a look of contempt, "Maashi, don't ever do that again. Tying a sheffrou may be something acceptable in your society but I'm a human female, and tying me is definitely not acceptable."

Maashi tilted his head sideways as if considering this for the first time. "I understand. It won't happen again."

I remembered the piercing pain I felt that day. "Why did it take you so much time," my voice cracked, "to respond when I cried out?"

He lifted his arms and shook his head. "Something happened during our encounter and you were hurt. My mind became disconnected with my surroundings. I couldn't hear you and you got hurt during that brief instant." His arms dropped on his knees and he stared at his hands. "I deeply regret it. I won't let my guard down again."

There was a faint buzzing sound, and the guard standing by the door let Lado in. He rushed over to Maashi and hugged him. "Are you feeling better, sir?" His voice was full of concern.

Maashi nodded, and Lado kissed his neck. He turned toward me. "I trust you are well."

"No, I'm not." I said, indignant at his lack of concern for me.

A gray tint colored Lado's face. "I am sorry to hear that."

My stomach growled. I couldn't remember the last time I ate. "I'm so hungry I could eat a seven-course meal," I said.

They both stared at me with a bewildered look.

"The last time you ate was three days ago." Maashi said. He pressed on invisible controls on the floor, and a whole tray of food appeared. I had a choice of puddings, fruits and nuts and two tall glasses filled with choun.

I attacked it with gusto and while I ate and drank, I listened to them.

"I have been in direct communication with Central Command and have participated in the analysis of the most recent data." Lado said in a serious tone of voice. He ran his fingers in his cropped hair.

I finished my first pudding, grabbed another then asked Maashi in between spoonful's, "Aren't you going to eat or at least drink something? Tomisho said they didn't give you food during your detention."

Lado took one of the glasses and offered it to him. "You should drink, sir."

Maashi held the glass and took one sip.

Lado said, "Security has detected several disruptions in space-time in sectors four and six of the Quitir quadrant."

The Sheffrou's brow paled and his eyes darkened. "Are the disruptions related to the upcoming Great Eclipse? The event has been associated before to these types of disturbances."

"Yes, sir, but there are far more disruptions than expected. Security is convinced our enemies are causing some of them. Central Command believes the Krakoran," Lado glanced at me, "the Untouchable, are planning an attack under the cover of those space-time disturbances. They are familiar with our customs. They know we will celebrate the eclipse and are more vulnerable during the festivities. Also, a reconnaissance probe has found a ship which matches no known vessel traveling at low speed in the outer boundaries of the quadrant. We have transmitted the coordinates to our allies, the Vizinem, to complete the identification."

Maashi put his glass down. His brow hardened, his hands opened and closed several times.

"We have increased security throughout the sector," Lado said, "and we will be on high alert in all the secondary sections."

"Have the Elders considered canceling the celebration?" Maashi said.

"I heard there was a debate, but Sawishas have unanimously rejected that option. As always, the Black and the Silver Guards refuse to be intimidated by mild changes in space-time. They will modify their surveillance only if we have undeniable proof the Untouchable have caused the changes."

Maashi bounced off his seat. "That's ridiculous," he roared, "I agree that our customs are important, and we should honor them, but security measures have failed to protect us before.

What makes them think they'll be adequate this time? Some rare Creams and Yellows and even Fanellas will be present at the celebration, not to mention several young Pure Colors."

Fanellas? I hoped I could see them. But I didn't like this discussion about attacks. Over the years, I had lived through several episodes of lockdown in the Emergency Room because of an imminent threat related to an active shooter or a person carrying another type of weapon and I hated the increased danger to the patients and the health workers. The medical staff was ill equipped to deal with violence and depended heavily on security.

"Is there a way to find out if the disturbances are a natural phenomenon or a sign the enemy is present?" I asked.

"There is," Lado said, "but it is a tedious process and we don't have enough time to complete it before the start of the festivities."

Maashi glared at Lado. "Security must be flawless," he said with a voice that left no doubt about the seriousness of the situation. "Any attack may lead to kidnappings and cause casualties."

"Shonava," Lado said, "I have discussed this at length with the one in charge of security, a black called Khon. His teams have been preparing for this event and they know the risks. Khon is optimistic but cautious. He stated they were ready to respond to any emergency. He expects the festivities will proceed without problems."

Maashi hissed for a long moment. With hands fisted, he said, "We should not underestimate the Krakoran. This would be a grave error."

Lado's big hand rested on Maashi's neck. "Everything will be all right, sir. We have no conclusive evidence of an imminent attack. These are only conjectures based on previous events."

"Nonetheless, I am not pleased to hear this. I don't trust our security,"

"I expected your reaction, sir, so I took the liberty to invite Khon to come and talk to you himself."

The door chime startled me.

Lado said, "This must be him."

The paneled door opened, and a tall wiry Chami wearing all black attire entered. His hair was charcoal and slicked back, and his thick brow was set in a stern expression. He bowed to Maashi and they both exchanged clicking sounds. This went on for a few minutes. Then Maashi spoke in English. "I wish to state that I do not approve your explanations and I think your security plan is flawed. Furthermore, I will make a formal complaint to the Elders about your lack of leadership and I consider your overconfidence and arrogance are not conducive to proper management of the situation. My statement on this matter will remain in the permanent record."

At this point, Khon pulled out a yellow bracelet hidden behind a crease in his shirt. Maashi sighed, and Khon put the bracelet on his wrist and something else in his hand. Then he left after a quick nod to Lado and an even quicker glance towards me.

"What was that all about?" I said.

"All the Chamranlinas will wear a personal shield bracelet," Lado said. "This measure will increase the safety of everyone involved."

Maashi produced a smaller one that Khon had given him. "This one is for you," he said. "All you have to do is press on it and it will create a personal protection field like this." He pressed on his, and a fraction of a second later, a clear bubble enclosed him.

I stared at it and touched the outer layer with the tip of my finger. "Impressive. Can you move around with this?"

"Yes, I can." He waved his arms and took a few steps. The bubble followed him. "I can walk without difficulty, talk and you will hear me, but nothing can touch me."

It was as though he was surrounded by plastic wrap. "How do you turn it off?"

"You touch it one more time. It will dissolve in an instant." He did so, and as he spoke the bubble disappeared. "It is similar to a force field, is connected to your magnetic field and can be released with a simple tap." He bent down and put an identical bracelet on my left wrist.

"A powerful gadget." I stared at it. I didn't trust gadgets. Computers froze. Batteries died. Backup generators failed. On Earth, I once bought an expensive car with multiple high-tech features. I was furious after I saw all the fancy gadgets break, one after the other.

"No need to worry. Only the one wearing it can turn it on or off. Try it," Lado said.

I pressed on the yellow bracelet with my right hand. I felt the same, but I saw the bubble around me. "Are you sure it'll work?" I asked, frowning.

"Yes," answered Lado. "We did a full scan while you were sleeping and, to our surprise, your personal magnetic field will offer the same protection."

On impulse I touched it again, and the bubble dissipated. "How many times can I use it?"

"There is no limit to its use," Maashi said, "and as long as you are alive, it will function."

"I see." I twirled the bracelet around my wrist. "When is the celebration?"

"In two days," Lado said. "We call it the Great Eclipse because Chitina's two moons, Ara and Kori, will align in front of the sun, and plunge the planet in darkness for most of the night; when at last, the orange sun rises there will be sunshine without interruption for a whole sequence."

"Scary." I pursed my lips. The thought of complete darkness with the possibility of an attack by the Untouchable was terrifying. I recalled how my youngest son Johnathan loved to watch horror movies whereas I hated them. What would he think of this scenario?

"The Great Eclipse marks the beginning of a new sequence," Lado said, "Spring if you like. A time of joy and renewal because after that event the sun will shine during the day and the evening for months to come. The event reminds us to pause and take a moment to reminisce about the past sequence and look forward to a brighter future. Do not worry Tamara, you will stay at the Sheffrou's side or mine at all times, and you will be under close supervision by the guards."

Before I could comment, a clear chime rang, the guard stood aside and Tomisho leaped in wearing a flamboyant blue and silver outfit.

With a broad smile, he kissed Maashi's neck and caressed his cheek. "How are you my friend?" he said.

Maashi hugged him back but remained silent.

"Good morning, Tamara." He nodded in my direction. "How are you?"

I glared at him. "I understand you're the one who put me to sleep for three days."

"It would seem I need to practice my kissing," he chuckled and bent his head toward me.

I raised both my arms, fisted my hands, and said, "Don't touch me. Don't kiss me."

Tomisho's eyes increased in size. "Why are you angry?"

"You're a careless individual." I got up to leave.

"Forgive me Tamara, I am truly sorry." he said in a gentle voice and bowed.

Maashi said, "Tamara, he meant no harm."

I ignored them both. I lifted my tray and settled on another couch further away to finish eating without interruption.

Tomisho turned to Maashi. "We should go swimming today. There are some new runs I want you to try."

"I don't think that's a good idea," said Maashi.

"Shonava," Tomisho said, "you must face the Sawishas, the sooner the better."

Maashi hissed. "They don't intimidate me. I don't care what they think." He paced the length of the room and stopped a few feet away from Tomisho.

"Then come with me." Tomisho strode toward Maashi and put his hand on his shoulder. "Shapinka, you cannot hide in your quarters. You must prove your courage. You must act according to your rank and treat with contempt the ones who dare criticize you."

Maashi clenched his fists, shrugged Tomisho's hand off, and walked to the other side of the room. He turned and in a harsh voice and eyes as dark as coal, he said, "I don't need to prove anything."

I cringed and swallowed hard. I had never seen him so angry.

Tomisho advanced toward him. "Shonava," he said, "I know it is difficult for you, but this is a crucial moment; the celebration is upon us. Assume your role as a high-ranking Sheffrou. Show the everyone you are not guilty of any wrongdoing."

Maashi turned his head and hissed. "I was negligent. I should have been more vigilant."

"Shapinka, we talked about this. It was an accident."

"No Tom Tom," Maashi said, "I had a lapse in judgement. For Tamara's safety and mine, I should have brought her in the encounter room. She was hurt and it's my fault." In two quick strides, he was at my side and kneeled. "I apologize Tamara. I put you at risk. Please forgive me."

"The recording didn't hurt Tamara," Tomisho said, "it was the device."

I understood what Tomisho meant and my face hardened. All the time Maashi and I were together we were being recorded. I glared at him. He didn't bring me to the encounter room that day because he wanted to broadcast our intimacy over all the compounds to boost his popularity and increase his chances to be chosen for mating. In a voice as cold as ice, I asked, "Who heard me? Who saw me?"

Maashi looked away. "No one saw you. Everyone heard your cries of pleasure," he paused, "and your screams when you were in pain."

"Damn it, Maashi. What's wrong with you? Have you no respect at all? When were you going to tell me this?"

He took a long breath, and said, "I planned to tell you after the celebration."

I swore between my teeth. My face burned in anger and shame.

"Shonava," Lado said, "Security examined the device, and someone tampered with it."

"What?" I launched upward and my tray went flying. Maashi caught it before it toppled and set it aside. "Who would do such a thing?" I said.

Maashi hissed. "Why would anyone hurt Tamara?"

"The matter is still under investigation," said Lado.

"All the more reason Shonava," Tomisho insisted, "to come with me and demonstrate to everyone you are a powerful Sheffrou and no one can intimidate you."

I crossed my arms and eyed Maashi with a hard stare. "You should leave. I'll need time to process this."

Defeated, Maashi sighed. "I agree," he turned to face Tomisho, "I will accompany you." To me he said, "I'll be back later. I'll make sure there's a guard on duty for your protection."

I didn't bother to answer.

He left with Tomisho and Lado followed close behind.

I plopped on the couch and stared at the unfinished food. Maashi's behavior, putting me at risk for his own personal gain, was inexcusable. He had seemed so different, so bitter, like someone I had never seen before. I munched on the last fruit and let its tangy juice linger in my mouth then poked at my last pudding.

The device had been tampered with. This meant Maashi had enemies among his own people. Were they so desperate to hurt him that they were willing to attack me?

On Earth, I had no enemies. Apart from the occasional heated discussion over procedures or the best approach to resolve a problem, I spent my life between my family, my friends and my responsibilities as a physician.

I couldn't imagine a world where the competition for mating rights created adversaries among friends who had been raised together since a tender age. Even though I strongly disapproved Maashi's action, I understood how the pressure from his peers, his superiors and his subordinates, pushed him to carry out his deed without consideration for the consequences. In my case, the experience I had acquired in the Emergency Room where we often dealt with crisis helped me to keep my emotions under control and not let them affect my judgement. Maashi's carelessness and my subsequent injury angered me, but I had to keep my feelings in check because, although I wished it were otherwise, the only way out of this world was linked with him.

There had been no mention of Earth in a long time. Was I doomed to live on Chitina forever? I shivered. I grabbed the closest cushion and held it tight.

Circumstances would surely improve after the Great Eclipse Celebration; if there wasn't any attack. I rubbed my bracelet, and the clear bubble appeared. Would this be protection enough? Should I be equally wary of the Untouchable and the Chamis?

# Chapter 17

After I finished my meal, I retreated in my quarters where Lado joined me a few hours later. His brown shirt and darkened brow indicated something preoccupied him.

"Is Maashi back?" I reclined in my chair and grabbed my pad feigning indifference, but I was eager to find out how the run with Tomisho had gone.

"The Sheffrou is sleeping in his receiving room with two Chamranlinas."

My heart skipped a beat. "Two Chamis? Who?"

"They joined him in his quarters after he returned from the swim."

"Do you know them?"

"I know one. His name is Rahma. He is the leader of a group of young Sawishas."

"When did Maashi meet them?"

Lado said with an unreadable expression, "I heard from one guard that when the two Sheffrous, Maashi and Tomisho, were getting ready to start the run, several Sawishas standing on the edge of the water hissed and insulted him. Chamranlinas do not forgive anyone who carelessly hurts a young female, even if she is of a different species. It appears the news of your recent injury has reached every compound."

I felt my cheeks burn. Maashi's little gadget and my injury were now the gossip of the day on the planet.

Lado continued. "Downhill, where the current slows and the water creates a tranquil pool, the two and their guard stepped out and saw a group of twenty young Chamranlinas standing by the edge of the water. They quickly circled the Sheffrous and blocked their way. Responding to their menacing stance and fearing an attack, the lone guard moved closer to intervene if necessary.

"Sheffrou Maashi confronted the group and examined the young Chamranlinas one by one. A few of them were sawisha. None approached to greet them and kiss their shoulders as is the custom, but none made any threatening move. Sheffrou Tomisho waited without saying a word."

I frowned. "What did they want?"

"Rahma, the leader, a sawisha wearing a dark brown wrist band, stepped forward and bowed to Sheffrou Maashi. He introduced himself and said he and his friends knew about his abduction by the Krakoran and subsequent rescue months later. They understood he was still recovering from his ordeal and admired his courage and resilience. They expressed their sympathy for the loss of his chowlis."

With raised eyebrows I said, "I guess Maashi didn't expect that."

Lado nodded. "The Sheffrou knew young Chamranlinas were unlikely to attack him but was surprised by such kind words. Rahma then stated that they would be honored to assist him in any manner and at a moment's notice if he so needed.

"Sheffrou Maashi took a moment to respond. He thanked them for their generous offer and said he would be pleased to meet each one in his quarters. An hour later, six of them came."

"Six? You said two."

Lado raised his voice. "I was present, and six young Chamranlinas came, including Rahma. The Sheffrou welcomed the group and treated them as guests, but he was tired and stressed. We all agreed he needed to relax so Rahma, with the help of his close friend Chopa, gave him a massage."

"I see." Chamis in general and particularly Pure Colors loved tactile stimulation. They said it increased their charissa. Maashi was no exception.

Lado stopped and chuckled. "I have to admit Rahma, although young, no more than ninety sequences old, is very skilled. As the others held him with firm but gentle hands to help him relax, Rahma massaged him, starting with the back, with long comforting strokes. I could see his body relax, his muscles unwind, tension slipping away.

"When the massage was completed, Rahma asked permission to transfer his saweya, his positive energy. It was a bold request since they had just met. He accepted so the young brown and his friend Chopa pressed their bodies over him."

I snorted. Maashi loved to hold me over his chest when he rested on his back. My hair stood on ends. "Wait. What's this body energy?"

Lado looked in my direction, and said in a condescending tone, "Have you not heard about saweya?"

"I think Maashi mentioned that word before, but I don't remember what it means."

He lifted both his arms. "Little female, saweya is life energy and even you possess this. Healthy adults can transfer it to others by close body contact. This is most important for Sawishas who can be sustained by their chowlis with breastfeeding and with intimate body contact." Lado paused as if the revelation meant something special to him.

He continued with his story. "The Sheffrou responded to their touch and completely relaxed after the massage and fell into a deep slumber. I stepped out, reassured he was safe with both Chamranlinas by his side."

I visualized in my own way the newcomers Rahma and Chopa laying over Maashi and I couldn't stand it. Pins and needles pricked my skin. "I need a shower. I'll see you later." I rose and darted off toward the water room.

Ripping my clothes off and throwing them on the floor, I jumped in the shower, and let the freezing water bombard me. The thought of Maashi in the two Chamis' arms drew angry tears that I fought hard to suppress. I wanted Maashi for me, only for me. Filled with jealousy, I stayed for the longest time under the cold spray with clenched fists.

I hated this place.

# Chapter 18

After a long nap I woke up with an oppressive feeling of doom. The fast approaching celebration and the persistent talk of attacks by the Untouchable filled my dreams with dark menacing creatures which hovered outside the door of quarters.

I couldn't shake my mounting fear. I played with the bubble bracelet, as I called it, and made the clear shield appear and disappear and this helped calm my nerves. I wrote a long note to Allison on my pad recalling happier times. I debated my emotions with her as if she could voice an opinion. Was my anxiety justified? Or amplified by listening to too many worried Chamis?

Maashi's behavior also changed. I was sure his own kidnapping one sequence ago right after the Great Eclipse Celebration weighed on his mind. He stayed busier than usual, inviting many Chamis, a few sporting colors I had never seen, creamy white and pure pink. Even the impressive green I had seen at the gym and at the recent gathering came to discuss the upcoming events. On the other hand, he clashed with Lado every time they saw each other.

The door chime announced a visitor and Lado strolled in the receiving room followed by two Chamis I had never seen.

"Tamara," he said, pointing to the first one, "let me introduce Rahma," then turning to face the other one, "and Chopa. They have met Sheffrou Maashi and bonded with him and will join us on the trip back to the Central Compound."

"Hello," I said. At first glance, they looked like brothers. They had the same hazel eyes and their hair was short and wavy, not unlike Maashi's, giving them a youthful appearance.

Rahma, the more muscular of the two, wore a dark brown sash confirming his sawisha status. He took a step toward me and spoke with a clear youthful voice. "It is a pleasure to see you Tamara Walsh."

"The pleasure is mine," I said, "and you can call me Tamara."

The taller and thinner Chopa tightened the knot of his milk chocolate sash speckled with pink, executed a formal bow, and said, "It is a pleasure."

Maashi strolled in looking more rested than in the last few days. "Tamara," he said, and nodded to the others, "we're leaving within the hour to return to the Central Compound. It's closer to the Rashandomora cave where the Great Eclipse Celebration will be held. Gather anything you want to bring with you. I will provide you with the necessary clothing."

"Good," I said. I was excited to get back to the Central Compound, closer to the place where I had arrived on Chitina. "Maashi, have you heard anything about the wormhole? You said the search party had found something."

"It was a false sighting," said Maashi.

I grumbled and fisted my hands. "Back where we started."

"The only new fact," Lado said, "is that the alien spaceship we were tracking which matched no known vessel in our databanks moved out of the area."

I stared at him. "Do you think it was a Krakoran ship?"

"No," said Maashi, "the Krakoran don't travel aboard spaceships."

"What do you mean?"

Chopa answered, "We believe the Krakoran live in an alternate space and that is why they are so difficult to trace. They can materialize at will in different locations and disappear in an instant."

"That's surreal," I said. "How about us? Are we traveling through the tunnels?"

"No, we will fly," Maashi said. "The weather is favorable today, and the flight will take less time than going through the tunnels."

We left a short while later. We took the anti-gravity elevators to the surface and boarded a large vehicle the size of a bus. It had a long, sleek design, and its color mimicked the dark reddish color of the planet's soil.

The guards and Maashi's group, Lado, Rahma, and Chopa, boarded dressed as they were but Maashi brought a nateet, a simple garment with a hood for me. "To keep you warm," he said.

"And you?" His cream shirt was so thin that his skin showed. "Are you going to wear something warm?"

"I don't need more clothing. We can tolerate extremes of temperature without ill effects."

I nodded. Needy and fragile humans. "Do we need luggage, provisions?"

"The ship is equipped for emergencies and the duration of the flight will be less than one hour. Everything we need is on board."

Wearing my light but toasty nateet, I followed Maashi. The pearl and blue interior comprised two sections: the pilot and copilot sat up front, surrounded by lighted panels and the other section was reserved for passengers. The seating consisted of groups of four aligned in two semicircles. I sat on Maashi's lap because I was too small for their seats. Lado accompanied us with Rahma and Chopa and four guards. The vehicle had small windows at each end but none where we were sitting; not a design I favored. I always preferred to sit by the window in an airplane to watch outside.

"Ready?" said Maashi.

"Yes, I'm ready." I said.

Chopa said, "We will experience mild turbulence on and off throughout the flight."

He wasn't kidding. The trip might have been uneventful by Chami standards, but it reminded me of a roller coaster ride. We flew with such an irregular pattern that in the end my stomach couldn't stand it and I almost threw up on Maashi's lap. At least the landing was smooth. What a relief when we arrived at our destination.

Maashi brought me back to my quarters. I dropped on a lounge chair that materialized when we walked in the receiving room. I sighed and propped my feet up on a cushion.

"Traveling on this planet is not for the faint of heart," I said.

Maashi smiled and caressed my cheek. "Feeling better?" he asked.

"Yes, but I think I'll rest here for a while," Then I asked him about something he hadn't mentioned but was important for me. "Do you dress up for the celebration?"

Maashi smiled. "I will send you a garment I have chosen for you." He stood up and left. His expression suggested he had something special in mind, but I was disappointed because I would've liked to choose my outfit myself.

I closed my eyes and must have dozed off because when I opened them, the lights were dimmed, a sign it was later in the day, most likely early evening. I rose from the couch and sauntered to the water room to shower.

I came back in my receiving room wearing only a towel and waited. Anticipation of the big event played with my nerves. I laughed. Look at me: jittery with clammy hands, nervous as if I was going on a date, without a thing to wear, and, above all, ignorant of what the celebration involved. Unable to stand it any longer, I got dressed in my usual khaki outfit and went to see Maashi.

I took the short hallway leading to his quarters and heard some loud snapping noises and countless clicks. Maashi's receiving room was crowded with Chamis, including Lado, Rahma, Chopa, and a few others I had never seen.

The room itself looked much larger. The couches were gone. Two muscular guards dressed in silver and black marched in through another door at the far end. Everyone stepped back and leaned against the walls.

Maashi called me, extending his arms. "Come, Tamara."

I trotted toward him, and he scooped me up.

"I don't want to bother you if you're having a private party," I said, "but you mentioned you would send my outfit, at least that's what I understood."

Maashi whispered, "Little one, you're always welcome to join us. We are in the process of doing a sweep in all the rooms. You must not touch the floor because there is a high level of static electricity."

Maashi still holding me in his arms, leaned back, and I heard a shrill whistling sound as each of the Silver Guards threw a black golf-ball size device in the air. The balls burst open like firecrackers and zigzagged with a sizzling sound, leaving yellow streams of light behind them. In a few seconds, they had twirled and zoomed across the entire room. They finished their strange flight with a comical poof and then dropped to the floor.

I laughed out loud and nearly applauded. "Wow, Maashi," I said. "What kind of sweep is that? Those balls exploded like fireworks."

Maashi answered with an amused glow in his eyes. "Tamara, this may seem like a game to you, but sweeping is a mandatory safety procedure. Security performs it over the entire sector to detect the Untouchable."

My jaw dropped. "Is everything okay?"

"Yes, chumpi," Maashi smiled. "The sweeping is complete, and we are ready to celebrate." With that, Maashi threw me in the air the way you would throw a young child. I squealed in surprise, and this was the signal everyone was waiting for. The Chamis made the furniture reappear, and they covered the walls with long, colorful, shiny banners with waves of blue and green with gold glitter. I watched as a thick flamboyant red and gold carpet appeared on the floor. The transformation was amazing as the receiving room, bare a few minutes ago, became alive with color.

"Come with me," Maashi said. "My presence isn't required here." He carried me to the encounter room, which had a red and gold diamond pattern matching the carpet colors in the receiving room.

"Why did you change the colors? What do they mean?"

"The red represents strength and power and the gold is a sign of fertility. These colors symbolize the Great Eclipse Celebration."

We settled on the rippling mattress, and Maashi smiled at me, "Shapinka, I am pleased that you will be part of the celebration. It is a very important event for Chamranlinas." He lifted my chin up with a long middle finger and dropped a quick kiss on my lips then he kissed my neck and my nose.

"I missed you," he said. "Are you feeling better? Is the pain gone?"

"It's all gone." I breathed a sigh of relief. There hadn't been any persistent ill effects. I watched Maashi. It was strange to see how he could be kind and full of concern when he was content and how he could blow up when he was angry. But then, weren't we all the opposite of ourselves when we were angry?

He laughed, and the crystalline sound echoed on the rippling walls. In one motion he removed his shirt and a sweet fragrance filled the room. Before I realized it, Maashi took my face in his warm soft hands and gave me a slow kiss. Something inside me melted.

His slender fingers slid down my neck. He opened my shirt and exposed my shoulders and pressed his lips on them. The kiss sent shivers of pleasure up my spine. I inhaled his sweet aroma and felt light as air. My body grew warm as he held me close. My shirt and undergarment gone, he played in my hair with his fingers and massaged my scalp.

"Oh," I inhaled a long breath.

Maashi whispered in my ear, "Chumpi, sweet one, let me hold you." He cuddled me in his arms like a babe. "You haven't been pleasured for days." He nuzzled my neck and nibbled my earlobe.

I sighed. How could I not forgive him? I wanted to forget everything and drown in this incredible feeling. He caressed me until I moaned in delight. He pressed his mouth on my lips and his long silky tongue slid in and went back and forth inside my mouth. The rush built until it reached its crescendo. I climaxed and sunk my fingernails in his flesh.

"Take it easy, Tamara," he whispered. "Breathe in and out."

His voice sounded as if it came from far away. I closed my eyes, inhaled, and exhaled. The pleasure wrapped me like a silk cocoon. I released my fingers and savored the fantastic feeling.

After a moment I came to my senses. I was resting on my back beside him. He had extended his arm on my stomach to keep watch over me. I turned to look at him. He was lying with eyes closed, glowing a sapphire blue.

I admired the curves of his lean muscular upper body and extended my hand to touch him when something unexpected caught my eye. He had removed his pants and unfastened his chemcha, his protective underwear. My eyes grew wide as I saw his genitals for the first time. I knew his size would be impressive. His member was more than a foot long and his two testicles were the size of mangoes but something else was different. Several precious stones shimmered on the tip of his penis.

"Oh," I said under my breath. These stones were embedded deep in the flesh. Whatever manner was used to implant them must have inflicted unspeakable pain. I breathed in short spurts and tears filled my eyes. Who would do such a thing?

Maashi's chest inflated. He stirred and fastened his chemcha. He turned and looked in my direction. His eyes focused on my face.

His brow darkened. "Forgive me," he said with a voice soft as honey. "I should have been more discreet. I didn't mean to upset you." He took my hands in his and kissed the tip of my fingers. "Don't be alarmed. They inserted the jewels a long time ago. The pain is only a memory."

"What happened?" I said with a strangled voice, "did the Untouchable do this?"

Maashi sighed. "They aren't the ones responsible. It is an ancient Chamranlina tradition. We call them the Draharma gemstones. I am a Pure Color, Tamara and all Pure Colors must prove their courage to gain the right to mate. There is a price to pay."

Before I responded, a chime rang. Maashi pressed a small depression on the wall and said, "Yes?"

"Sir," said Rahma, "forgive me for interrupting but, it is time."

"I will join you in a moment." He glanced at me. "We shall discuss this matter later." He bent forward, took my face in his hands, and kissed my forehead.

I frowned.

"You should go to your quarters and get ready. We have prepared everything for you."

I cleared my throat. "Do you think we'll be safe tonight?"

Maashi paused before he answered. "I think we should try to enjoy the evening as much as possible without letting down our guard."

"I practiced making the bubble appear and disappear."

His brow softened. "Tamara," he said in a more serious tone, "that's not what I meant. Many Sheffrous will be present. Their combined holomas will fill the cave and create intense emotions and wild, irresistible desires which could affect your behavior. If you find that distasteful and you wish to leave, you may ask Lado or a guard to accompany you. Do not leave alone."

"I'm not one to take unnecessary risks. Don't worry."

Back in my own receiving room, I found a beautiful turquoise color top with a pair of flowing pants on the couch. The material was as soft as silk, and the edges were embroidered with a delicate cream-color lace. I tried it and it fit perfectly. A pair of golden sandals completed the outfit.

I sighed as I waited to join Maashi. What I had seen earlier in the encounter room brought back memories. On my world, I was shocked the first time I examined women who had been subjected to genital mutilation. One young woman, a refugee from Sudan, had been in my office accompanied by her American husband. The sight of her mutilated genital area had overwhelmed my usual composure to the point I had to step out of the room and hold back my tears. Now seeing Maashi's genitals, the memory of that unfortunate woman still vivid in my mind, I retreated on my couch and held my knees with both hands to stop their shaking.

Rahma came a short while later and led me to Maashi's quarters. He was smartly dressed, with a dark brown fitted shirt and sash which accentuated his muscular physique.

I was curious to see what Maashi would wear. Lado looked solemn with a unicolor olive-green outfit with a chartreuse sash; he was adjusting the Sheffrou's sash when I walked in.

My expression must have betrayed me. "You look so," I searched for the right word, "regal."

Maashi smiled. "You are quite endearing. Turquoise is the hue favored by young Sheffrous." He added with a small grin. "Pardon the comparison."

I circled around him, admiring his outfit. He wore a light, cream-color shirt with an ample royal blue sleeveless coat and matching royal blue trousers with a gold stripe along the outseam. The coat had an intricate gold and silver design on the chest and on the upper back. A cobalt blue sash with specks of gold completed the ensemble.

A moment later, a guard came in carrying a small package wrapped in a red and gold cloth.

"Special delivery for you, sir, from Sheffrou Tomisho," the guard said.

Tomisho sent him a gift. I pursed my lips and suppressed a grunt.

Maashi opened the package. It contained a long cordelet made of gold strands woven together. Lado put it over Maashi's neck and it hung beautifully on each side of his chest. He fastened it on both sides of his collar with two brooches with a figure-eight design. The cordelet strands separated at the ends and shimmered with the slightest movement.

"Congratulations on your gift, Shonava," Lado said, "It befits your rank."

Maashi's lips formed a timid smile. "Thank you." He bent over, opened a small box, and picked up a short sash with a royal blue wave and tied it around my waist. "Tamara," he said. "I would be honored if you wore my color."

"I'll wear it with pride," I said.

Chopa stood by the door. His outfit was a striking milk chocolate color with minute pink dashes and pink wrists and collar. "Shonava," he said, "we must leave now."

"We will stand at your side sir," said Rahma as he and Chopa positioned themselves on each side of Maashi.

A cold chill of fear and excitement ran up my spine.

# Chapter 19

The Great Eclipse, a remarkable celestial event, marked the beginning of each new sequence for the Chamranlinas. Chitina, where the Chamis had sought refuge after their home world Chamtali became inhospitable, had two moons, Ara and Kori. Once every sequence, about two human years, the moons aligned their orbits and positioned themselves precisely one behind the other shielding the planet from the orange sun and creating a total eclipse that lasted for several hours. Symbolizing a time of renewal and rebirth, the celebration brought hope for a better future in a brutal world. Chitina had been full of promise for a new and secure life, but like a reluctant mistress, was remiss to deliver its gifts.

The trip in the tunnels to the immense cave where the celebration was to take place took an hour, longer than I expected. Accompanied by several guards, our group composed of Maashi flanked by Rahma and Chopa with Lado and I close behind advanced at a slow pace. Even though I insisted I could walk, Lado carried me all the way.

"Little female," he said, "it is safer for you."

Tonight, there was no arguing with him.

I shivered with trepidation during our trek, but my worries soon dissipated when we arrived at our destination.

Six Black Guards stood in front of a grand arch twenty feet high, sculpted out of white marble veined with silver and gold. Pillars of the same white marble, eight feet wide, flanked the arch on each side. A shimmering, silvery material hung from the top of the arch and covered the entrance like a curtain before a grand stage.

The guards wore peculiar headgear made of black triangular pieces topped with large gold feathery spikes reaching high above their heads, and were dressed in black except for a gold stripe, originating at the left shoulder and traveling down their shirts to their waist. Although their attire was eccentric, their fierce expressions left no doubt about the seriousness of their function. I couldn't forget however Maashi's scathing remarks about security's lack of effectiveness and wondered how well prepared they were.

One of them stepped forward and assessed our group. He scanned each one of us with a small hand-held device no bigger than a cell phone. His calm demeanor reassured me, and my trembling stopped. He bowed to Maashi and let us through the wide entrance. Lado released me from his arms so I could stand by Maashi's side.

The place was grandiose, much larger than I could ever have envisioned. The ceiling, high and wide, adorned with glittering gold and vibrant red patterns all the way to the front of the cave struck me as the most impressive structure I had seen on Chitina. Every hundred feet, large columns carved in reddish brown granite rose like tall obelisks. The towering columns curved towards the center of the cave where each joined a similar column rising from the opposite side. Intricate designs hewn in the stone decorated the walls at shoulder height and coursed all the way to the ceiling.

Our group gathered at the entrance. I observed the scenery and tried to memorize each detail, each color, as if I could keep the image forever etched in my mind. The Sawishas sat in the lower areas, close to the broad central aisle, and the Multicolors were scattered high above them. The wide seats, carved in the granite, progressed as high as the eye could see, and overlooked the central area.

In awe, I watched the Chamranlinas dressed in brilliant costumes, each group seated in their own section corresponding to the colored banners hanging from the ceiling. The rows of spectators continued all the way from the back to the front of the cave. This allowed everyone present to observe each new guest upon arrival.

Silver Guards were stationed in different locations throughout the cave. I spotted them from afar by their stunning outfits with bright silver and burgundy designs. Standing guard with unapproachable arrogant expressions, they saluted by raising their right arm and turning their palm upward, as Maashi and his entourage entered.

Our group paused for a moment as we waited for the official introduction to the assembly. An impressive red stepped in front of us, and the booming rumble of a massive drums echoed throughout the cave. The crowd hushed at once. Lado whispered beside me, "The red will introduce Lord Maashi Torrenadanga, first Lord of the Central Compound."

The official announcer bellowed a resounding series of clicks and bowed to Maashi. All eyes focused in our direction. The spectators stilled in their seats. Maashi lead the way and, one by one, the seated Chamis rose and stood at attention as we passed.

Maashi slowed his advance and stopped after fifty paces. He scanned the assembly from side to side. The frightening silence filled the room as effectively as a loud roar. I followed behind Maashi, feeling infinitesimal, all my limbs shaking. I wondered how the Chamis would greet the Sheffrou. The recordings, accessible to all, broadcasted every detail about his life. Did they consider him a hero who survived a terrible ordeal or a despicable being who performed dreadful acts to save his own life? What did they know about me? How did they judge him after the recent incident where I was hurt?

A deep sound, slow and rhythmic, low in intensity at first grew louder and louder. I held my breath and watched in awe as the Chamis stomped their feet in unison. The thundering sound echoed throughout the cave and drowned all other noise.

Lado bent down and said, "Do not be frightened, Tamara. Thousands of Chamranlinas are paying tribute to Sheffrou Maashi. Every one of them has learned of Shonava Maashi's plight: his capture and relentless torture by the Untouchable, and his ultimate rescue. They stomp to express their pride and admiration for the Sheffrou." Lado's face glowed. "Tamara, Chamranlinas are a forgiving people and will overlook multiple trespasses by an individual as long as he shows remorse and remains humble and ready to serve both males and females. They are thankful for his rescue and wish to honor him for his strength and courage. They are also expressing compassion for his misgivings."

Taken by surprise by such an extraordinary display of support by the Chamis, Maashi stopped and stared at the crowd. His expression changed and relaxed, and his almond eyes grew larger as he proceeded down the aisle. The Chamis had demonstrated their generous nature. I would never forget this special moment.

I walked by Maashi's side with my heart overflowing with pride and delighted at the sight of Sawishas dressed in incredible tunics and gowns each more elaborate and festive than the other. The stylish Pinks wore attire ranging from dusty rose to vibrant fuchsia while the Yellows dazzled and babbled without cease like wonderful exotic birds. The animated Browns and the sociable Oranges hugged and chatted together. The noble Creams, located between the Yellows and the massive Greens, mingled with all the other colors.

Green Chamis, loyal supporters and consummate allies of Sheffrous, ranged from bright apple to dark olive green, but most were a deep emerald, and all were husky muscular individuals. The Purples followed the Greens, and they represented all shades, from lavender to eggplant, including some with gold accents that shimmered with the slightest movement. Small, long-limbed humanoid creatures with curly hair accompanied their mentors. They were just a little taller than I and emitted clicks like the Chamis.

Lado whispered behind me, "They are the Loloyan. Chamranlinas adopted a large number when a prolonged drought spread over their planet, killing the adults and leaving a great number of orphaned offspring."

I nodded. I could see now why the Chamis would mistake me for a Loloyan.

At the other end of the cave, a wide stage held a group of older Chamis dressed in gold and silver. Lado explained they were the fourteen Elders who formed the Council of Elders. On their left were the Sheffrous. On the right, a small area of empty seats caught my attention.

"Lado, why are these seats empty?"

"When all the Chamranlinas have arrived, the Fanellas will walk in through a door behind the stage and take their rightful place beside the Elders."

"Nice." I had been waiting to see females for a long time.

Maashi took his place among his peers. He got a bear hug from Tomisho, looking quite the hunk in his royal blue attire. Maashi held and kissed Sheffrou Choban, the one I remembered meeting at the pool ages ago. Lado left us to join a group of Multicolors assembled high above our section. Rahma and Chopa served as guards and didn't stray far.

Dasho, Maashi's friend, smiled at me and kissed my cheeks. "How are you, Tamara?" he asked. He wore an elegant sky-blue outfit with an ivory shirt decorated with lace. A sweet fragrant aroma reminiscent of gardenias floated around him.

Younger Sheffrous dressed in turquoise or powder blue sat in the back behind the more powerful sheffrous like Maashi and Tomisho. They seemed both curious and amused to see me. Among them stood another Chami that Dasho introduced as Ashani, a young sheffrou 8 who was Maashi's pupil. He smiled and bowed in our direction. Intermingled among the group were five sturdy figures wearing dark blue outfits with midnight blue sashes.

I tapped Dasho's arm and in a low voice asked him who they were.

"They are the formidable Sheffrou 6. There are only a few."

All the Elders nodded and acknowledged Maashi's arrival. I knew he held an important position in Chamranlina society, but this was beyond anything I could have pictured. Overwhelmed, the only human in this assembly, my knees shook hard. Did they expect me to address them? I didn't relish any kind of public speaking often required in my profession and wasn't prepared to say anything.

Maashi picked me up in his arms and sat me beside him. "Relax, Tamara," he said. "Slow down your breathing. All you have to do is observe."

Grateful he read my mind, I flashed him a quick smile.

The crowd stirred and high-pitched clicks erupted. All eyes watched as the last group entered through a side entrance close to our section. Preceded by several Black and Silver Guards, I held my breath as the last group graciously paraded in.

Wearing only translucent shimmering gowns, the Fanellas advanced one at a time, each one more stunning and exotic than the other. Slender compared to the males, they had emphasized their striking oval eyes with gold, silver and blue glitter. The sixteen females proceeded to their assigned section. All took a seat except the first one which remained standing in front of the crowd.

This first Fanella wore a full-length gown decorated with a delicate vine-like pattern which descended from the shoulders to her hips. Her hair, a light honey color, braided with dainty white flowers cascaded down her bare back. Her intense turquoise eyes speckled with gold glowed like jewels. She turned toward the Sheffrous, and they all approached to greet her. One after the other, they kissed her palms. She smiled and clicked to all.

The Fanella had a special smile for Maashi. She said a word, took a necklace of lavender and white flowers from one of the Silver Guards and placed it around Maashi's neck, never taking her eyes off him.

Maashi took her hands in his and pressed his lips on her palms. His solemn expression and longing gaze made my heart flutter. Memories of a time long ago flashed in my mind, when my husband Nate would look at me with those same eyes. Now I wished for Maashi's longing eyes on me, but I thought it would never be so.

Maashi and the Fanella clicked to each other. I understood he knew her. Perhaps he had mated with her in previous years?

A moment later, she rejoined her group and the Sheffrou did the same. Everyone settled in their seats. Dasho, who sat on my left, said, "The ceremony will begin now."

The first speaker was introduced to the Elders, and I listened in a daze, my hands clenched in my lap. I concluded that if I had ever entertained thoughts of Maashi and me becoming a couple, it was clear now it would never occur. His longing eyes for the lovely Fanella took away any doubt. She had stolen his heart.

One after the other, the speakers addressed the crowd with long speeches in their clicking language. Dasho brought me back to reality by translating. "The speakers praise the immense progress the Chamranlinas have accomplished since they have established a colony on this planet and remind us of how living underground on Chitina has been both a blessing and a hardship. By hiding in the large caves, we have offered more effective resistance against the attacks of the Krakoran. We have created four Fanella sections and they are producing offspring. Feeding everyone is still a challenge since access to sunlight on the surface of the planet is dangerous and therefore, we must limit the outside excursions to short periods of time.

"The last speaker, a towering dark green, explained how we have developed a fleet of vessels capable of attaining extreme speed for interstellar travel. These have enabled us to track and intercept our enemies who hide in another dimension and rescue the unfortunates who have been kidnapped and faced torture and death. Sheffrou Maashi Torrenadanga is here today, living proof of one of these successful rescues."

As the speaker stated this, the crowd hissed and shrieked, and the foot-stomping resonated like thunder throughout the cave.

I waited anxiously for the last speech's completion. An uncomfortable tension grew inside me. I felt hot and queasy.

"The dark green finishes with a more ominous evaluation of the situation," Dasho said. "He states that the Fanella compounds are still vulnerable to attacks. The females experience a high level of stress and they either cannot conceive, or their pregnancies end prematurely, and the offspring is lost to everyone's great sorrow and dismay. He concludes that our species is still threatened with extinction. The Chamranlinas must work with renewed energy to ensure their continued survival in a hostile world."

I sighed. I had learned more this evening about the Chamranlinas and Maashi than in all the time I had been here. The somber picture drawn by the last speaker saddened me. The Chamis faced a terrible enemy and were up against incredible odds in a life and death struggle to survive.

Unable to forget the look I had seen in Maashi's eyes I was crestfallen. I understood now why his pride prevented him from disclosing any details of his horrible ordeal with the Untouchable. How could he? I was a human from a totally different world where overpopulation, pollution, and dwindling resources were becoming great sources of concern. My heart went out to him and his kind.

A loud booming sound filled the cave. Then another. And another. The fourteen Elders stood, saluted the crowd, and left through a side opening accompanied by Black Guards. The Fanellas soon followed. Maashi's eyes followed the last one to leave, the one his heart favored. His eyes grew darker and his lips became a thin line. Dasho put a hand on his shoulder and clicked to him. His tense expression softened, and his face changed back to usual as he hid his true feelings.

A shrill whistling sound filled the air, and the cave went pitch black.

I gasped.

Maashi took my hand. A second later, a large white globe appeared high above. One by one, gigantic globes as big as a vehicle appeared and floated throughout the cave. They emitted something like black light. The spectators' clothes lit up under the strange fluorescent lighting.

While the Chamis themselves were invisible, some part of each one's attire glowed in the dark. Their intricate headgear, capes, decorative breast plates, shoulder pads, arm or leg bands shone and created imaginary creatures moving about and mixing in a crazy kaleidoscope. The hem of my outfit and the sash Maashi gave me before we left glowed white and purplish blue.

Overcome by the strange sight, I broke in a nervous giggle, then burst in laughter at the unlikely mix of walking colors. "Wow," I said. "This is awesome. I've never seen anything like it."

Maashi's only response was to bend down and kiss me. Pleasure zipped through my body and exploded in little bubbles under my skin. I felt elated and lightheaded as though I'd been indulging in too much champagne.

Standing wide-eyed, I took in the spectacle as thousands of small petal-shaped droplets fell from the lighted globes. They floated down, twirling and dancing like snowflakes and landed on heads and shoulders. The amused Chamis laughed and licked them off each other. I tasted one, and it melted on my tongue, leaving a fresh fruity taste.

The spectators, glowing and contrasting in all colors of the rainbow, coalesced in small groups, separated and then re-formed, creating bright, ever-changing patterns.

The giant glowing mass moved towards the Sheffrou area. An affectionate group of shiny red, bright green, shocking pink, dazzling yellow, creamy white and flashy purple creatures soon invaded us. The ensuing chaos of laughter, kisses, and hugs overwhelmed the Sheffrous. The warm and fragrant aroma radiating from their holoma saturated the surrounding air.

I inhaled the fragrant perfume heavy with pheromones. A powerful hunger stirred deep within me. Maashi turned in my direction, took my face in his hands and kissed me. I smiled back at him, but a group of bright purple and neon green individuals competing for his attention already surrounded him.

One large green sawisha encircled Maashi's waist and licked his neck. I recognized him by his hands. He was the one who had intervened when Master Kokin had intimidated him before the swimming competitions. In a warm husky voice, he said, "Shapinka, I am delighted to see you again." He parted Maashi's lips with his long middle finger and touched inside his mouth. He removed his finger, licked it, and kissed Maashi for a long moment.

Seeing them kiss made me dizzy and warm.

I didn't notice the approaching purple and gold hunk until he lifted me up in his arms. He kissed my neck and licked my cheeks. His strong earthy fragrance was overpowering. His body felt firm and muscular and, on impulse, I touched his shoulders. He chuckled and caressed my breasts with long fingers.

I shivered with pleasure. I raised my head and lost myself in his mesmerizing golden eyes. He opened his mouth displaying his purple tongue. Fascinated, I watched as he bent down and pressed his lips against mine. Something inside me fought to pull away, but I was helpless and couldn't resist its soft wet touch. He slid his hand between my legs and pressed it going back and forth. My willpower evaporated. I could not extricate myself from his overreaching fingers. I gasped, arched my back, and moaned from the unexpected pleasure.

Someone else put a hand on my shoulder. As if in a dream I heard clicks, and then Dasho said, "Come with me, Tamara."

"Oh," I said, "I was just starting to enjoy myself." I felt hot and tipsy and held on to the purple. More clicks, and Rahma and a guard appeared.

The sawisha released me.

Dasho took me in his arms and kissed my forehead. "You are a sweet little female, but I think it is best for you to leave now."

Dasho smelled like a bouquet of garden flowers.

"Mm. You smell good," I said. I buried my face against his shoulder and hugged him.

He smiled, "Shapinka, you are sensitive to holoma. Maashi told me to send you off with Rahma when the time came."

Before I could reply, he had transferred me in Rahma's firm grasp who said: "As soon as we enter the tunnels you must activate your protective shield."

"The bubble bracelet? Sure." I laughed at his joke.

We left through a side door, accompanied by the guard. We made swift progress in the dark hallways and Rahma brought me to my quarters and we hid in the encounter room.

The rippling mattress made me woozy and I released the bubble surrounding me. I rested my head on his chest. He smelled fresh like an ocean breeze. I slid my hand in his shirt and caressed his soft skin. It felt leathery, more so than Maashi's, but inviting. I had the irresistible urge to kiss his chest.

"Ah, you're nice." I kissed him and shivered with pleasure. I moaned and rubbed my face on his skin.

Rahma remained immobile and stared at me. He held me and caressed my back in long smooth strokes. That's the spark I needed to light the fire smoldering in me. With a grunt I climbed up on him and reached his neck. I kissed him fiercely and licked his face. I moaned and wrapped my legs around his waist and clung to him.

He untied my sash and loosened my shirt. I promptly removed all my clothes. Naked, my senses fully aroused, I held on to him and brushed my chest with abandon against his. The hunger I had felt growing in me all evening spread to my every pore. In the privacy of the encounter room I could shed all reserve and put out the raging firestorm roaring in me.

I licked and nibbled his breasts and bit him. I could feel his chest heaving with each deep breath he took. He whimpered, and his hands slid down my waist and rested on my hips. I grabbed one hand and put it in between my legs. He touched me, removed his hand then licked his fingers. With a firm grasp, he laid me on my back beside him. He slid his long slim fingers in between my legs and licked them again and again until he breathed in loud spurts and grunted. Then he caressed me until the pleasure engulfed me. All my frustration exploded in this single moment. I screamed and bit him hard, rolled over him and rocked back and forth until my breathing calmed down and the pounding in my head stopped.

Exhausted, I went limp in his arms. After a few minutes I retreated deep into myself. My body was like an empty shell and I drifted in a state of semi-consciousness. Oblivious of my surroundings, I sank in a deep slumber on the rippling mattress.

# Chapter 20

I woke up hours later. My eyes adjusted to the low light of the blue and beige diamonds of my encounter room. My head throbbed and my mouth felt dry. The events of the previous evening floated back in my conscience. Like different pieces of a puzzle, they appeared one by one and locked together, creating a shocking picture.

I growled at the vision. I couldn't explain my actions. All my life I had been a mature, levelheaded individual, a physician, wife and mother of three, the kind of person who stayed in control of herself even if the others lost control.

What happened to me last night? Not only was I in a personal relation with an alien, but during the celebration, the temptation to indulge (how else would I call it?) with a Purple Sawisha overpowered me. Held in his arms, enticed by his strong earthy odor and his muscular body, I had lost all inhibitions. If Dasho hadn't intervened, I would have succumbed to my desire. I shuddered at the thought.

What about the wild sex with Rahma? I held my head in shock and disbelief.

I had to admit I knew why. This surprising behavior could be related to the crazy atmosphere of the celebration and to the holoma, the fragrant pheromones radiated by Sheffrous. Both aroused my senses to such a level my body felt on fire and I lost touch with reality. Thrilled and delighted by the overall exhilaration of the Chamis and the incredible spectacle of the walking fluorescent colors, I didn't heed Maashi's warnings and was snared by the holoma trap like an overconfident fourth-year medical student who thinks he knows everything but has never examined a patient.

As much as I would've liked to put all the blame on the pervasive holoma, I knew I should be held accountable for what I did. These last few weeks, I had become increasingly irritated with Maashi. I had watched with jealousy his developing relationship with Tomisho. I envied the close contact he shared with Rahma and Chopa, who were constantly by his side. Yesterday, I saw he had more than a passing attraction for the beautiful Fanella, who kept her eyes locked on him, and he seemed to enjoy the attention of Benshimu, who gave him much more than a friendly kiss.

Anger simmered in me. During the celebration, it became clear I would never develop an exclusive connection with Maashi. Was there even hope for a close relationship? Maashi played a dominant role in Chamranlina society, and I would forever remain a small part of his life. I would never be able to compete with Sheffrous, Sawishas, and especially not the green-eyed Fanella. Maashi's heart belonged to her.

I thought of my family back on Earth, my husband Nate and my children, David, Allison, and Jonathan. Pain and remorse filled my heart. How easily I had tossed memories of my previous life aside and hidden them in the deep recesses of my mind. It had been simple to ignore my own world, but I had forgotten who I was: a human female, with a family and a real life on Earth. My life here was a dream and now the dream was changing into a nightmare.

The powerlessness and sadness were equaled only by the guilt I felt. This wasn't my world. Whatever it would take, I resolved from now on to find a way home. Maashi would never be for me.

Thinking about him brought conflicting emotions: regret, shame, anger. Rahma would reveal what had happened between us, or the Sheffrou would find out the truth in my own mind. He would plead innocence by saying the human female had jumped on him, and he found himself powerless to resist her advances. True. I couldn't deny it. Would Maashi be angry, jealous, or worse, indifferent?

I had seen his anger before, seen how he had paced the room, his body tense, his arms ready to strike. I remembered how his amber eyes had become furious dark slits and my hair stood on ends.

I growled and punched the wall of the encounter room, creating a series of alternating blue and beige ripples. Why did I behave like a mad woman?

All this debating compounded my headache. I drank some water, covered myself with the blanket, and made my way to the water room.

I took a quick shower, got dressed, and was ready to face Maashi. Dizziness overcame me. I leaned against the wall. I needed food. I had tried to follow Lado's instructions and order some myself before but was unsuccessful, something about the flick of the wrist. I set out towards Maashi's quarters. Odd. I thought the entrance was closer to the water room. Those annoying hallways were so long....

An unusual foul odor like rotten meat lingered in the air. A draft of foul air breezed beside me and made my head spin. After a moment the nausea subsided, and I proceeded down the hall to the third door on the right and pressed a small round area in the middle to open it. Nothing happened. I pressed again. Nothing. A yellow light flashed above me, signaling it was locked. I wrinkled my nose in disgust. What was going on? The Chamis never locked the doors.

I knew a simple solution, another entrance further down the hall. This would take me the long way around, but I could still get in Maashi's quarters.

Ugh. That disgusting smell again. It was worse now. Halfway down the hall I stopped. I thought I heard something. I strained to listen. Behind me the hall was dark as the lights automatically shut off after I went through. A low growl came from yards away. My blood froze in my veins. What was that? The Untouchable?

I scampered away as fast as I could without making any noise and reached the last door. My heart thumped in my chest as I pressed the door to open it. Nothing. Again. Again. Nothing. Damn.

Another growl, this time louder and closer. I needed a moment to think. Forget that. I ran as fast as I could down another hallway, tripped, and landed on my knees. For an instant, the walls danced around me. Breathless, I stood up and trotted down the hall to my right, struggling to keep my head clear. I pushed on each door I saw. All locked.

My knees shook hard. I stopped and listened. I couldn't hear anything. Was this a good sign? I inched forward with my body pressed along the wall. I followed it and at the end, I turned left and froze.

A huge black feline as big as a tiger, its small ears flattened back was crouched in the hallway. The beast snarled and exposed rows of enormous teeth. I stood still, petrified.

I forced a breath in and took one step back. As I did, a stern voice bellowed behind my back. "Raah, eschtaway." The beast lowered its head in a submissive posture, but not without a warning growl. A long brawny arm lifted me up in one sweep and black eyes set under a wide brow reminding me of Neanderthal men glared at me. "You are the Sheffrou's Chimitanga," he said with a resounding voice. "What are you doing here?"

Shocked by the sight of the cat and its master, I couldn't utter a single word. The giant black held me with a firm grip against his chest and said, "I will bring you to Lado's quarters. They are the closest. It is too dangerous out here."

Lado greeted the guard with a courteous bow. "Thank you for bringing Tamara back."

He retrieved me and said, "The compound is on high alert because of last night's attacks by the Untouchable. Security is patrolling the halls and tunnels with the Raah Azan, the black felines trained to detect the enemy. Everyone must remain in their sectors." He added, "I didn't notify you because I thought you were still asleep."

He set me down.

I took a deep breath and tried to calm my nerves. "What attacks?" I stared at him and noticed the grim expression on his face: the irregular wrinkled brow and the dark elongated eyes. He wore steel color clothes, a dull shade even for him, and his sash hung loosely around his waist.

Lado's eyes became much smaller. "You should sit down, Tamara," he said in a voice cold as the grave.

I sat down beside him. "Is Maashi all right?"

"Sheffrou Maashi is safe." He sighed. "A few others have not been so fortunate."

I swallowed hard, knotted my hands together on my lap, and locked my eyes on him.

"There were several attacks last night." Lado looked stricken.

"What?" My heart skipped several beats.

"Sheffrous Dasho and Choban were traveling together, and they were ambushed." He inhaled. "There was a fight. Sheffrou Choban tried to protect Dasho from being captured and was killed in the struggle as well as two guards." He stopped, closed his eyes and lowered his head.

"I'm so sorry." I breathed in with difficulty and heard a wheezing sound deep within my chest. I thought of Choban, his gentle ways and musical laugh echoing in the pool. "Is Dasho okay?" I held my knees with my hands to stop their shaking. How could this happen?

"Sheffrou Dasho has been injured. He is in shock and being treated for his injuries."

"Are they life-threatening? Will he recover? Can I help?" I blurted out all at once and stood abruptly but Lado's hardened expression stopped me.

"Thank you but there is nothing you can do. We expect him to survive but the healing process will be long and arduous."

I blinked a few times and dropped back to my seat. "Is everybody else all right?"

He took a moment to answer. "There were two more attacks and a dreadful fight took the life of nine guards. A young Sheffrou called Ashani was captured." He stopped. His face had grown pale, his eyes half-closed. "It is a sad day for Chamranlinas."

Ashani, the gentle one I had seen for the first time the night before had been kidnapped. The news would devastate Maashi.

My eyes filled with tears. My mind flashed back to what I did last night. Did Lado know details about my night with Rahma? I swallowed hard and focused.

"Why so many attacks? Where was security?"

"I cannot explain how all this could happen." Lado rubbed the back of his neck and stared at the floor. "There is something else."

"Oh?" I gasped. "There's more?"

"Sheffrou Tomisho is missing. We fear he has also been taken by the Untouchable."

"What? Are you sure?" I inhaled abruptly, chocked and started coughing and wheezing. I coughed so much I saw stars. Lado handed me a glass of water. With shaky hands I brought the glass to my lips and took two sips.

"We are on lockdown," he said, "We will find out later."

"This is terrible. I can't believe it." I was crestfallen. I put a hand on the cushion beside me to steady myself. "Where is Maashi?"

The door opened and Rahma lumbered in. Wearing steel gray clothes, he sat down with slumped shoulders, absent-mindedly scratched and rubbed his forehead, and ran his fingers through unruly chestnut hair. He said to no one in particular, "Sheffrou Maashi has locked himself in his encounter room. He refuses to let anyone in." He glanced at me.

I bent my head and avoided his gaze. The attacks had been devastating. Some nightmarish scenario was unfolding as if the worst predictions had come true. I sat there numb with disbelief.

"Lado," Rahma asked, "I have been informed security has been tracking a strange spaceship."

"We still haven't identified it. They told me it does not appear threatening."

"Still," Rahma said. "I will inform my group to follow with the unit in charge of surveillance until we find out more."

Lado nodded.

Did Rahma mention our night together to anyone? Was Lado able to read my thoughts right now? I felt my cheeks getting warm. I didn't dare ask anything more about Maashi. The encounter room was the only place where he could grieve in private the loss of his friend Choban and ponder the fate of the other unfortunates, Ashani and Tomisho. I wanted to be close to him and offer comfort, but I didn't want to divulge my transgression just yet. He had too much grief to deal with already.

My head pounded, and I felt lightheaded the same as when I sensed the onset of a migraine. "I'll go rest in my quarters for a while."

I stood and stopped in my tracks. The door wasn't in its normal location. I turned around and stared at them. "Something odd happened earlier this morning; I was sure the door had moved, and now, this one isn't in the same spot. How can that be?"

"Security has mixed the parameters to confuse the Untouchable," Rahma said.

I looked at them and said, "Can you explain what you're saying?"

"Chamranlinas live in caves," Lado said. "Only the bigger caves are what you see."

Rahma pointed to the wall with his arm. "The smaller ones are holograms and your senses cannot detect the difference. We can change their design at will."

"As a rule," said Lado, "Chamranlinas refuse to modify the physical environment. Instead, we have developed ways to create illusions which appear as real as reality itself. Also, in the next few days, make certain a guard or one of us accompanies you between your quarters and anywhere else in the compound. This is for your protection and to ensure you don't get lost."

Rahma added, "You should report anything suspicious."

"The only thing I noticed," I said, "was an awful smell of rotten meat in the hallway where the guard and that huge cat found me."

They both jumped from their seats.

"Well? What does it mean?" I said, irritated because I realized they hadn't been forthcoming about the lockdown, the holograms or the attacks.

Lado ran his fingers through his short crew-cut hair. "The Untouchable," he said, "smell like rotten meat. It means they are still in the sector."

Rahma added, "They were close to you."

My jaw dropped. I had been within their grasp. That's why the huge cat growled and followed me down the hall.

Lado bent his head sideways and stared at me. "The Krakoran did not understand what or rather who you were."

The color drained from my face. I thought my legs would buckle under me.

Rahma said, "Let me accompany you back to your quarters."

Shocked and rendered speechless by this information, I nodded. We walked back together accompanied by two guards. I held back any comments for fear that I might burst out crying.

When we arrived at my quarters, he said, "You should remain in the encounter room. It will be safer. I will bring you food and water."

I mumbled a thank you.

He lingered at the door. "Tamara," he said, "I must inform Sheffrou Maashi about our encounter."

I stared at my feet.

He added, "But not today."

There was nothing more to say. I knew Maashi would find out eventually what happened between us.

Rahma left. I settled on a pillow and with an idle finger tapped on the carpet every few minutes or so and watched the delicate ripples travel all the way to the wall. I recalled how I had been overwhelmed by a dreadful feeling of doom before the celebration. Sometimes things could turn out so wrong. Memories of horrible nights in the Emergency Room when we were faced with multiple bad outcomes invaded my thoughts. Last night, intense lust had overpowered me. I had jumped on Rahma, bit and licked him, and rubbed my body against his. Never in my whole life had I behaved that way. It was as if an unknown force had taken control of me.

The multiple attacks by the Krakoran occurred at the same time. A mere coincidence? Or had the celestial event of the Great Eclipse affected all creatures causing chaos throughout the Chamis' world?

# Chapter 21

The next morning, the door chime rang early. I let Chopa in.

"These are dark times," he said. "I will accompany you to the Sheffrou's quarters."

I stared at his outfit. His somber attire, steel gray shirt and black pants, was a sharp contrast from the pink and chocolate outfit he wore at the celebration.

He smoothed his shirt and noticed I was staring at him. "These colors represent mourning for the dead and respect for the unfortunates who suffer."

I nodded. Everyone's thoughts were on Ashani and Tomisho. "Any news of Tomisho?"

"We have no further information on his whereabouts."

I stepped out in the hallway. He took off in long strides and I scurried beside him.

"How is Maashi?"

Chopa stared straight ahead. "The Sheffrou has spoken publicly only once and expressed hope for his friends' safe return," he said. "Several Sawishas including Shonava Benshimu came to offer condolences for Sheffrou Choban's demise and Sheffrou Ashani's kidnapping. They also offered support in the search for Sheffrou Tomisho."

"Do you think they will find him soon?"

"My opinion matters little."

We arrived to Maashi's receiving room. The two panels slid apart, letting us in. The Chamis had changed the colors of the carpet and walls to a dull gray and the couches were charcoal or burgundy color.

A crowd filled the room, all wearing dark clothing, their own colors visible on the bracelets they wore on the right wrist. Some sat idle, others stood in small groups. A few of them exchanged low clicks. The scene reminded me of a wake where the only sounds are those of hushed condolences and quiet sobs.

Maashi sat on a lounge chair at one end, his back against the exterior shape of the encounter room. He also wore gray but with a midnight blue sash. Rahma sat close to him with stooped shoulders and a brow thick with worry. Lado sat across from them on another couch, his face looking harsher than usual. Maashi held in his hand the gold cordelet he had received as a gift from Tomisho before the celebration. He was rolling it back and forth between his fingers, lost in thought.

"Come, Tamara," was all he said.

I trotted over to him and we hugged each other. My throat tightened as I saw his large colorless eyes now hollowed out from pain, a look I had seen many times among victims of a major trauma, especially those who had no memory of the events preceding the accident. He kissed my forehead and my neck and took me in his lap.

"Maashi," I whispered, "I'm so sorry about Choban."

"Thank you." His empty gaze locked on mine. "Did you eat?"

"A little. I wasn't hungry."

Maashi turned to Rahma who produced a tall cup of choun. I took a sip. The white liquid tasted fresh and creamy. I held it tight to keep my hands from shaking.

The main door opened, and everyone turned as Khon the black in charge of security stomped in the receiving room. His dark eyes scanned the chamber. His stone-like face revealed nothing.

Maashi put me aside and stood. Khon walked over to him and bowed. A cold silence spread throughout the room. The crowd waited.

Khon's clicks were short and harsh.

The color drained from Maashi's face. He stood motionless and hissed for a long moment. He twisted around and slammed his fist on the wall so hard clusters of ripples rushed to the other end of the receiving room.

Lado, Rahma, Chopa and a few others jumped at his side. They put their arms around his waist, kissed his shoulders, patted his back, and clicked to him. In one wide sweep of his arms Maashi pushed them away and leaped out of the room. The others stood in place, dumbfounded. Khon watched him go and his lips thinned. He left unnoticed by the crowd.

I sat there, clasping my glass, my chest tight with anguish. What did Khon say? Was the news so bad Maashi had to leave and hide his pain? The room spun faster and faster, and the walls disappeared.

I regained consciousness a while later. I was propped up against firm dark green cushions in Lado's receiving room. In this warm quiet setting, for the first time since the celebration, I inhaled and exhaled without wheezing. In the last few weeks, I had noticed with increasing irritation and concern that I couldn't tolerate stressful situations. In the Emergency Room, I used to deal with trauma cases, patients in pain thrashing about, or out of control psychiatric patients, and never experienced any respiratory symptoms or fainting episodes. Was it a sign of some alien illness?

Dressed in slate gray, Lado was the only one present. He had prepared a generous tray of food: several puddings, different fruits, including my favorite, the toughi that tasted like honeydew melon, and a lumi of choun. He had set the food on an olive-green table shaped like a cube beside me.

"Tamara," he said in a low voice, "You are weak. You must eat. Sheffrou Maashi will not be pleased to see you are not getting enough food."

"Tomisho?" I said.

"They captured him. It has been confirmed."

Was he alive? I swallowed hard as tears blurred my vision. Lado set a light hand on my shoulder and handed me the glass of choun. After a few sips, I felt better.

The door opened and Maashi walked in, followed by Rahma and Chopa all dressed in gray. Maashi dropped on a couch close by, keeping his back straight and stiff. His eyes were smaller and dark, and his jaw was set. Rahma and Chopa settled together on another couch.

Maashi glared at Lado. "Khon has informed me that fewer guards accompanied Tomisho and Choban's group compared to mine when everyone returned back to their quarters."

Lado kept his head down. Rahma and Chopa stared wide-eyed and silent at Maashi, then at Lado.

"Khon said that you requested more guards to cover me and that decision decreased the guards available for the others."

Lado did not respond. Maashi hissed.

"The enemy attacked the two groups who lacked adequate coverage with terrible consequences."

I held my breath. My fingers clutched the glass of choun.

Lado rose keeping his shoulders low and bowed to Maashi. "Shonava," he said, "I made a solemn oath to the Elders to use any means necessary to defend your life. I told Khon to give the utmost priority to your protection."

"Not by depriving others." Maashi jerked his lean frame upward and exploded. "They should have received the same level of protection as I." He glared at Lado. "Leave now." He turned his back to him, his hands balled into fists, ready to strike. He said, "Do not come back. I don't want to set my eyes on you ever again."

Lado didn't respond. With head low and expression unreadable, he left the room.

Maashi stood immobile with his fists clenched tight. "I will be in my pool area. I don't want to be disturbed by anyone." In one long stride he reached a side door and exited.

They canceled the lockdown the next day because there had been no further attacks.

During the following week, back in my quarters, I paced my receiving room over and over, ate a little, and waited for Maashi. I wrote to my daughter on the little computer Maashi had given me. I debated on and on with myself about the situation. Was Maashi still angry at Lado, at everything that happened? Did he get more news about the captives? Did Rahma inform him about what happened between us? How did he react?

One morning, I couldn't wait any longer. I went to Maashi's quarters. Rahma, Chopa, and three others, one light green, a light purple with a long scar above his left eye, and a short-haired chocolate brown and pink sat together in the receiving room. I observed them and understood by their slow and deliberate conversation and their steel gray clothing that they had no news about the two missing Sheffrous.

I sat beside Rahma on a long burgundy couch. Following Maashi's orders, they spoke in English when I was present. No one sat in Lado's spot.

"Have you seen Maashi?" I said.

Chopa answered, "Shonava Maashi left three days ago. He will be back next week."

I heaved a long sigh. Gone again. He didn't come to visit me before he left.

"Will we ever see Lado again?" I said.

"It is unlikely. The Elders transferred him to another sector," Rahma said.

"A friend told me the Sheffrou forgave him the third time he offered apologies," said the young Chami with the light green sash, settled on a couch beside Chopa. He was the first Chami I had seen with silky black hair.

Rahma explained, "Custom dictates we must forgive any offense within three days, otherwise it will never be forgiven." He addressed the group. "Sheffrou Maashi showed kindness. I do not think I would have been so lenient."

They all clicked in unison.

I looked at him. "Why not? Lado has been close to the Sheffrou for months."

Rahma raised his arms up high. "His decisions endangered Sheffrous. We lost three the night of the Great Eclipse."

"And we have none to spare," said the short-haired Chami with the chocolate brown and pink sash.

Clicks again.

"How many Sheffrous are there in total?" I asked.

"About fifty at last count," said Rahma.

"Exactly fifty-one," said Chopa.

"This includes the Sheffrous level 4, 6, and 8," added the short-haired Chami. He adjusted the knot of his chocolate pink sash.

"But you have younger ones who will become mature in a few years," I said. "I saw some at the celebration."

Rahma sat back and sighed, "The ones you saw are the only ones we have."

"It has been many sequences since any male offspring were born," said the light green. "Without more male offspring, the number of Pure Colors will not increase."

"You should have a lot of female offspring by now," I said.

"Most Fanellas are not able or willing to mate every sequence. It is unacceptable to coerce them to mate against their will," said Rahma, "so their numbers remain low."

"The Elders recognized and honored Sheffrou Maashi several times for his success at mating," said Chopa.

They all stomped their feet in unison.

His success didn't surprise me. Maashi possessed a seductive physique and was also gentle and kind. The females surely enjoyed his company, especially the lovely green-eyed one. I sighed.

I asked the group, "How many females are there?"

"The Council keeps the exact number secret for security reasons, but I think there are fewer than forty adults," said Chopa. "No one knows how many offspring there are."

"So few," I said. No wonder many young Chamis had never seen one up close.

We sat there in silence for a moment, as if everyone realized these meager numbers bestowed a grave new importance to the recent kidnappings.

"Rahma," said the Chami with the light green sash, "do you have any news of Sheffrous Tomisho and Ashani?"

"The search teams have been deployed," Rahma said. He addressed the group, "We hope to have information on the captured Sheffrous in two to three weeks. The plan is to recuperate them as soon as possible, before they are damaged."

I took a deep breath to squash the anguish growing within me. "What do you mean? What damage?"

Chopa said with unexpected vigor, "For Sheffrous, being kidnapped is a horrible experience. Stories of torture and atrocities abound."

My chest tightened. I didn't want to listen to any gruesome details and steered the conversation away from this painful subject. "What about Maashi? How is he coping with the loss of his friends?"

"It is a very difficult time for him," said Rahma, "so the Elders sent him to the Eastern Compound where Dasho and Choban used to live to meet Sawishas and service the males. He asked me to stay here since he took Pini with him."

They grinned at each other. Even Chopa's expression changed and his face eased into a little smile.

"Who is Pini?" I said.

"Pinishinilongtida, or Pini for short," Rahma said, "is a young pink member of our group. Sheffrou Maashi took him along to train. He will act as his personal aide for the duration of the trip."

They all smiled like they shared a private joke. I frowned in irritation.

The Chami with the purple sash who had not said a word yet asked, "Why was the Sheffrou sent away? Is it not when the sequence begins that the chosen Sheffrous establish first contact with the Fanellas?"

"You forget that Sheffrou Maashi," said Chopa, "was third choice for mating. Only the first two chosen can initiate first contact."

So Maashi wasn't the favorite. "Third choice is still good, isn't it?" I said to them.

They all stared at me.

"The one chosen third is allowed to mate only if the mating was unsuccessful with the first two," said Rahma.

"I see. And what kind of business does Maashi have in the Eastern Compound?"

The Elders frequently sent Maashi to other sectors for a few days, but he never explained what he did there. I thought he traveled to perform diplomatic functions.

They all stirred in their seats and chuckled except Chopa who kept a serious expression.

"Did I say something funny?"

Rahma turned towards me and bent his head sideways. "Little female," he said with a mocking smile, "one would have expected you to know the answer to that question by now."

I hated when they made those types of comments. Right then, his condescending gaze reminded me of Lado. "Rahma,"

I said in a dry voice, "if I knew the answer, I wouldn't be asking the question."

"I did not mean to offend you," Rahma said, his brow darker.

"The Sheffrou performs his usual function. He is servicing the males," Chopa said.

"I don't understand what you're saying."

"To be more precise," said Chopa, "he pleasures the Sawishas and the Multicolor males. His role is to fulfill whatever they need for their sexual gratification."

I sat there and could feel my face blush a deep red. "What?"

Chopa explained further in a monotonous voice, as if talking to a child, "Tamara, there are not enough Fanellas. They only mate with Sheffrous to produce female offspring. The other males have the right to be sexually fulfilled. Sheffrous are skilled in the erotic arts and can satisfy their needs. Their role is to service them and mate with the females."

A light breeze could've toppled me over. Everyone in the room understood this except me. Maashi had tried a long time ago to explain what his work consisted of, but I couldn't grasp what he meant.

"For the sake of completeness," said Chopa, "I must add Sheffrous are forbidden to mate with females of any other species. If Sheffrou Maashi ever attempted to mate with you, he would be subjected to a severe punishment."

My cheeks burned like someone had slapped me. They knew Maashi was pleasuring me. They knew everything. Maashi had mentioned nothing about . . . those rules. I sat there pinned to the couch, thinking of all the males he was servicing at this moment.

I recovered in a fraction of a second, jumped off my seat, and glared at them, "You and your Sheffrou are all a bunch of hypocrites," I said, fuming. "With luck, they will find the wormhole in the next few weeks, and I'll leave this forsaken world forever. It won't be soon enough."

Rahma eyed me sideways and said in a taunting voice, "Sheffrou Maashi had to cancel the search for the wormhole a few weeks ago. The Elders decided he should concentrate on more important things. He had no choice but to obey to regain their trust and to have any chance at mating this sequence. It would seem you will have to bear our presence longer than you had intended."

Checkmate. I felt tricked, used, a mere pawn in a chess game. Anger boiled in me, ready to explode. I stormed out of the room so they wouldn't see me choke on my tears.

I ran to my encounter room and locked the door. I sat down and wiped my face. What had I done to deserve this? Such cunning, such deceit. I could see it all now.

I hated to admit the fact, but I had fallen in love with Maashi. Could I still accept him now that I knew about his secret life? He serviced the males, Sheffrous, his chowlis, the females, everyone.

He was Sheffrou and this complicated everything.

He was also my only chance to return home.

Was the search for the wormhole an empty promise, a simple ruse to exploit me?

If I acted like I didn't care for him anymore would he tire of me and send me home?

# Chapter 22

I got up the next morning and dragged my achy body in the receiving room. I took a bite of a leftover fruit. It tasted bitter and I spit it on the carpet. I dressed without conviction, sat down on a low couch and stared at the wall. Its dull color mirrored my life in this world. During my eighteen years as a physician, I had never suffered such hurt and humiliation. No words could describe the emptiness in my soul.

I ached for my life on Earth with all its joys and pleasures even though I had experienced serious difficulties in my relationship with my husband Nate. His overbearing attitude and his constant complaints had brought dissatisfaction and disillusionment. We lived together, but without the closeness and intimacy I longed for. Passion and fire had long deserted our couple. What was for me as necessary as the air I breathed had become for him a mere physical exchange. Where I hungered for excitement and adventure, he wished only for a quiet retreat. He had agreed to move to the South to be close to our children whom I adored thinking it would be an acceptable compromise and would satisfy my needs, but our relation hadn't improved.

Now far away in this world, I saw things in a different light. We both had changed, and I had done my best to save our marriage, but I realized I had been avoiding the inevitable. The only acceptable path would have been separation.

My children were the ones I missed the most. The sadness and guilt I felt weighed on my heart. These last few weeks I had been so immersed in the Chamis' world I had almost forgotten my family, but I couldn't imagine a life without them.

My oldest, David, strived to succeed in the harsh and competitive medical world. Although he possessed a strong character, he still needed my guidance and support. He had planned to be engaged this summer. Now I feared he might postpone this important event until they found an explanation for my disappearance.

Jonathan, the youngest, would soon start his senior year in high school. I wanted to be there for him. I wanted to attend his graduation and encourage him to pursue his goals.

How could I forget the golden glow of my beautiful daughter Allison? She enjoyed life to the fullest and dreamed of a future as an artist. Now, alone and grief-stricken, who would cherish and comfort her? Who would share her sorrows and successes? I swallowed hard. Tears rolled down my cheeks.

On Earth, I was an individual with a purpose, the leader of a team of professionals. I led an ordered life and was a respected member of my community. My work as a physician had been demanding, overwhelming, but it also brought joy and the immense satisfaction of helping others. I had considered changing my career, moving on to something else, something which would give me more freedom. But, I knew, deep within me, I would never choose anything different. My work as physician was an intrinsic part of my life.

I sat and stared into the emptiness of my quarters mirroring the void I felt. Tears rained on my clothes. I sobbed without restraint letting go of weeks of false hope. My former life had been reduced to an illusion. The wormhole had ripped me apart from my family and sent me far into an alien world unlike anything I had known before. Would I ever see my house and my neighborhood again now they had called off the search for the shiny circle? Would I ever gaze upon Earth's blue sky? The thought brought renewed anguish and I wailed louder.

In this world, I was a little female, living under the long shadow of a powerful Sheffrou, with no identity of my own, one among the many who were part of his life. I had spent days waiting for his affection without questioning his motives and wondering what my own role ought to be. Here on Chitina, everything revolved around Sheffrous. Maashi divided his time between his chowlis, the Sawishas, the other males and the females. His work consisted of generating pleasure for himself and everyone else.

What if he kept me here for his pleasure? He could make sure I would never find my way back. Was this the real explanation for calling off the search for the wormhole? Perhaps he didn't want me to go home.

Without his help I couldn't go back. My journey led to a dead end.

Despair filled my heart.

The door chime rang.

"Who's there?"

"It is Chopa."

What now? I wiped my face with my arm. "Come in," I said.

He stepped in. "How are you, Tamara?" He executed a light bow. "I bring a message from Lady Ileana," he said. "The lady would be honored to have a meeting with you."

I stared at him not understanding. My eyes burned and I had to clear my throat. "Who is Lady Ileana?"

"You have seen the lady at the celebration. She is the Fanella who put the garland of white and lavender Tishi around Sheffrou Maashi's neck."

The beautiful green-eyed Fanella. The one Maashi favored. I hesitated a short instant. "When does she want to see me?"

"In two hours of your time." He waited a moment then said, "What shall I tell her?"

"Tell the lady I accept her invitation."

"Very well," Chopa said. "I will come back and take you to her." He nodded and left.

A meeting. Was this going to be the same type of meeting I had with Maashi when I first came to this compound? Did she speak English? Why did she want to see me?

I showered, put on my favorite cream shirt and a pair of fitted khaki pants with my turquoise sash and prepared mentally as if I would meet royalty. I was ready early and twirled with my sash while pacing the room.

Chopa came as promised. "Lady Ileana will meet you in a secluded area. I will carry you there. Two guards will accompany us."

We left for the tunnels, one guard walking ahead, one closing the rear. After what seemed an hour-long trip, we walked into a small room no bigger than a large closet, with two sets of wide doors facing each other.

Chopa set me down and said, "This door will open. Go inside. Lady Ileana will join you."

"Does she speak English?"

"She will find a way to communicate with you."

Two oval panels slid apart. Intense white light flooded the area. I blinked and shaded my eyes with my hand.

Nothing could have prepared me for what I saw. I stood with my mouth open. If I had ever imagined heaven, this would have been it. This world was as different as possible from the dark caves where the Chamis spent their lives.

Under a cotton-candy pink sky, a breathtaking multicolored world stretched as far as the eye could see. Dominating the landscape was a tall tree with a broad canopy which reminded me of an acacia. Delicate white flowers mixed with pale green leaves cascaded down its branches. Dainty green and darker wine-colored plants, overgrown with patches of yellow, lavender and fuchsia petals covered the ground. Bushes of white, trumpet-shaped, fragrant flowers emerged from wide circular leaves and reached way above my head. Ferns covered with small blue berries grew in the shadows beneath the tree. Everywhere I looked, I saw more color, more exotic shapes. Then, between a group of butter yellow bushes and hanging iridescent flowers, I saw her.

Lady Ileana sat on a flat moss-covered rock at the base of the tree. She bent her head sideways and gazed at me. Her honey-colored hair studded with white pearl-shaped flowers framed a perfect oval face. Her light skin shone through her translucent gown, revealing small round breasts. With her thin waist and long slender legs, she appeared as delicate as a porcelain doll. Green eyes smiled as she studied my reaction to her world. I stood there amazed by her beauty and the delightful spectacle before me.

"Good afternoon," I said. "I am pleased to see you." I smiled at her. Did she understand my words?

Her face glowed like a jewel in the sun. Her eyes became larger and shimmered with flecks of gold. She extended her arm and pointed to the rock beside her.

"Thank you," I said, intimidated by her perfection as if she was a character out of a fairy tale. I approached and sat beside her on the spongy surface of the rock.

She clicked, and her fingertips touched my arm, my shoulder, then my thigh. I raised my head, looked at her, and lost myself in two green oval pools. She clicked again and cradled my face in her hands. With no further preamble, she kissed me.

"Oh," I said, startled.

She kissed me again, this time using my surprise to slide her sweet tongue in my mouth and lick me provoking an unexpected shiver of pleasure.

I raised my arms in protest.

Ignoring my reaction, she smiled. "It is a great pleasure to hold you and kiss you," she said and erupted into a crystalline laugh. She hugged me against her, then released me. Her fingers caressed my head and traced the contour of my jaw.

"You are shapinka, little Fanella," she said in a soft voice. "I yearned to meet you ever since I saw you at the celebration. I have wondered about your world, wanted to know what kind of person you were. I sense a kind heart but also much sadness."

It took only a moment for me to divulge how I grieved the loss of my home and family and wished to return to Earth. I told her also how I suspected the Chamis including Maashi had deceived me.

She focused on my words and, when I stopped, hugged me like we had known each other for a long time and shared a kindred spirit. "Tamara," she said at last, "I would love to see your world and meet your sisters. I am told Earth is a unique planet filled with wonders. I am sorry that you are apart from your family and can feel how much you miss them.

"You appear to live in a place where Fanellas enjoy a degree of freedom we will never know. Alas, our lives are interconnected with our duties to mate and we raise our offspring under the harsh reality of the Krakoran threat." She lowered her head and rested it against mine.

"I wish," I whispered, "things could be different for you and your children."

"As you can see," she extended her arms encompassing all the beauty surrounding us, "our people have created a world as perfect as possible for us but although we live confined in our compounds for our security, fear and sorrow still infiltrates our lives." She paused, joined her hands and her eyes lost their color. Her face paled so much she reminded me of a Japanese geisha.

She knew, more than any other, the price to pay to survive separated from the one you loved. But the intensity of her reaction surprised me. The acute color change of her face was a sign of profound pain and I suspected something much more crucial caused her anguish.

"What's wrong?"

"As we speak, an unknown illness has stricken two of our youngest offspring."

"An illness? Perhaps I can help. May I see them?"

"Thank you for your kind offer but our best physicians are caring for them." She sighed. "I may be overreacting. I worry all the time."

"Just the same, don't hesitate to call me if they don't get better. Sometimes a different perspective can help find a solution to a challenging problem."

"These are difficult times," she said with a faraway look. "I hope someday we will be free of the claws of our enemies and the sadness they bring," She took my hand in hers. "I hope you will see your world again. Finding the gateway that brought you here will be very difficult. You should adapt as much as you can to our world and not despair." She smiled a sad smile. "As for Sheffrou Maashi, you must understand he can bestow affection and love to many at the same time. You must trust him. He will be true to his promises."

My mood sank at the mention of Maashi. I blinked back tears.

"What did I say to bring you such sadness?" she said and kissed my cheeks. Talking about Maashi brought back some color to her face.

I closed my eyes and fought to regain control of my emotions. Her affectionate kisses and hugs were melting my heart. I took a deep breath, and soon as I opened my mouth, she slid her tongue inside. This time I took her face in my hands and gave her a firm push back.

She looked at me with kind eyes. "Forgive me," she said, "I had to know more. Sheffrou Maashi could not tear his eyes away from you during the celebration. I could tell he is quite fond of you."

Did she say that to flatter me? "On the contrary, he appeared to be enthralled with you."

She caressed my cheek with a long slender finger. "Little Fanella," she said, "Sheffrous possess an unquenchable need to give love and be loved in return. Without constant affection, they lose their charissa and they fade away." She sighed. "Dearest one, I wanted to meet you in person to learn more about your world and see if you had feelings for Maashi. I have searched your soul and found your love for him."

Her delicate brow darkened. "I envy you. You spend time by his side every day." Her breathing deepened for a long moment.

Her comment troubled me. I sensed the pain in her heart. I wanted to comfort her but couldn't find soothing words.

She put her arms around me and held me close. "Shapinka," she whispered, "your mind searches for answers but just listen to your heart. It will not lead you astray."

A light breeze rustled the tree leaves. The air felt cooler. "Dusk is upon us. I must go. I hope to kiss you again one day." She pressed her lips on my forehead.

Lady Ileana stood, took a few steps, and disappeared behind the tree. I heard a sliding sound and the door to the Chamis' world of tunnels and caves opened. I took one last look at her magical kingdom and left.

Chopa and the guards were waiting for me. We went back to my quarters in silence. The halls seemed darker than usual. Chopa set me down in my receiving room and said, "Stay safe shapinka." He left without another word.

I stood there, overcome by emotion. She loved Maashi and I also loved him. Did he love her more? Was she his soulmate? Did he long to hold her slender body in his arms and dream of her kisses?

What an unfair and mind-boggling situation. Anger rose in me. I clenched my fists. How could I share Maashi with so many others also attracted to him? I screamed and cried out, wanting to rip this horrible world apart the way an angry child would destroy a rag doll.

I threw the bigger cushions lying on the couch and kicked them all over the place and tore the smaller ones. I punched the walls and hurled my little computer with such force that it broke in small pieces.

Standing there, panting, I was stunned by my rage. I didn't recognize myself.

The door opened. It was Chopa.

I glared at him. "What do you want?"

He scanned the room and didn't answer. His face remained expressionless. He then took a few steps and sat on a couch. He looked at me and said, "Do you want to talk about it?"

As soon as he said that, my anger evaporated. I dropped beside him, dejected. I held my head with my hands and asked in a shaky voice, "Do you think Maashi loves me?"

"What I think is not important."

"Stop that, Chopa. I want to know."

"The Sheffrou does love you." His eyes enlarged as if a sudden thought popped in his head. "Tamara, our world is different."

"I hate it." I threw another cushion, and it bounced and missed the couch and landed sideways on the floor.

"You will have to share him with others." He looked away. "We all do."

I stared at him. "You too?"

"I am only a spotted brown, not a Pure Color, but I have feelings."

"How can you say this? Don't you hate that you have to share him?"

"No Chamranlina, not even another Sheffrou, can satisfy his intense need for affection."

"How about the Fanella? Could Lady Ileana satisfy his desires?"

Chopa's brow widened. "I do not know. But even if she could, the Elders would never allow them to live together and the Chamranlinas would be totally against it."

"But how can Maashi, you know, enjoy females and males alike?"

"He has been trained to do so."

I frowned.

"Sheffrous are not born bisexual. Deep Purples teach them to enjoy males."

I shook my head. "This is too much."

"When Sheffrous are young adults and develop their characteristic skills, they must bond with a purple or green who will train and prepare them for the three Draharma trials. Only then will they be recognized by all and may be chosen to mate."

"This makes no sense."

"Tamara, Sheffrous possess a tremendous libido. In the past, this has led to open conflict with the other Pure Colors and Sheffrous. The Pure Colors attacked anyone who dared challenge their right to mate with incredible ferocity. I know this is difficult to understand but the training process has been the rule for hundreds of sequences and has prevented many conflicts. It was a compromise meant to satisfy both Sawishas and Sheffrous."

I hissed between my teeth. "You manipulate and take advantage of them when they're young to satisfy the needs of all the other Chamranlinas." I shook my head in disgust. "You should leave. I can't deal with this."

Chopa continued. "Survival of our people depended on the satisfactory resolution of the conflicts created by Sheffrous. They were the only ones who produced female offspring, but they were also uncontrollable. The mandatory training and the

Draharma trials were the only solution." Chopa stood and said in a softer voice, "You seemed uninformed of the Sheffrou's obligation to service the males. I thought you should learn more about our customs before you judged Sheffrou Maashi too harshly."

"This is the second time someone has mentioned the Draharma trials. What are they?"

"They consist of three rigorous trials that all the fertile males who wish to mate must complete. All the candidates must show courage and humility in excruciatingly painful and humbling tests."

I frowned. Those trials probably had something to do with the jewels on Maashi's penis.

"Chopa," I said with an exasperated voice, "I've been struggling to understand your weird customs ever since I got here."

He took a few steps toward the door, paused then turned. He extended his arm and handed me a small square device the size of a lighter. "Take this," he said. "If you need me, press on it and I will come."

I took the device.

"Stay safe, Tamara," he said. He stood at the door and pressed on discrete buttons by the doorframe. The room changed back to its original design, furniture and cushions alike, except for my computer which was scattered in multiple pieces. He looked at it and said, "I will find another one for you," and left.

That night sleep took a long time to come. Hundreds of thoughts flashed through my mind. Maashi had always showed

kindness even the one time when I got hurt during an encounter. Was this why I had been blind? Was I just a toy for
him or was his attention and affection for me genuine, as Chopa
and Lady Ileana said? If I never went back home, having learned
about his secret life and knowing what I knew now, could my
connection with him and my love remain the same?

With a heavy heart, I lay motionless until my exhausted
mind surrendered to sleep. Even then, I searched for Maashi in
my dreams. I still longed for him, I wanted him to hold me, to
feel his arms around me, his soft fingers on my skin, his gentle
lips on my breasts. Without him, my life had no meaning.

I woke up with a start. At this hour of the night the sky-blue
ceiling was filled with grim shadows. I held a soft cushion
against my chest. My fingers caressed its silky material and traced
its delicate pattern. My mind searched for answers. Was Maashi
also a victim in this strange world? Did he need to feel cherished so much he had to search incessantly for love? Was it an
intense hunger he couldn't satisfy? Or a bottomless well which
he couldn't fill?

The thought that Maashi was suffering had never occurred
to me before. If that were the case, his pain made my pain even
more unbearable.

Dark thoughts invaded my mind. I remembered an incident that happened years ago. I had been involved in the care of
a patient who fought with tremendous courage a terrible disease
which consumed her life. She moved away and months later, I
found out she had committed suicide. The news shocked and
saddened me. Over time however, I came to understand her
choice. She had made a conscious decision to end her miserable
life. A decision to be free.

I breathed in deeply. I had to clear my head. I got up, put on some clothes, went out and told the guard I was going to see Chopa. He let me pass without protest.

# Chapter 23

I walked the length of the hallway and then I knew what I had to do. I turned around, went back to my quarters and took my pad with me for directions and a few bottles of water. I wore the warm garment with a hood, long pants and boots; this time I would avoid contact with the germs and parasites lurking in the dark.

I marched through familiar tunnels at first, then through others where dust made the path slippery and the sound of my footsteps no longer echoed off the walls. Lit by oval globes the size of my hand every twelve to fifteen steps, they meandered far underground.

As I entered an impressive cave the size of a ballroom, I marveled at the intricate carvings on both sides of the large portal. My fingers traced the deep grooves one by one. This was such a different world, with rigid rules and weird customs. I had never taken the time to learn their language. Did it matter anymore?

I wanted to reach the tunnels where darkness enveloped everything and leave bottles of water for a possible return in a few days. Then I would find a way to get to the surface and seek the area where I arrived.

Twice I hid behind boulders so the patrolling guards wouldn't see me. At some point I rested and sat down. Here, the ground was no longer covered with dust and felt cool. I smelled the dampness in the air. Soon I heard the roar of the Gorganna gorge. I swore under my breath. I must've made a wrong turn somewhere. I noted my position on the pad for future reference.

Memories of swimming with Maashi and Choban came to mind. My eyes watered and my vision blurred as I remembered with sadness Choban's smile and his clear musical laugh. I thought of Tomisho and Ashani kidnapped by the enemy. Were they still alive? Would they be rescued soon? I shivered in the cool air.

A hint of foul odor permeated the area. I thought the Krakoran weren't interested in me, but it was unsettling to think there might be one close by. I sniffed, listened carefully for any unusual sound, and looked for a clue in the tunnel behind me. Nothing. Seconds later, the odor of rotten meat was unmistakable. An Untouchable was approaching. I broke out in a cold sweat and ran in the nearest tunnel. It was covered with pebbles and the floor sloped abruptly downward. I flew ahead, not paying attention to my heading. I wanted to put as much distance as possible between the creature and me.

I peeked behind, tripped, caught myself, slipped, and fell anyway. My nose hit the ground so hard I saw twinkling lights. My right knee was bruised and bloody from the fall even with the thick pants. Damn. I scrambled up, ignoring the pain. I listened for the guards but heard nothing. With a sore knee and an achy right ankle, I limped along, biting my lips to avoid crying out. I strained to reach the end of the tunnel, which led to a cavern a short distance away. I was sure one of the secondary tunnels connected to the pool so when I reached the intersection, I stopped and looked both ways. My breath caught. About forty feet on the right, I saw it.

The shapeless translucent creature hovered in mid-air. Long filaments projected out from its core as it moved about. It reminded me of bacteria seen under the microscope. It must've noticed me because it shimmered and cast a greenish glow.

My blood iced in my veins. Fear propelled me forward down the left tunnel. I shook from the effort and dizziness forced me to stop. I looked behind and couldn't see it anymore. I progressed as fast as I could, all the while being careful to avoid another fall. The walls were damp, and the ground more slippery as I approached the pool. The sound of rushing water was amplified a thousand times in the deep tunnels. The Gorganna gorge loomed ahead.

I saw a faint light where the path ended. I remembered the creatures always attacked the Chamis on the surface of the planet or in the dry tunnels. Perhaps they feared water. If I made it to the pool, I would be safe. My right ankle was swollen now, and the pain slowed me down. One last sprint and I reached open space.

I took a few steps forward and stood on a narrow ledge overlooking the gorge. The swift water sped up and plunged in a dark opening right below. I stepped back, panting, terrified of falling in the fast current.

Making sure my footing was secure, I paused and controlled my breathing and my pounding heart. The mist soaked my skin, and soon my clothes were drenched. Standing on the ledge, I stared at the void under me and felt its powerful pull. Surrender would be so easy. The end would be swift, painless. I watched the water run by. I hesitated. Unlike the first time when I almost drowned, this time I wouldn't fight back. I would let my last breath escape, and the Gorganna gorge would swallow me. The search for my world would be over.

I shook my head in disbelief at these harrowing thoughts. All my life I had worked hard to enter medical school, to survive the endless hours and heavy workload of residency, to repair the broken bond between Nate and me. Now, with sadness and despair in my soul, was I going to forsake my life or fight for it?

I breathed in a long breath and clenched my hands. I had always been level-headed and determined. In critical moments I never chose the easy way out, refusing to surrender until I was certain there was no other option. Fighting for my life was the only choice for me. Whatever the outcome with Maashi, and even if I never went home, I would stay the course, find the strength and the joy I needed to survive.

The foul odor of the Krakoran infiltrated the air. The stench grew stronger and the shapeless form materialized to my right, less than ten feet away. I watched it, mesmerized. My skin crawled and my hair stood on ends. Standing on the wet ledge with nowhere to go, I pressed my back to the wall.

"Get away from me," I yelled. Anger boiled in me. Being captured by some shapeless alien creature was out of the question. That would not happen. I held on tight to the slick rock. The form moved closer, and one filament stretched out as if feeling or smelling the air. The creature pulsated as if ready to strike.

"Don't you dare touch me," I said. I moved further away and in one swift move turned to face the wall, holding on to the damp rocks, and kept my eyes locked on the undulating shape. Part of the narrow ledge broke off. I slipped and screamed. I grabbed the sharp edge with my hands. My body hung in mid-air for a few seconds. Using all my strength, I pulled myself up on my knees and hugged the wall.

The Untouchable hovered on my left just a few feet from me. Its smell overwhelmed my senses so much I could taste it and my stomach felt queasy. I advanced carefully on my knees, wincing from the discomfort caused by my scraped leg, keeping my body as far away from it as I could. The ledge got even narrower, but I saw an opening to another tunnel a few yards further. I eyed the small path and clenched my teeth. One false move and I would fall thirty feet. The open mouth of the gorge beckoned. Between two evils, if I had to choose, I would prefer drowning rather than being captured by that alien.

I pushed my body up and inched away from the creature, hoping it wouldn't notice. Perhaps it was analyzing me and if I appeared still, it wouldn't make any aggressive move. I took a small step, and a chunk of rock gave way under me. I screamed, held on with my hands, my feet dangling in the void. Struggling to secure my feet, I managed to gain one foothold.

The spray bombarded me from below as I hung precariously over the deadly current. I looked down and gasped in fear.

I released my right hand and reached in my shirt for Chopa's device, the one he had given me in my quarters. If I signaled him, he would come to the rescue. I groped in my inner pocket and tried over and over to get it out, but my wet fingers couldn't get a good grasp. Suddenly, it popped out. I pressed the device once and cried out as it slipped away and fell in the fast-moving water.

I checked on the creature hovering a few feet away. It hadn't moved.

I couldn't get my other foot against anything solid on the sheer rock wall. Damn it a thousand times over.

What should I do? I couldn't hang on like this much longer. I pleaded in desperation, "Maashi, if you can hear me, help me! Please help me." Tears stung my eyes. I held on with all my strength, but my hands were slowly slipping.

To my horror, the Untouchable floated toward me. One long tentacle stretched out from its side. Its light touch immediately produced an intolerable burning sensation. I screamed, pulled my hand away and lost my balance. I hung for a millisecond with my other hand then grabbed the ledge again with my injured hand. I cried and hiccupped with the pain.

"Hold on, Tamara." From deep in the thick mist I heard a familiar voice.

I looked over my shoulder toward the sound. Through my dripping eyelashes, I could see his shape. He stood just a few feet away within reach of the creature.

"Watch out, Krakoran," I yelled above the roar of the waterfall.

"Tamara, do not let go." Maashi said.

He crouched low on the narrow ledge and crawled toward me. "Hold on." With his jaw shut tight, his eyes dark as coals, he pushed his body close to mine. His face paled to ivory when he got within arm's length of the Untouchable.

Without taking his eyes off me, he said, "Tamara, the ledge is too weak to support my weight. You must come closer." He struggled to keep his body stable on the narrow rock. "I will distract the Krakoran and you can move toward me." He hissed and threw a few pebbles at the creature.

The Untouchable got bigger and brighter. It hovered and then advanced ever so slowly toward Maashi as if reluctant to leave me. Maashi stretched his body and extended his right arm along the rock.

"Come, Tamara. Come now."

My fingers were numb from the cold water, and I could barely hang on. I gripped the rock with my hands, but they were slowly slipping. My eyes watched powerless as my grasp weakened. I gritted my teeth and moved my left hand a few inches closer to Maashi.

"Good," Maashi said. "A little more."

I moved my hand again, but this time could not hold on. My fingers were slipping. I screamed at the top of my lungs.

Maashi cried out, "Tamara!"

He boldly lunged downward and caught my left arm. Half of his body hung over the edge. My feet dangling, I stared at the foaming water under me and desperately tried to grab on to the rock.

A loud hissing sound startled me. The creature had extended a wide tentacle and had pressed it on Maashi's right arm. His skin burned and a wretched odor of charred flesh filled the air. Maashi hissed and breathed hard.

"Hold on," I said to him. "Please!"

Maashi's body heaved with each breath he took. The burning continued.

"What can I do to help? Tell me," I said as loud as I could.

"Throw some rocks at it," he said, his voice choking with pain. "If you crack its crystalline casing, it will disappear. We will have a few minutes before it appears again."

Without letting go of my left wrist, his burning arm crawled on the slippery rock and brought me much closer to the ledge and I got a foothold on the wet wall. As soon as I did, with my free right hand, I took a loose rock and threw it at the Untouchable. The clang clearly resonated above the roar of the water. The creature shrank a little and stopped glowing. Encouraged by my first try and worried about the unrelenting burning of Maashi's arm, I took every rock and pebble I could reach and flung it at the Untouchable. I missed my target a few times, but I hit the outer shell several times. A white line appeared and ran lengthwise along it like one you can see on an egg about to crack open. In an instant, the creature disappeared.

Maashi sighed and rested his head on the smooth rocky ledge. I closed my eyes and tried to calm the drum beating in my chest.

I heard loud clicks and snarls. Rahma and Chopa, and two Black Guards, each one with a Raah Azan, appeared behind Maashi. The guards immediately threw long flexible cables that stuck like spider's silk around me and Maashi. With a slow and concerted effort, they brought us back to the safety of the tunnel.

Maashi's face and chest were white and his body shook. He pulled me to him, held my head in his left hand and said, "What happened, Tamara? Why are you out here?" His eyes were dark with concern and anger and his neck muscles tensed under the strain he felt.

I stared back at him and didn't answer.

Rahma was to first one to reach Maashi. He clicked in soft soothing noises, hugged him and kissed his neck. He tore the sleeve off Maashi's charred arm and aided by Chopa, applied a thick layer of white cream and sprayed it with bubbly foam. Then he covered the entire arm with a thin clear sheet like a plastic wrap.

Rahma turned and said, "I am glad you are safe, Tamara. Let me take care of your injuries." He applied the same cream, foam, and wrap on my injuries. The guards surrounded us and clicked at Maashi.

I touched my arm and bruised fingers. The foam had erased the pain and replaced it by a soothing cool sensation.

"Come," Maashi said. "We must leave this area." He picked me up with his left arm and held me close. Rahma and Chopa stayed by our side and the two guards, flanked by the Raah Azan, accompanied us back to his quarters.

# Chapter 24

Maashi carried me to the compound without another word. When we arrived in his quarters, he signaled for everyone to leave. He set me down and slipped in the encounter room. I followed right behind. Although the light colors of the room were calming, conflicting emotions seethed in me.

The Sheffrou's face and neck were as pale as alabaster. He sat and put his shaky hands on his knees. He breathed in spurts then his breathing decreased to his normal low rhythm. He bent his head sideways and looked at me. "Why were you out in the tunnels late at night when you knew it wasn't safe?" He extended his arm to touch my cheek.

"Don't touch me," I pushed his hand away.

"You were hanging in a most precarious position over the falls. I feared for your life." He shook his head and swallowed. His eyelashes were wet. He blinked and said, "What happened? What were you thinking?"

I wasn't going to let him lay guilt on me. I blurted out in a harsh tone. "You never told me what you do with the males." I sprang up. With my right ankle still sore, I shifted my weight on my left leg and clenched my fists. Heat crept up my neck, flushed my cheeks. "You betrayed me."

"Tamara—"

"You never said you were having sex with the males. Did you also have sex with Tomisho, the sawishas, the other Sheffrous, everybody?" I asked, my voice increasing in volume.

His mouth opened, but no sound came out.

"I want an answer, Maashi." I glared at him and fisted my hands.

He closed his eyes and turned his head away, then opened them. They were big and dark like thick clouds on a rainy day. "Tamara, I am Sheffrou." He took a long swallow of saliva. "I am different. I wanted to explain my condition, but I wasn't sure you would understand."

"Maashi," I said, insisting on each word, "you lied."

"I had no intention of betraying your trust."

Too angry to put my feelings into words, I just stared at him.

"I was waiting for the right time to tell you." He paused. "I realize now there is

no right time to explain the role we play. Please forgive me. I didn't mean to hurt you."

"So, it's true."

"Yes."

I sat down, defeated, a bitter taste in my mouth. I looked up at the blue and khaki diamond shapes on the walls with a lump in my throat. We were both silent. My hands held on tight to my knees. I had hoped he would deny my accusations, but he had acknowledged his eccentric behavior as if it were normal.

"And I guess you were waiting for the right time to let me know about Lady Ileana." I waited for his reaction, but all he did was tilt his head sideways. "I met her while you were gone. You're in love with her, aren't you?"

He stared straight ahead, and his body stiffened. In an instant, his chest paled so much he looked like a wax mannequin.

"Maashi?"

He swallowed but didn't say a word.

"Are you all right?"

He shook his head from side to side then stared at his hands. Were his feelings for her a secret?

"I'm sorry," I said, surprised by his distress, "I upset you." Could he understand I was jealous of her?"

Maashi kept his gaze downward and spoke in a low voice. "Tamara, it is forbidden to love a Fanella. If anyone knew my feelings, I would never be allowed to see her again." He turned his head away.

"Don't worry."

Maashi reached for my hands and held them in his. "Only my chowlis know my feelings for her. I have tried my utmost to conceal them." He blinked and his eyelashes were wet. "You know my heart well, much more than I thought."

"Your secret is safe with me." It was impossible to stay angry with him, but I silently cursed the day I stumbled into that evil wormhole.

I couldn't help being in love with him, but this didn't mean I wasn't jealous of the Fanella. I thought if he truly cared for me even if he loved her, this would be enough to content me. Lady Ileana said Maashi could love many. Was this true or did she tell me that to lift my spirits?

Maashi straightened, rubbed his brow, and his face regained a little color. After a moment, he said, "Rahma told me about his encounter with you. I am pleased you spent an enjoyable evening the night of the celebration."

I shook myself away from him. "Is that all you have to say? Don't you care about me?" I slammed the closest cushion on the wall and watched wave after wave of ripples travel from one side of the encounter room to the other.

"Tamara, I do care." He put a comforting hand on my shoulder. "Little one, on that night, the Fanellas' presence and the gathering of such a great number of sawishas stimulated the Sheffrous who produced an incredible amount of holoma, and this flooded the cave with pheromones."

"You knew this would affect me?"

"Yes, it is a known fact that the powerful holoma creates an erotic environment for all present. The Pure Colors and the Multicolors met and exchanged intimate thoughts and desires and connected physically at a level never achieved in an everyday setting. That's why I told Dasho to watch over you. If he noticed a significant change in your behavior to the point you would be offended by it in normal circumstances, he should make sure you left under the safety of one of my chowlis. You left with Rahma. I trusted him but he lost control and overstepped his boundaries. He wasn't at liberty of touching you. I have reprimanded him for that."

Maashi lifted my chin with one finger and said, "Tamara, caring doesn't mean exclusive possession. You may experience pleasure with other males as much as you want. I am delighted you enjoyed yourself. I would have preferred to be the one with you, but you were pleased so I am grateful." He pressed his lips on my forehead.

His concept of relations reminded me of the swinging couples of the nineties. I decided to go ahead with my last question. "Who is Pini?"

"He is a young pink."

"Rahma said he's your new friend, and he accompanied you on your last trip."

"Yes, I took him so I could teach him."

"Are you having sex with him?"

"With Pini?" Maashi bent his head sideways and made a funny sound with his throat.

"Don't mock me, Maashi."

"I know this must be confusing." He signed. "I admit Sheffrous possess a tremendous libido and have encounters with any consenting adult."

I crossed my arms in front of me and said with a mocking tone. "I know that now."

He ignored my comment. "Pini is only thirty-four sequences old. He is very young." His eyes changed and shone deep amber. "I would never consider having any kind of sexual contact with him until he is much older."

"You didn't hesitate to make love to me." Calling it sex made it sound offensive.

"Tamara, you are younger than Pini, but you are an adult female. Pini is just a teenager. He will not be mature until forty-five sequences."

"Whatever," I grumbled. "What are you teaching him?"

"I wanted to spend time with him to inform him about you so he could become your companion."

"What?"

"Little one," he whispered, "you need a companion to watch over you and keep you safe when I'm not available. Lado is gone. Rahma and Chopa aren't suitable candidates. Pini's youth and energy make him an excellent choice and Pinks are very gentle. He'll take care of you, make sure you have everything you need, and teach you our language and our customs."

"I can take care of myself."

"I doubt that after what just happened." Maashi's eyes locked in mine. He moved closer, and whispered, "You scared me."

I turned my head away.

Was he telling the truth?

Trying to keep my voice cold and detached, I asked him, "How did you know where I was? How did you find me?"

"I left the Eastern Compound early. I missed you and I was worried." Maashi blinked. "I went to your quarters and the guard said you had left hours ago. Several guards were tracking an Untouchable and saw you in the tunnels. We searched all over." Maashi stopped, looked at me sideways. "Then we discovered that Chopa's detector had been swept away in the Gorganna gorge. I thought I had lost you." His voice fell silent. His face paled as he shook his head in disbelief. "I finally connected with you through your thoughts and located you."

He bent forward and put his right hand just below his chest. His eyes were glistening with tears. "Please, do not leave like this ever again," he whispered. "I have already lost my dear friend Choban. I don't want to lose you."

I believed every word he said. I was sure he would be devastated if something happened to me but there was something else I was determined to ask. "Why did you cancel the search for the wormhole? Were you going to tell me, or was it also something too difficult to explain?"

Maashi avoided my eyes.

"Why did you bring me here to your compound? Why do you keep me here?"

He shook his head. "I am not keeping you here. I would never do such a thing." He frowned and said, "Why were you out there, Tamara?"

I stared at him. "I want to go home Maashi."

"Tamara." He bent down toward me and brought his face close to mine. "Please believe me when I say I would let you go back to your world a thousand times rather than see your life end here."

I swallowed. His words rang true.

He straightened up. "The Elders canceled the search for the wormhole because of the threat of the Untouchable. The search has resumed, and we are now looking for any anomaly and over a broader area."

He took one long breath and held my fingers in his. "Many months ago, before you came, I was kidnapped by the Krakoran and it took months for my people to rescue me. I felt abandoned, in pain, and I thought I would die." Maashi's voice broke. He gazed away and whispered, "The first time I saw you, I understood how lost and alienated you must have felt. Your plight brought back sad and painful memories. Your courage touched my heart and I vowed to help you any way I could."

"Maashi, my situation is different," I said. "No one knows where I am and even if they did, they wouldn't be able to rescue me."

Did he understand that?

"I will continue the search for you."

I blinked my tears and bit my lip.

"Little one, we cannot undo what happened and we don't have enough information to send you back to your world. I don't know what the future holds for you. I can't say if you will ever go home."

I felt defeated, tired, chilled to the bone.

If I couldn't go back, could I accept a life here with him, with all that this implied?

Maashi took me in his arms. "Come."

Exhausted, I couldn't find the energy to protest.

He stepped out of the encounter room and carried me to his private pool where the water was so limpid its surface created a perfect reflection of the blue walls speckled with gold.

"Come in the water with me."

He stepped in the pool and slowly lowered me in. The water enveloped me, seeped into my every pore, soothing my soul. Maashi's skin felt warm and his sweet aroma radiated all around us.

He cradled me, held my head close, his cheek resting on mine. He kissed my neck and my shoulders. I breathed and sighed. His intoxicating perfume filled my lungs and my mind. I admired how his shirt clung to his body, showing every muscle, every curve. His skin glowed. I wish I could be held like this forever.

"I missed you, little one," he said, his voice a mere whisper. His fingers massaged my scalp until all tension seemed to evaporate from my body. He removed my clothes one by one and took off his shirt. He pulled me close. I rested on his velvet skin. I was in heaven.

"I missed you too." I stroked the back of his hand with the tip of my fingers.

Holding me securely with his left arm, he swam around the pool. Gliding on my back, I admired the delicate gold swirls carved in the ceiling. Safe in his embrace, I reveled in the smooth feeling of warm water flowing over and under me.

"Mm," I said.

Maashi's eyes softened and he smiled. "I know it has been hard for you. How alone and sad you have felt these last few days."

"Maashi, you know I can't stay here. I have to go home." I spoke the words, but they didn't sound convincing.

Maashi bent his head and stretched out his long blue tongue. He slowly licked my neck and shoulders.

"Oh, so sweet." I moaned. What an exquisite feeling. His tongue felt gentle and silky.

He whispered in my ear, "From the first day in the miner's quarters when I held you in my arms and kissed your tears, I knew you were precious. I sensed your fear, but I found in you an incredible energy and determination to survive. From that moment on, I was compelled to protect you from harm and take care of you."

Right then, I wanted him. I wanted his love even if it meant sharing him with countless others. I was aware it wouldn't have made any sense on my world but in his arms, I felt happier and more alive than I had ever felt. All I wished was to remain close to him, his body, his touch.

Maashi lifted my chin and brought my eyes level with his. "Tamara," he breathed, "You bring light into my life. I care for you. I can make you happy. I want you to be my Chimitanga, my little friend. I will care for you, cherish you, and always keep you safe." He kissed my face and clicked softly in my ear. He swam to the side of the pool and pressed on a small panel and an iridescent blue bracelet appeared. Maashi placed it on my left wrist with the other bracelets.

I looked at him through wet eyelashes, "I love you," I said. "I don't understand how I can feel this way for you. I never thought this was possible. Thank you for caring for me, for this beautiful bracelet, for everything."

Could I be happy with Maashi and stay true to myself?

"Come with me."

He stepped out of the water, lifted me, and carried me back to his encounter room where black and gold diamond patterns rippled in slow waves from one wall to the other. The low ceiling and smooth elliptical shape of the room sheltered us like we were laying inside an oyster.

I inhaled deeply and nestled in his arms. I touched his cheek and lost myself in the liquid amber of his eyes. He played in my hair and massaged the nape of my neck, and his lips parted in a smile. "You are shapinka Tamara. One I can hold and kiss until she sings with pleasure. One I can lick until my body glows and my mind travels to a magical world."

"Kiss me, Maashi," I whispered. I hungered for his lips on my body.

His face softened. He bent over me. I opened my mouth and he slid his tongue inside and licked me. His mind and my mind were one.

"Welcome to my world," he whispered in my mind.

His voluptuous holoma encircled us in a protective veil and I surrendered to him. My spirit soared with translucent wings. Maashi's blue glow filled the room and bound us together until the walls vibrated in unison with our energy.

My pain and anguish disappeared replaced by a profound sense of calm. I drifted away on a vast turquoise ocean, lost in blissful oblivion.

"Sleep well, little one. Tomorrow's problems do not exist."

I closed my eyes and breathed deeply.

A few hours later, I woke, plopped back on the velvety cushions and watched the ever-changing patterns of the diamonds on the ceiling. So many events had occurred in the last few days: the celebration, the Untouchable's attacks, my meeting with Lady Ileana, my rescue at the Gorganna falls, and my renewed connection with Maashi.

I smiled as I recalled how Maashi offered the honorable title of Chimitanga, which translates into 'little friend of a Pure Color'.

I tool one of the smaller cushions embroidered with gold strands and held it against my chest. On Earth, my life was filled with boredom and dissatisfaction. Neither my husband nor I had noticed the subtle changes in our relationship until it was too late. Nate had volunteered for extra responsibilities at work, and I always seemed to have an important meeting to attend. Time spent away from each other was more important than time spent together. I thought it was a phase and we would readjust later.

After a few years we became two strangers living together in the same house and soon arguments popped over trivial things. We tried and failed to rekindle the closeness and intimacy we shared in our first years of marriage. Only now did I understand our relationship had been disintegrating for a long time.

I sighed and turned to my side. I had been close to my daughter Allison. Like two sisters, we had shared secrets and special moments together. At night, when only silence surrounded me, I remembered the jasmine scent of her favorite perfume, her bubbly laugh, and my fingers playing in her silky golden hair. I missed so much her presence and her friendship. A lone tear ran down my cheek. I might never see her again.

The boys, David and Jonathan, were strong and would support each other and would survive my absence but my daughter was sensitive and prone to depression when faced with challenging situations. Would she be able to cope with my dis-appearance?

I sighed. Sadness filled my heart. One day I might have to face an extremely difficult decision if the Chamis found the wormhole.

# Chapter 25

The door chime rang and Rahma entered in the water room just as I finished getting dressed.

"Congratulations," he said as soon as he saw me. "You are now Chimitanga. The Sheffrou is most pleased with you."

"Thank you," I said. I smiled. I realized Maashi's young companions were eager to serve him but were also curious of his private life. Sheffrous and Sawisha had more privileges and possessed a higher social status than the younger Chamis and the Multicolors. Now, as Maashi's Chimitanga, I had gained status in Chamranlina society.

"Come, we must go see the Sheffrou," he said.

Maashi was sitting alone on a lounge chair. He was rolling the end of his sash between the thumb and third finger of his right hand. His eyes were deep amber. He seemed lost in his own thoughts.

Rahma strolled in the receiving room, kissed Maashi's shoulder then his neck, and settled beside him. I sat on the other side.

Chopa walked in, bowed low, and sat across from Maashi. A few others came in, clicking and chatting. They were part of Rahma and Chopa's group of friends: one with a chocolate brown sash with a pink wave, another with a light green sash and black hair and a third one with a light purple sash and scarred face. They all bowed to Maashi, nodded at me, and sat.

The last one was a new Chami I hadn't seen yet. He bowed to Maashi and to me. Slender with turquoise eyes and spiky chestnut air, he wore a pearl-gray shirt and a pale pink sash circled his waist.

"Good afternoon Shonava. I trust you are well rested," he said in a young voice.

Maashi looked at him with gentle eyes. "Good afternoon, Pini." He turned then said, "Tamara, this is your new teacher, Pinishinilongtida. He will be your guide in the compound and will help with anything you may require."

Pini murmured, "How do you do?"

"I'm well, thank you." I suppressed a smile. This Chami, with chestnut hair and green eyes, looked stunning yet when he set his hands on his knees, I noticed they were trembling.

"Sir, do you know that one of the search parties has pinpointed Sheffrou Tomisho's location?" Rahma said. "I heard they are attempting a rescue as we speak."

"Yes, I heard," Maashi said and patted Rahma's shoulder.

A new Chami came in, carrying in one hand a tray of tall glasses filled with choun. He moved with the calm assurance of an athlete and provided everyone including Maashi, with a glass of the creamy liquid.

There was something familiar about him although I was sure I hadn't seen anyone with a rust-colored sash before. He handed me a glass and bowed. "Chimitanga," he said.

"Tamara," said Maashi, "Chustan was a participant at a wrestling match I attended weeks ago."

I nodded. He was the one who helped Maashi back up after his fight with the red.

"Sir," Chustan said, "I bring great news. The Black Guards have confirmed one of our vessels has rescued Sheffrou Tomisho from the enemy's lair. He is alive and being brought back to Chitina as we speak." He raised his glass. "May his life always be as sweet as choun. May he live long and mate every sequence." Chustan raised his glass, and everyone took a sip, clicked together with enthusiasm, and repeated for a second and a third sip.

Maashi took one swallow of his choun but his expression remained serious. Everyone quieted down and turned towards him.

"Sir," Rahma said, "is there something wrong?"

Maashi pulled out of his shirt the gold cordelet he had received as a gift from his friend Tomisho. He stared at it and rubbed it between his fingers. He took a deep breath and said, "We must be ready for Tomisho's return. He will be under close supervision until his health is restored."

"To a swift recovery," said Rahma as he raised his glass and drank. The young Chamis clicked and patted each other and emptied their glasses.

"The guards will prepare special quarters for him," Maashi said. "The Council will assign two chowlis and a physician to his care, and I will assist them. Chustan is older and more experienced and will remain with me. You will not see me," Maashi looked at me, "for a few weeks."

"Sir," Rahma said, "do you think he is injured?"

Maashi's eyes darkened. "I do." He rose. "I must leave now. I will see you tomorrow."

"Sir?" said Rahma.

"I must go to Dasho," Maashi said. "The injuries he has suffered during the attack by the Untouchable aren't healing well."

>————<<●>>—————<

I spent the day in my receiving room, drawing animals on my new tablet, the one Chopa gave me after I broke the first one. Pini came twice to see if I needed anything. I didn't know what to expect from him and sent him away.

The next morning Pini was at the door. He looked elegant with a camel-colored shirt and a pair of light brown pants tied at the ankles.

"Tamara," he said, "Sheffrou Maashi would like you to join him. I will accompany you now if you are ready."

"Sure." I had finished eating breakfast and was eager to see him.

We arrived in his receiving room. Maashi was sitting alone on a couch working on his virtual computer. He signaled me to sit. Pini sat on a couch across from us.

Maashi's eyes were small and dark. He took my hand and kissed it. "How are you, Tamara?"

"I'm doing well," I said. Maashi kept opening and closing his hands as if to stretch his fingers. "You look worried. Is everything all right?"

Maashi made a sound between a sigh and a hiss. "Dasho is depressed and suffers from extreme exhaustion. He might not recover the use of his right arm." Maashi paused. He grabbed the end of his sash and rolled it back and forth between his thumb and his long middle finger.

Pini shifted in his seat and his brow darkened.

I asked, "How sad."

Maashi turned toward me and said in hushed tones, "During the attack, the Krakoran burned part of Dasho's face. He will be permanently disfigured. There is nothing I can do."

"Oh." I shuddered, "that's awful."

Maashi swallowed and stared straight ahead. "It's a grave problem. His abnormal appearance will prevent him from mating with the young Fanellas. The Council will not consider him a suitable candidate unless he achieves a complete recovery."

"What if he remains scarred?"

Maashi didn't answer. He closed his eyes.

Mating was the most significant thing in a Sheffrou's life. If Dasho couldn't mate, would he be considered a second-class citizen and lose his privileges in Chamranlina society? Someone not worth protecting during an attack. The thought was disturbing.

A chime rang, and Chopa came in. He bowed to the sheffrou and sat with Pini. Chopa always looked serious, but his expression today didn't show any emotion at all. He didn't even acknowledge my presence. Rahma followed him in and his brow was broad and dark. He also bowed and sat alongside Chopa.

"What is it?" Maashi said.

Chopa responded. "I have been keeping in touch with Khon, the chief of security, to stay updated with the latest news as you requested, sir."

Maashi stared at him.

"I have been informed we have lost contact with the rescue ship which carried Sheffrou Tomisho. They were attacked by the Rodenegad from the planet Dagoon. Security thinks they are hiding in the Karkanian nebula which means it will take several days, possibly weeks, before they can return to Chitina."

Maashi rose in one swift movement. His eyes were black slits. He paced the room back and forth and hissed between his teeth. "This is not good. Tomisho needs to come back soon. He will suffer needlessly."

"Shonava, there is something else."

Maashi stopped in his tracks. "What?"

Chopa clicked a few times, then clicked faster and faster. Maashi paled, his brow thickened. He took one step back and emitted a low hissing sound. Rahma and Pini looked at each other. They clicked and hissed, raised their arms and in my direction.

"What is it? What's going on?" I said. "Did you find the wormhole?"

"No."

"What then?" I stood and crossed over to sit beside Chopa.

Chopa clicked and Maashi nodded to him. Chopa looked at me. "You are not alone."

"What?" My heart started to beat like a drum. "Did someone else come through the wormhole?"

"Not through the wormhole," said Chopa.

"Where then?" I cried out. "What did you find?"

"The rescuers have been out in several sectors to find the kidnapped Sheffrous," said Chopa. "One team tracked a signal less than a light-year away from here, but the signal was lost then they caught another faint signal from a bigger ship from much further away." Chopa stopped.

"Continue," said Maashi.

"The signals came from two types of ships we have never seen before." He gave me a furtive look. "We identified the first signal. It came from a vessel orbiting a planet slightly larger than Chitina. There were two alien life forms aboard. The vessel was trapped in a decaying orbit around the planet. The rescuers retrieved it, and it is being brought back to Chitina. They have determined the aliens are alive and in a protective casing designed for prolonged suspended animation."

I stared at Chopa and held my breath.

"The aliens are two human males."

"What?" I jumped from my seat. "That's not possible." It couldn't be. I searched in Maashi's eyes, looking for an explanation. They were wrong. Dead wrong. I looked at them one by one, willing them to tell me it was an error, a horrendous mistake. All eyes were fixated on me.

That's when I understood. Maashi's world was far away, but also in a different time.

My former life flashed before me, my children, my husband, my parents, my home. My beautiful planet with its people, blue skies, green forests, deep seas, now lost somewhere in the past, forever beyond my reach. Like witnessing an illusionist's sleight of hand, the world I had known had vanished before my eyes.

My chest tightened and my breathing became labored. I opened my mouth to cry out, but no sound came. My vision became blurred and a moment later, everything turned black.

When I regained consciousness, I was nestled in Maashi's arms. I could smell his fragrant body. He bent down and kissed my neck and my cheeks.

"Are you feeling better?" he said in a soft voice.

My mouth was dry, my vision blurry. It was as if every little bit of energy had drained from me.

Humans. Humans traveling in deep space, far from Earth. How could this be?

Warm tears ran down my cheeks before I realized I was crying. I was lost, completely lost. My family, my world, gone.

Maashi kissed my head and caressed my hair. "Little one," he said in a soothing tone, "Your wish was to go back to your world, to your people. You are close to success. You can reconnect with your own species."

A cold chill of fear ran up my spine. My blood iced in my veins. "Maashi, you don't understand, they are not my family. They aren't even from my time." I said, my voice quivering. "Humans aren't like Chamranlinas. They don't all work well together. They may not even accept me." Did he want to get rid of me?

Maashi frowned. "Tamara, there is a possibility we may never find the wormhole. I would be most pleased to keep you here, but this might be your only chance to live with humans."

I swallowed, confused. What about my feelings for him? What about us?

He lifted my chin and said, "I would never send you away if you didn't want to go."

My lips trembled. A heavy weight had settled on my chest. I shook inside. I couldn't take a deep breath and couldn't find the inner stillness and tranquility I needed to think straight. The same feeling of fear and dread that overwhelmed me when I first came in this world was back, and if it hadn't been for Maashi's comforting presence, I would have been totally lost.

"Little one, do not let fear control your mind. We will learn more in a few weeks."

Perhaps I was overreacting. They might be normal decent people. Perhaps they would be overjoyed to offer me a new life with them but was I willing to leave the Chamis? Did I want to leave the one I cherished above all? I looked up at Maashi. His amber eyes were staring into nothingness. He appeared lost in his own thoughts.

How was it that some days I felt so strong I could face the universe and other days it was quite the opposite? Today was one of those days. Conflicting thoughts swirled in my head and my emotions rocked out of control.

I sat alone in my quarters and considered what the news about these humans meant for me. I had found a place in Maashi's world. The possibility of locating the wormhole that brought me here was slipping away, but I had adapted to the Chamis' world and discovered love in the Sheffrou's arms.

The arrival of other humans changed everything. I stared at the blue ceiling with the puffy white clouds and clenched my fists. That damn wormhole had hurled me into an alien world and turned my life upside down. Now a new challenge lay before me. My future was uncertain once more.

<The End of Book 1>

If you enjoyed *I Am Sheffrou* please post a review
and find out what happens to Tamara and the Chamis next in
*Sheffrou Betrayed*.

# Glossary

Ara: the smaller moon of Chitina.

Chamtali: original world of the Chamranlinas.

Chamranlinas: name the aliens call themselves.

Charissa: "joie de vivre".

Chati: edible molluscs.

Chemcha: protective underwear.

Chimitanga: a Sheffrou's little friend.

Chitina: planet where the Chamranlinas live.

Choun: Chamranlina breastmilk.

Chowli: close companion to a Sheffrou or a Sawisha.

Chuckie: colored candy containing psychotropic drugs.

Chumpi: sweet one.

Chututu: a water-polo game played by the Chamranlinas.

Dagoon: planet of the slave-traders called Rodenegad.

Draharma trials: three trials all Sheffrous and Sawishas must complete to gain the right to mate.

Encounter room: small oval room designed for intimate meetings and sexual encounters.

Fanella: female Chamranlina, smaller and slender than the male.

Ghouli Ghouli Chamranlina: Group of multicolor Chamranlinas which are fertile.

Googlian: glow in the dark worms that live in certain tunnels and caves.

Great Eclipse celebration: important celebration marking the beginning of the time of renewal and the total eclipse of the 2 moons, Ara and Kori.

Holoma: fragrant aroma produced by mature Sheffrous when they feel pleasure.

Ishkibu Sheffrou: a Sheffrou who can travel through wormholes.

Karkanian nebula: nebula where Chamranlina ships can hide.

Kori: the second moon of Chitina, larger than Ara.

Krakoran: also called Untouchables, aliens, enemies of the Chamranlinas.

Lichi: edible fungus.

Loloyan: humanoid aliens who lived on planet Koronos.

Lumi: sweet drink served in a long slim glass.

Nateet: sweater with a hood.

Onumdum: a unicellular organism used to treat electrolyte imbalances.

Quatay: characteristic markings on the chest of Sawishas and Sheffrous.

Raah Azan: large black feline.

Rashandamora cave: cave where the Great Eclipse celebration is held.

Rodenegad: slave-traders who live on planet Dagoon.

Rue Kish: intense desire to mate.

Runshama: recurrence of suppressed memories.

Saweya: life energy.

Sawisha: part of the elite group of Pure Color Chamranlinas, their tongue is unicolor.

Schloppies: testicles.

Sequence: one year or 712 days. The year is divided in 17 months: 16 months of 42 days and one month of 40 days. One day is 26 earth hours.

Shapinka: Precious one, a term of affection and respect.

Sheffrou: third gender, may be male or female. Sheffrous are Pure Colors, their tongue is blue.

Shonava: lord.

Shoshans: large like antelope-like quadrupeds.

Talinda: Chamranlina.

Tishi: White trumpet-shaped flowers.

Toughi: fruit tasting like blend of pear and apple.

Tousanoo: healer, therapist.

Vizinem: aliens allies of the Chamranlinas.

# Acknowledgements

I would like to thank my family, my friends, and my fellow writers of the Surfside Chapter of the South Carolina Writers' Association, especially Trilby Plants and Richard Lutman, for their continued help and support.

# Meet the Author

    As a child, I dreamed of becoming an astronaut and traveling to faraway worlds.

    Born in Montreal, I currently live in South Carolina and enjoy reading, traveling, and I'm still fascinated by stories about alien worlds. After a successful career as an obstetrician-gynecologist and four children, I divide my time between my family and creating my own science-fiction stories. When not busy writing, I ride my tricycle around the neighborhood or work in my bee and butterfly friendly garden.

I would be delighted if, after reading book 1, *I Am Sheffrou,* or book 2, *Sheffrou Betrayed*, you would consider leaving a review on Amazon and Goodreads or any website of your choice. Book 3, *The Sheffrou's Gambit,* will be published in 2024.

Good Readings to all!

*Cami Michaels*

Website: CamiMichaels.com

Email: CamiMichaelsscifiauthor@gmail.com

Facebook: Cami Michaels Sci-fi Author

Printed in the USA
CPSIA information can be obtained
at www.ICGtesting.com
CBHW022308201024
16154CB00018B/160